ournal
of an Awful Good
aladin
BOOK ONE

Written by Mick McArt
Cover Art by Matthew McEntire

MICK ART
PRODUCTIONS LLC
PUBLISHING
WWW.MICKARTPRODUCTIONS.COM

Journal of an Awful Good Paladin, Book 1
All Rights Reserved
Copyright © 2020 Mick McArt, Mick Art Productions
V1

ISBN: 978-1-948508-05-6

Published by
Mick Art Productions, LLC
www.mickartproductions.com

PRINTED IN THE UNITED STATES OF AMERICA

For my kids,
Micah, Jonah, and Emerald.
You three make me laugh
on a daily basis and remind
me to look at the world
with a renewed sense
of wonder.

REVIEWS FROM THE REALMS

"This book is top of the heap!"
– Swilliam Muckabout, Trashman's Quarterly

"I laughed my head off!"
– Hackett Danecky, Realmsian Block Party

"I like the short story format,"
– Dee Stracted, Littleread Publishing

"I gobbled up every delicious word!"
– Nibbles the Werehamster

"It's even funnier than I predicted!"
– Crystal Bull, Minotaur Fortune Teller

THANK YOU'S

God, my wife Erica, my sons Micah & Jonah, & my daughter Emerald. Matthew McEntire for the amazing cover art and giving the Unremembered Realms a great visual identity. My mother Marilyn McArt; Curt "Spaceburt' Coker; Kristen Coker; Chuck Bailey; my father Mickey McArt; Brian Green; George P. Burdell; Sara Jesse; Eric Abbott; Nick Belton; Randy Pearson; Dave Wehner; the Bila family; The Amazin' Mitten; Bruce Shields; Dave Robishaw; Eric Allison; Tom Adams; Andy Schiller & Family; Randall David Aasted; Tom Vasel; Eric Summerer; all of my Kickstarter supporters; Justin Andrew Mason, Larry Elmore; Scott Fleishman; Luke Gygax, Jennifer Bouchard who is an editing wizard, and a huge thank you to the evergrowing fan base of the Unremembered Realms who inspire me to keep building this world!

Mick Art Productions Publishing
www.theunrememberedrealms.com

Journal of an Awful Good Paladin - Book 1
Written by Mick McArt
Cover Art by Matt McEntire
Map by Justin Andrew Mason
Editing by Jennifer Bouchard
Proofing by Erica McArt

PROLOGUE

Standing in the atrium of the giants castle, we could see the over-sized staircases going up and door. The dozens of doors line the hallways that could lead to anywhere told us one thing. It was going to be a long night of sneaking, searching, and fighting. "Getting this ancient artifact isn't going to be easy team," I told my party as I waved them forward.

"Look! A sign," our mage Garrot said as he walked to it, "it's even lit up!"

"You are here," Kellepto read, while pointing to the big red arrow and running her finger over the words.

"This could be a trap," I warned. "Don't touch anything!"

That's when I heard a loud bell ringing. When I looked over, our dwarven monk, Footpalm the Elflinger, was removing a bell from Garrot's hand, stopping the noise. "Are you daft!?" shouted the dwarf. "Why are you ringing a bell?!"

"It was just sitting here," Garrot explained. "And the little sign says ring for service! There's no point in being rude."

"It's a trap," Aiden, our cleric said doing a facepalm. "Hidden in plain sight."

Dozens of monsters of all sorts started coming out of the doors. They were yawning and stretching but carrying deadly looking weapons. "Did you take a number?" a large slobgoblin commented as he approached, pointing to a number dispenser by the sign. "We like to kill all invaders in the proper order."

Garrot pulled the little number tab. "It says 212," he said smiling.

"Is there a wait?" I asked the foul smelling creature.

"Today's you're lucky day, paladin," he replied lifting his sword. "Because your numbers up!"

Entry 1

Being a paladin isn't easy; sometimes you have to face things you never thought you would. I was called upon to apprehend an elderly woman who was causing trouble in a market square. I was told that she kicked a leg out from under an apple cart, spilling all of its contents. Then, she threw an apple at the owner, giving the surprised dwarf a black eye. Next, walked around, booing all the street performers, making them lose tips. It seems the aging menace woke up on the wrong side of the nursing home and it was my job apprehend this cane-wielding maniac!

My former training with the Redeye Knights did not cover this kind of situation, so I just figured that I should play this one by ear. I raised my hands up in front of me and approached the octogenarian looney with a friendly grin.

"Are you lost, ma'am?" I asked.

"Scram, paladin!" she yelled. "Or I'll clean your clock, old school!"

With an incredible amount of strength, she stomped my foot, and then roundhouse kicked my head, sending me crashing through the cart of a cake vendor! "I'm bleeding!" I said shocked, as I looked at my hand after rubbing my face.

"That's just the icing from the cake," the vendor stated, while looking distraught over his crushed wares. "What kind of paladin are you? Can't you even stop an old lady!?"

That style of kick wasn't from just any elderly woman. She was a Rhuddist Monk! Those are monks who love to stir up trouble for no good reason at all. Their motto is "Inner peace, through outer chaos!"

I stood back up and cautiously approached this deceptive lady, who threw down her cane and immediately went into a praying mantis-style fighting pose. A crowd had now gathered around to see what she was going to do next. Much to their disappointment, it was a short show. She let out a battle cry and ran at me at a surprising speed. Unfortunately for her, she slipped in some frosting and crashed to the ground at my feet, knocking herself unconscious!

I spotted a small glowing ring on her finger and removed it. It must have been magical, because she immediately transformed into a petite, raven-haired beauty! She did not look happy when she woke up in a Neverspring jail cell!

"I'm too old to be in here," she yelled, rattling the bars. "My knitting circle is going to hear about this! It's a travesty of justice!"

I held up her ring and she looked at her hands. "I'm too young to be in here," she yelled, switching gears all of a sudden.

"From the list of charges I've seen," I began. "You might just be too old to be in here, after all, once your time is actually served!"

Entry 2

People often ask me how I met Aiden the Cleric. I was traveling from Broke Ridge to Miftenmad in the Province of Elderwhelp when I came across the nervous-looking fellow tending a campfire. He breathed a sigh of relief after noticing what I was a paladin. "I thought you were a small ogre, at first," he commented, before inviting me to sit down.

We had been chatting for a while when Aiden revealed to me that he was on his way to a small island off the coast of Farlong, called Lecturus. "They put out word that they were looking for organ donors," he explained. "So the high priest at my temple has been sending out acolytes, such as myself, to let them know we have an extra one at the temple that plays music wonderfully."

That's when he got up and started nervously pacing around. "The problem is, I'm the third one they've sent. Nobody has been returning. All we get is a thank you note after a couple of weeks. It doesn't make any sense. They've never even picked up the organ!"

This situation seemed a bit odd to me, so I volunteered to go along. "I go by Stormcloud," I said, standing up and holding out my hand. "but my real name is Nimbus Slumberdim. I can accompany you if you wish."

The cleric smiled and returned the handshake. By the break of dawn, we put out our fire and headed out. Luckily, when we reached the water, we spotted a small rowboat that the people of Lecturus must have left for visitors to their island. We could see the island in the distance, so we got in the boat and started rowing across the water of Dunkenbay. As we got closer, we spotted the village. There were only a few huts surrounding a much bigger one. The whole place was encompassed by a lush, blooming garden. "They must be druids," I told the young cleric. "They sure know how to stay in touch with nature."

There were about a half-dozen of the druids milling about the place when we approached. Most smiled and waved, showing off their crooked, browning teeth. One, wearing a blue robe with some moss growing on it, approached us. "Are you here for the organ donation?" he asked.

Aiden nodded his head. The druid pointed to the largest of the huts. "You need to see Cowclay," he said. "He's in charge of all the donations."

"Thank you, sir," I said, shaking the druid's hand; which, I noticed was quite sticky.

I made a mental note to wash that hand, later. Strangely, the druid was now sniffing his hand and smiling. "We can't wait to have you for dinner!" he cheerfully stated, while walking away.

"These druids seem kind of off," Aiden said, warily. "That one sure acted suspiciously."

"I'm sure everything will be just fine," I boasted. "You have to believe in your fellow man."

With that said, I felt a pinch on the back of my neck. I looked at Aiden, who gave a quick "ow", while reaching behind him to grab at something. "It's some kind of darrrrr...." I said, as I fell to the ground.

When I woke up, I noticed Aiden stirring as well. Then, I saw a druid doing some stirring with a large-sized ladle! We had been tied up and thrown into a large pot of hot water. "I think we're in hot water," I told Aiden, trying to be funny.

I could see a few vegetables floating around us, too. "Whoa, whoa, whoa," Aiden shouted. "I was sent here to donate an organ! Let me talk to your leader!"

A large druid stepped up from behind the cook and said, "Welcome to Lecturus! We are the CHUDs, which stands for Cannibal Holistic Unwashed Druids! My name is Cowclay."

"I'd say it's nice to meet you. I'd shake your hand, but I'm a little tied up right now," I said, while trying to wriggle free of the ropes that tied my hands together in front of me.

"No need," Cowclay laughed. "I'm sure I'll get to your hand by the second course. I just adore finger food."

"I can see what your favorite is," Aiden said, looking at my chest.

Looking downward, I could see they had drawn lines on me. Right over my heart, there was a star drawn. Down my ribs, it read "hearty vittles." "I don't know," I said to Aiden, trying to think quickly. "I'm pretty tough. I don't think his rotting teeth will do a good job. He has too many cavities."

"My teeth can tear through your rib cage!" Cowclay spat, angrily. "You're just lucky my men like stew!"

"You know," Aiden interrupted. "Part of Nimbus's training as a paladin was in Dentology. There are only a few temples that teach that, you know."

I looked at him, puzzled. He quickly gave me a wide-eyed stare, and then I realized what he was trying to do. "Can I take a look?" I asked, wobbling as I stood up in the slick cooking pot.

Aiden had struck a nerve, because the druid hesitated. "Are you sure?" Cowclay asked. "I have been having shooting pains in one of my grinders…"

The large druid stepped forward. "Open up and say 'ah'," I said as he stepped closer.

He waved over a few other druids who held their staves out by my face. "If he tries anything, beat him and his friend to death!" Cowclay ordered, before opening up his mouth so I could look in.

It wasn't a pretty sight. The cavities were numerous; some teeth had even started to turn crooked. I swear one was even fizzing! His breath was horrible... like he had swallowed a dead fish.

"Tsk. Tsk." I stated. "This is going to be painful!"

With that said, I headbutted him in the face and wrapped my bound hands around the back of his neck. I pulled him into the pot, head first! At the same time, Aiden cast an Invisible Hammer spell and bashed two of the druids in their faces, before they realized what was happening! The remaining druid looked like he was going to hit me with his staff, but I yelled out, "You hit me, and your leader drowns!"

Cowclay struggled underneath me, but he was no match for my strength. The cook nervously said, "I told him we should stick to eating rogues! I told him that the eating of clerics would only attract paladins!"

I signaled for the druids to cut Aiden loose first. Cowclay was starting to go limp, so I pulled him out of the pot and pushed him to the ground. Aiden cut me free next, and we both climbed out. I pulled Cowclay up, put him in a chokehold, and demanded that his men bring me our gear.

He ordered the rest of the druids to stand down while Aiden put his armor back on. I let him go and he took deep breaths. "You can go," he panted, then spit. "But don't ever come back."

Then, he paused before looking at Aiden. "You don't suppose we could still get that temple organ, do you? All we have is an old flute that's cracked; it's out of tune and sounds awful!"

Aiden shook his head at the audacity, and then we started marching off. After getting on the boat, we rowed for a little while before I asked. "You're not considering delivering that temple organ, are you?"

"Are you kidding," Aiden laughed. "Those guys couldn't even cook a decent stew! I could only imagine the music they'd make!"

Entry 3

I decided to start keeping a journal after an adventure near the city of Dankpond. I was traveling with Aiden, the Cleric, and Footpalm, the Elflinger. Footpalm is a dwarven monk who loves to throw elves around violently, he says it helps him find "inner peace".

We had heard rumors of an undead horde building up in a cemetery by a den of evil clerics. I figured that with Aiden's help turning the undead, and between Footpalm's and my fighting skills, we could quickly bring these lawbreakers to justice.

It wasn't long before we were at the evil cleric's hideout. It was a massive crypt with a thick wooden door. I was just about to smash it in with my shoulder when I noticed a little sign had fallen on the ground. I bent down and picked it up. It read, "No Turning Symbols allowed on-premises. By order of the Dankpond Village Council."

I couldn't believe it. One of these evil clerics must have had a corrupt member of the council issue this. "Are we going to smash the door in or what?" Footpalm asked. "I don't like hanging around in cemeteries."

"We can't," I said, "that would be breaking the law. That would make us like them."

"Are you kidding me!?" the dwarf stated, throwing up his hands. "That's the dumbest thing I've ever heard!"

Aiden just shook his head and placed his Turning Symbol back into his pack. He knew I wouldn't go against my personal code, but without being able to turn the undead inside, it would be a much harder fight. "So, what now," the cleric asked.

"We'll go to the town's judge and get a special writ to access the facility," I explained, "I'm sure it won't be a problem."

On our way back through the woods, Footpalm thought he heard someone talking, so we all hid in some bushes; which, were thick in this area. Two travelers walked by. One was a tall rogue who appeared to be human. It was hard to tell because he wore a cowl, but I did notice he had a distinctive green glowing eye; which, I found odd. The other was an incredibly beautiful female wood elf with long silvery hair.

I held Footpalm back with my hand, so he wouldn't jump out and fling her into a tree. After they passed, we made it back to Dankpond, where we found a courthouse and had all the paperwork signed and cleared out after three short hours.

By the time we reached the crypt, we were disappointed. Its door had been picked open and all the evil clerics inside were slain and robbed. Undead were also scattered about, looking like they had been deeply sliced open by a sword or incredibly sharp dagger. Any treasure worth taking had been stolen, so I poked around until I found a document that was shuffled into the paperwork of one of the cleric's desks. It revealed the corrupt person on Dankpond's Village Council.

On the trip back, Aiden and I had to listen to Footpalm's whining about missing all the action. "It was probably that rogue and that elf," he lamented. "I knew you should have let me fling her into the trees!"

He calmed down after I promised to buy them dinner at the Tuckshovel Tavern, a popular place to eat in Dankpond. When we got there, I noticed the rogue we saw earlier sitting at a table by himself writing in what appeared to be a journal. "That's a good idea," I thought to myself, I should do that, too.

I was going to say something, or introduce myself, but he looked kind of worse for wear and a little beat up. I decided it was best to leave him alone.

Although my party and I hadn't got any of the gold from the crypt, there was a nice reward given to us for revealing the council's traitor. Keeping the realms safe was a reward unto itself, but a few coins in my pocket never seems to hurt, either. I wondered if that journal writing rogue thought the same thing.

Entry 4

The authorities in Neverspring hired my party to catch a screwball cleric who was using an unorthodox way of curing his patients. This so-called healer was a half-orc named Hassan Chopp, and his methods of healing involved removing troublesome appendages by chopping them off!

Luckily, the mage in our party, Garrot the Asphyxiator, had a clue as to his whereabouts. This knowledge was because our spellcaster wasn't that fond of using reliable clerical healing magic. He liked to try every unorthodox treatment he came across; which, would also probably explain why he was always sick with something until Aiden would corner him. Garrot was always recommending some goofy lotion, talisman, or edible monstrosity.

"He's totally legitimate," Garrot griped. "If you have a problem, Hassan gets rid of it!"

The phony cleric was traveling with a fly-by-night carnival that had set up on the outskirts of the city. Hassan had a tent set up and claimed to be an expert in holistic techniques. Earlier that week, Garrot went to this charlatan with a hangnail seeking a cure.

"Did he take care of your problem," I asked Garrot, as we walked out of the Neverspring constable's office, on our way to the carnival.

"He sure did," the mage replied, holding up his right hand, showing me the bandaged nub of his ring finger.

"I thought the hangnail was on your left hand," I said, now looking down at the infected, swollen finger.

"Hassan said that removing this one would provide balance and restore health to the other one, it just takes a couple of weeks," Garrot stated, smugly.

"Didn't you have an expensive ring on that finger," I asked, remembering the gold, jewel-encrusted ring he used to wear.

The mage's face was beginning to turning red. "Hassan is an expert," he said, curtly. "His assistant told me so."

"People are going out on a limb whenever they visit this psychotic cleric," I whispered to Kellepto, our party's elven rogue.

"Yeah," she agreed. "Then losing it! Do you mind if I run ahead and talk to this creep? Maybe I can convince him to give Garrot's ring back."

"Good," I replied, feeling a little better over our duped mage. "Remember to be polite!"

She waved at me with her dagger before running off. Footpalm shook his head as he looked at Garrot's missing finger. "Man, I'd hate to see his cure for a headache!"

<hr />

Entry 5

When you're a paladin, most of your adventuring work comes from jobs recommended by temples that are seeking a percentage of the loot for a tithe. That's why my party and I were shocked when entering the town of Skipstone. We found it half-destroyed and their temple in ruins.

A humongous tar dragon named Niccodyrmus had flown into town, killed a bunch of townsfolk, raided the temple's coffers, and left a small, shakey cleric named Stogey. "Niccodyrmus ate all my brethren," the distraught halfling claimed. "Then, he belched in my face and flew off!"

Stogey had sent word out that Skipstone needed help and we were the first ones to arrive. "Let's find this foul dragon and crush him out," Aiden stated, furiously.

We invited Stogey to join us. He was a bit reluctant at first, but then he spotted my magical sword gleaming in its sheath. "Is that magic sword powerful?" he asked, looking awestruck.

"Sure is," I said, pulling it out. "My claymore's named Abbott. It was once owned by Lucky Striker, a fighter of incredible skill. Legend has it that he fought alongside a powerful cleric by the name of Abbott. Lucky wasn't so lucky when he was hit with a Disintegration spell from a powerful Lich named Thunderskull. Abbott, already wounded and desperate, picked up the magically sharp sword and impaled the lich from behind. The stab disrupted another powerful spell the lich was trying to cast."

"Whoa," said the halfling. "Did it kill Thunderskull?"

"Yes," I continued, "but before dying and turning into a pile of red ash, the powerful magic that the lich was about to cast drew the soul out of Abbott. It captured him in this blade. That's why my weapon also contains some healing magic."

"Are we going or what?" Footpalm asked, impatiently. "Enough with the yapping, I want to kill something."

The impatient monk was right; we had to stop this menace before it had an urge to strike this town again. "I can show you where the dragon lives," Stogey said. "I've been monitoring his activities for a while."

The halfling led us to a massive cave in the side of one of the Hoktu Mountains. It was a bit of a climb, and there were a few kobold guards there, but we dispatched them pretty quickly. They were fast, but not fast enough. Footpalm beat them like dirty rugs against the cavern walls. A kobold captain managed to slip through our clutches and run down deeper into the cave.

We took off after him at full speed. We wanted to finish him off before he could alert the dragon. By the time we caught up to the kobold, we realized he had led us into a trap. We had entered a cavern filled with gold, gems, and oddball bits of fantastic looking treasure! The problem, before we realized it, was that we had all sunk ankle-deep in warm tar!

"That's just great," Kellepto complained. "I just got these boots at the Dragondrop Mall! It took me over two hours just to settle on these!"

Stogey shushed us, and things became quiet, except for the kobold captain who was standing on a rock and pointing at us yelling, "They're over here!"

"Looking for anything in particular?" a deep raspy voice intoned.

It was the dragon, Niccodyrmus. It's glowing green eyes shown from the dark of a shadowy cave. He stepped forward, allowing us to see his full head, murky black scales, and toothy grin. "Such a fine selection of morsels," it purred. "I'm going to chew each one of you, slowly, enjoying each bite and…eww, a dwarf."

"What's wrong with a dwarf?" Footpalm stated, becoming upset. "Not good enough for you!?"

"Dwarves give me gas," Niccodyrmus said, coming out of the cave and into full view. "Perhaps I'll just step on you!"

Footpalm started in on the giant lizard with some pretty bad insults; which, distracted the foul beast. "Should I hit him with a Ball of Fire?" Garrot whispered to me.

"We're stuck in tar," I replied. "Chances are, we'll burn to death with him, or at least die from the smoke inhalation."

I couldn't reach the dragon to hit it with my sword, and Kellepto's crossbow bolts just bounced off its scales. Garrot and Aiden were going to hit Niccodyrmus with some electricity-based spells, but he was now picking up Kellepto out of the tar. We were helpless! Then, just as the huge dragon was about to throw our elf into its mouth, it paused, and then started to cry. "I can't do it! I just can't do it anymore!"

He sat Kellepto down on some rocks and loudly wept. "I'm trying to quit eating people, but it's so hard!"

We looked at each other in shock, not knowing what to do. "Um... okay," was all I could say.

"The dragon priestess has warned me that my blood pressure is too high, and I need to be on a vegetable diet," he confessed. "But I've been eating people since I was small and I don't think I can stop!"

"No, no," Aiden said, nervously, "She's right. You want to be around for your younglings, don't you?"

"Of course," Niccodyrmus whined. "Oh, I wish I had never started eating everyone in the first place. But all the other young dragons were eating people and it looked so cool!"

"Have you tried quitting cold turkey?" I suggested, hoping it would buy us some time.

"I eat flocks of turkeys at a time," the dragon replied. "Warm or cold."

"No," I said, "I mean, just stop altogether. Take a long look into a reflective pool and say 'I can do this!'"

"I could do that. I mean, I think I could!" Niccodyrmus said through sobbing breaths.

"Are you guys serious about helping this creature?" Stogey said. "It just destroyed half of Skipstone!"

"We're trying to save the other half," I told him. "If this is the only way, then we have to help!"

"If you help me, I promise I'll never bother Skipstone again," Niccodyrmus promised.

Stogey didn't look happy, but death was our only other option. Plus, I think the cleric in him couldn't turn away a desperate creature. "Okay, okay," the halfling said, reluctantly.

Niccodyrmus happily freed us from the tar and we coached the ancient dragon about self-control techniques for the rest of the day. The lingering kobold captain kept giving us dirty looks. It was obvious he didn't like that we were helping his master.

By nightfall, we stood outside the cave wishing the dragon well.

"Thank you so much," Niccodyrmus stated. "You've given my grandlings a chance to play with me a few more centuries."

"Do you mind if we take some gold back with us?" Stogey asked.

"Don't push your luck, kid," the dragon said, sternly.

The kobold captain walked out from behind the dragon, fingering its blade. I think Footpalm had had enough of this little creature. "One more thing," the dwarf stated. "If you ever start jonesing for some flesh, just stick a little kobold between your lip and gums!"

"You mean like this?" Niccodyrmus asked, before picking up the captain and doing just that.

The muffled scream ended after a few seconds. "Mmmm," the dragon said. "You're right, dwarf, this works like a charm!"

Entry 6

The Unremembered Realms is a strange place, filled with all sorts of bizarre creatures and unpredictable situations. Speaking of bizarre creatures and unpredictable situations, I'll never forget the night I got lost in the Tanglewood Forest.

I was still a Redeye Knight at the time, so traveling with no sunlight did not bother me. If I got sleepy, I'd just chew on a few coffee beans and march on. I kept quiet, for the most part, because I knew Tanglewood was notoriously dangerous and many had disappeared in here, never to be seen again! My eyes quickly adjusted to the dark, so walking wasn't that bad; I just had to be careful not to alert any Shadowlings of my presence. These evil and vicious halflings lived in this part of the forest and did not like intruders.

I kept my hand on the hilt of Abbott, my magic sword, as I walked. Shadowlings were hard to spot in darkness, because of the blue color of their skin, but they did tend to talk a lot, so if you listened, you could hear them chattering if they were close by. My thoughts about them were interrupted when I spotted some firelight ahead of me.

I decided to investigate. I hunched low and moved toward the source of the light. I paused behind a bush and saw three figures sitting around a campfire.

One was a large human with some kind of hook for a hand and

wearing an eye patch. He could have been a half-orc, but it was hard to tell because of his wide-brimmed, worn-out looking hat. Sitting on a tree stump next to him was a humanoid wearing a white mask and cradling a large machete on his lap like a baby. The third creature appeared to be some kind of goblin I've never seen before. He wore a red and green striped tunic and these metallic claw-like weapons on his hands.

I crawled forward in the thick brush, hoping to hear their conversation, so I could tell if they were friendlies or a threat that I should avoid. To my surprise, two would listen as the other would recall a scary story. The first tale I caught was being told by the one with the claws. "The Hero of the Woods crawls around looking for unwary campers," he paused, listening for a moment, before continuing, "just like us!"

The other two looked around the woods, timidly. The one wearing the mask clutched its machete even closer. "They say he has spilled so much camper blood, that his beard has turned red!"

The goblin-clawed guy jumped while making this last statement, startling the other two, nearly causing them to fall off their seats! He just smiled as they composed themselves while he retook his seat.

"They're telling ghost stories around the campfire!" I thought to myself, smiling. I remembered doing that at campouts, myself. It was a common thing in the Unremembered Realms, apparently, even among monsters! "My turn," the oversized man with the hook for a hand stated, leaning himself closer to the fire, so his remaining eye became shadowy.

He began a tale about two orcs, a guy and a girl, whose wagon had broken down, not too far from this very spot. "They were young and scared, jumping at every noise, no matter how small!"

It was about that time that I felt a horrible itch on my leg, so I reached down to scratch it. This movement caused a small twig under me to snap! The three became quiet and looked in my direction, but not directly at me. I could see their fear, but still, I did not move, again; I did not want to be killed by these three oddballs.

"They didn't know the Shining Knight lived out in the thick brush of the Tanglewood Forest," he explained, slowly moving his hooked hand across his throat. "Until it was too late!"

The other two nervously laughed and looked around. I grinned at this trio's naiveté for a moment, but that's when I spotted something out of the corner of my eye. It was some Shadowlings, and they were crawling all over the traveler's wagon, stealing their supplies!

I itched my arms, wondering what I should do in this situation. I knew these were horrible monsters, but I couldn't just let them get robbed. As far as I knew, they hadn't broken any laws. While I was thinking about the situation, the humanoid with the white mask was on his feet, gesturing like a wild man in front of the two others. It was obvious that this fellow couldn't speak, so he was doing some kind of charades, hoping the others would understand. They had no idea what was going on behind them.

My throat was growing tight, as I considered yelling out, but then I realized something. I was laying in a patch of poison ivy! I couldn't lay in this spot, anymore; my throat had started to swell! I had to warn the monsters about their predicament! "Wath oud fortha Shabbowlingsth!!!" I yelled out, as I ran toward the three, my armor clanking, noisily.

The horrified trio must not have understood me, due to my throat being swollen, and nearly fell into the fire as they got up screaming like school girls. I tried to stop them, but the burning sensation on my skin kept me from being able to catch up. The Shadowlings all took off, too, not knowing what was going on. At least I was able to help the oddball trio to not lose their gear; I thought they would appreciate that. Especially, considering they left three wet spots where they were sitting, they would be needing some dry pants very soon.

Entry 7

One of the things I like most about being a paladin is all the ways that I get to help people, and sometimes it's beyond just rescuing them. For example, my crew and I had been hired to hunt down and kill a yellow-skinned water troll that was swimming around in Purgewater Lake, gobbling up vacationers. So, we hired a local Purgewater ranger named Donderay.

On the first night of tracking the aquatic beast, we made camp by the water's edge. I had noticed Donderay didn't seem very excited by what he was doing, and he seemed lost in thought most of the time. Kellepto finally broke the ice with the ranger, and he admitted that he wasn't that fond of his job.

"I want to go into marketing," he explained, nervously smiling. "To advertise and sell products in news scrolls all across the realms."

"Why don't you?" I asked.

"I need inspiration," he sighed. "I just don't have any ideas."

"Just do it," Garrot the Asphysiator stated. "Think big!"

"I agree," I interrupted. "There is no substitute for living your dream; you can't think small."

Donderay looked strangely at us for a moment, then fished around in his tunic for a writing quill. "Can I quote you on that?" he asked.

"When I discovered that flinging elves was my favorite thing to do," Footpalm chimed in, "I just kept going, and going and going. I'm always lovin' it!"

"I don't know," the ranger said, "What if I'm no good; what if I fail?"

"Success is a mind game," Kellepto said, taking a bite of the chicken we had spit-roasted. "You should always have things your way. Man, this chicken is finger-licking' good."

Donderay kept writing and was now grinning from ear-to-ear. I did-n't know what he was writing, but it seemed to pull him out of his glum spirit. "Got milk?" I asked Garrot, who was pouring out some water into a cup.

"What is it with you and milk, Nimbus?" he answered, uncorking another container and pouring me a glass.

"It gives him strong bones," Aiden the cleric, stated. "…and it does the body good."

"Wives tales," replied the wizard, as he handed me the cup. "That's all, make-believe."

"There is no substitute for doing something you enjoy," I told the ranger, while downing my cup of milk. "Mmmm, mmmm, good to the last drop. Hey, maybe this job truly isn't for you; it's okay to think different."

"You are right, "Donderay said, standing up triumphantly."I am what I am, and that is an Ad Man! I'll help you find this troll, but then I'm off to Neverspring to start a new journey!"

"Where's the beef?" asked Footpalm, who interrupted Donderay's speech to complain. "I'm so sick of chicken."

I heard the feisty ranger became successful after helping us locate and exterminate the water troll. I guess Donderay was a madman at com-ing up with catchy slogans. I have no idea what we said that inspired him so much, but I was glad to hear that he was in the happiest place for him in the realms, being all he can be.

Entry 8

I'm glad Kellepto is in the party, but sometimes I swear she does not understand personal space. One time, after a large meal in the Fool's Dish Tavern in Tidepool, I excused myself and headed out back to the out-house for a little time alone. As I sat there doing a bit of pondering, I heard her voice from outside the door. "That's disgusting," she commented.

"Of course it is," I shouted. "I'm going to the bathroom!"

"Can't you be more discreet," she asked.

Frustrated, I threw a corn cob at the door. "No, I can't. Now go away, you're making me nervous!"

"A big guy like you, gets nervous," she asked. "I find that hard to believe!"

"Can we have this conversation later," I asked, getting angry. "I'm trying to accomplish something here."

"Fine," she stated. "I'll just wait here until you're done."

"Go away," I shouted. "You just keep talking!"

"Fine, I'll be quiet," she said.

"That's the point," I yelled. "If you're quiet, then you'll hear me, and then I can't finish what I came in here to do, and I'll be miserable all day!"

"Well, hurry up then," she said, hitting the door a few times.

"Argh! Go back to the tavern. It's your presence that's bothering me!" I shouted through the door.

"I didn't bring any presents, Nimbus," she replied, sounding perplexed. "Is it your birthday?"

"No, it's not my birthday, Kellepto!" I yelled, exasperated. "But I'm trying to leave a package, if you know what I mean!"

There was a moment of silence from outside the door. I thought she left, and I let out a sigh of relief and started to relax. "Is it a surprise?" her voice spoke again, piercing the silence.

"Is what a surprise?" I asked, clenching up again.

"The package, silly," she answered. "Is it something we can all use?"

"Believe me," I replied, angrily, "it's not something you'd put in your pack!"

It was no use, at this point. Kellepto just kept jabbering on and on about the upcoming dungeon delve, so I just gave up and went back to the tavern. I felt off through the whole raid, and eventually had to have Aiden distract Kellepto, while I snuck off to a dark corner of an orc barracks. In the end, Kellepto was right; it would become a surprise for any orcs that returned later!

Entry 9

One of the strangest things I ever encountered in a dungeon was when I got separated from the rest of my party and entered into what I call, "The Haunted Maze." Being lost wasn't as bad as being chased around by the four ghosts who floated throughout the place.

The four would chase me around, relentlessly. What was even stranger, was when I would be exhausted from running or feeling hungry, I'd find some strawberries or a bowl of cherries on random tables. After consuming the mysterious fruit, it would give me the energy to fight back, but only temporarily. Eventually, I did find my way back out, but not before I grabbed a bunch of strawberries and cherries to fill my manpack.

Entry 10

My team had been hired by a cartographer out of Eaglespaw to protect him as he traveled around, mapping out uncharted areas. He was an unpleasant fellow named Shinburr, but he was rich, and we needed the money.

Surveying the land in Eaglespaw was beautiful, especially around Trippenfalls. Shinburr drew on his scrolls with the utmost care, before rudely demanding we take him to the next place. The whole trip, he would criticize all of us for one thing or another, but he seemed to relish taking shots at Kellepto, who would react to him the most.

The cocky cartographer did seem to cool out a bit with Kellepto when she started telling him about the legend of the "Gold Faerie." Kellepto explained the magical little creature finds favor with someone special, takes a bit of their gold, then replaces it with a lucky rock.

Believe it or not, that's precisely what started to happen; Kellepto was right! The Gold Faerie showed up almost every night and started taking the cartographers gold!

Shinburr was thrilled to get a new lucky rock every night on our adventure. "The faerie surely favors me," Shinburr bragged while sitting by our campfire, holding up a stone for us to see. Garrot was extremely jealous that the rest of the party wasn't getting a lucky rock. He wondered if we had offended the faerie, somehow.

I had my suspicions as to what was going on. I could see that Kellepto was in a much better mood after more days passed and more gold disappeared. Garrot, frustrated, began collecting rocks by the sackful, hopeful that one of them would turn out to be lucky. I asked Kellepto what she was up to, but she'd shrug and laugh. Finally, I put my foot down when Garrot asked me to help him carry his rocks because they became too heavy for him.

Kellepto reluctantly confessed and gave Shinburr back his gold, and he fired us on the spot. "Oh, well," I said that night around the campfire after he had left. "I suppose he was kind of unpleasant anyways."

Garrot poured out his rocks earlier that day. Even though he knew it all fake, he seemed a little sad. When we woke up the next morning, I noticed he was whistling and chipper. "What's up with the wizard?" I asked Kellepto.

She just smiled and showed me a gold coin, "I know you don't believe in the Gold Faerie," she explained. "But he does. I figured if this is all it costs to buy him a little joy, why not? He's now got a lucky rock, and we can donate the coin to charity."

I didn't like the situation, but I couldn't argue that this made Garrot happy. "So be it," I sighed. "Why couldn't you make up something more useful, like the Hot Breakfast Faerie?"

Entry 11

No matter how skilled, brave, or lucky you are, when your time is up, it is up. This concept was on display when we got hired to clear out the fiery volcanic dungeon of Windbelly the Mad. We had fought everything you could think of- ash ghouls, cave trolls, one nagging harpy, and an endless army of orcs. I used Abbott, my magical sword, to slice through many of these beasts. Footpalm, on the other hand, crushed many orc skulls with his trusty bone staff. Kellepto and Garrot kept to our marching order and fought from the back with arrows and various spells. To top things off, we had a local legend traveling with us, whose name was Clickchain.

This impatient warrior was a fighting force and I learned a lot from him as he fought beside Aiden the Cleric. He would handle each challenge with bravado, and a "never say die" attitude. His chainmail armor showed that, too. It was slashed, rusty, and blood splatted. That is, except for the insulated plate mail glove he wore on his left hand; which, he lovingly called Sparky. A few times a day, he told us he could grasp an enemy and send a high voltage charge through them, causing them a great deal of harm, if not outright death.

Clickchain seemed to have it all, but then, as I said earlier, it seemed his time was up. After battling a trio of fire skelementals, we came upon a gorge that was twenty-feet wide overlooking flowing lava and with stalagmites shooting up from molten orange liquid. "There has got to be a way across that," I said, looking around.

"Maybe there's a lever or button or something that will open up a secret passage," Kellepto commented, scanning the wall. "Everyone, take a look."

Clickchain brushed past the elf and grunted, "Let someone who knows what they're doing take a look."

She wasn't too happy about him doing that and shot me look. I just gave her one my confident smiles, and she rolled her eyes, as if to say "whatever." "Give me a hand," Footpalm said, while standing on the ledge of the gorge. "I think I see something up on the wall."

He laid down his bone staff as I walked up to him. That's when Clickchain quickly brushed past me, "I'll get this," he blurted.

Before I could blink, the impatient fighter tripped on the bone staff and slipped over the edge! Talk about a bad roll! "My staff!" shouted Footpalm, as he quickly grasped for his weapon, barely catching it.

I, on the other hand, grabbed for Clickchain. I caught his left hand, but it sent a high voltage of electricity through me that set my hair entirely on end! During this haze of energy, I almost blacked out, but when my vision cleared, I realized that my hand was still clasping Clickchain's glove, but the brash fighter's hand was no longer in it!

We couldn't believe it. The impatient fighter we stood by only moments ago was now gone! Pulling myself up and away from the edge of the gorge, with hair still smoking, I slipped Sparky on my left hand. I was determined to finish the mission with, at least, part of Clickchain still involved. "I can't believe it," Aiden said, shaking his head. "He didn't even die in battle. I'm shocked!"

"Not as much as I was," I stated, patting at the smoke coming from the top of my head.

We finished the adventure, even though Windbelly the Mad escaped by turning into a vaporous cloud, before disappearing. I swore I'd find him and bring him to justice for Clickchain. I didn't like the thought of his memory disappearing into a puff of smoke.

<hr />

Entry 12

One of the craziest things about living in the Unremembered Realms is that, sometimes, you don't have to look for adventure, it finds you. Like this one time, my party stopped in Hollowood, the realms' biggest city of entertainment, for a bit of rest and relaxation. We had all parted ways and agreed to meet back up at the Planet Hollowood Tavern after a few days.

When we all met at the agreed time, we noticed that our mage, Garrot the Asphyxiator, hadn't shown up. "That's unusual," Footpalm said, while pushing away his unfinished stew. "It feels weird eating a meal without him hovering over my shoulder, asking for the leftovers."

We waited until noon. Then, we decided to look for him. The mage was not only handy to have in our party, but he had become a good friend. After an hour of looking around, we cut through an alley behind a large theater and appeared on Hollowood Boulevard. Hundreds, if not thousands, of realmsians were going about their daily business. I almost gave up hope of finding the magic-user, but then Kellepto grabbed my shoulder and pointed across the street. "There he is," she stated.

"All I see is a couple of cult guys passing out flowers," I replied.

"I know," she said, "and he's one of them!"

I couldn't believe it! It was our mage, alright. Garrot had shaved his head and was wearing orange robes. He was even wearing some kind of crown made up of plants! As we approached him, he turned to us with a dazed expression, before giving us a broad smile. "At last!" he joyfully exclaimed, "You've come to join me!"

"What in the realms are you talking about, you fool," Footpalm replied, already angry at the mage. "You've joined a cult! Are you out of your spell casting brain!"

Aiden the Cleric chimed in. "Is this what you've been doing? We were looking all over for you! And what's that on your head?"

Garrot smiled and gave us a slight bow. "It is the Vision Plant. It helps us to see tomorrow."

"It's parsley," Kellepto said, plucking a leaf off one.

"Hey," Garrot complained. "You're clouding my visions!"

The other cultist standing next to him placed a hand on his shoulder and smiled. "Be at peace, my brother. We are here to show them to the Trail of Enlightenment."

"Oh, yeah," Garrot said, calming down. "Do you mind if I take your reading?"

"A reading?" I asked. "What is that?"

"It's to see if you're worthy to walk the trail," the other cultist said. "Help them, brother G."

With a quick flick of his wrist and a small grunt, Garrot cast something that made a small glowing aura around us. "Whoa," Footpalm shouted, jumping back. "That better not be some kind of charm. Cuz' I hate charming people!"

"It's just an Aura cantrip," Aiden laughed with a smile. "Every eight-year-old in magic school learned that one."

"It is not," Garrott protested. "It's an Enlightenment Tracker."

"Is too," Aiden said, a bit more determined.

"Is not," the mage shot back.

"It is not about who is right," the other cultist interrupted. "It is about who is wrong."

Garrot looked awed at the wisdom of his fellow cultist. Kellepto shook her head. "You just said the same thing, only backward."

"Did not," the cultist shot back.

"Did too," Kellepto said, getting back in his face.

"Hold on, everyone," I finally cut in. "I want to know what you see in this thing, Garrot. I know you have good intentions, but this isn't the first time some cult has duped you."

"The Blankminds are not a cult," our mage explained. "It is led by Tookus the Bigg, an all-wise ogre who promises to help us find our way to the Belly of Paradise."

"The big Tookus?" I asked. "I've never heard of him."

"It's Tookus the Bigg, you dolt," the other cultist snarled, nearly dropping his parsley crown.

"Well, if he's that big, you think I would have heard of him," I explained, trying to calm the bald man down.

"He's so big, he can't get out of bed," Garrot explained. "The chosen Prophets of Tookus bring him his food, and he gives them wisdom, or allows them to enter in the Belly of Paradise, where we all hope to be, someday."

Kellepto motioned for me to bend down, so she could whisper in my ear. "Let's play along," she said, quietly. "We'll never get Garrot back if we don't go see what's going on and expose it."

"I hope we can," I whispered back. "I'm not wearing parsley on my head."

After whispering our plan to Aiden and Footpalm, they reluctantly agreed, and we all pretended to be impressed with our auras being read. Garrot and his new friend were thrilled and led us out of town and down a hidden trail that led to a small compound with a few homes and some other cultists mulling about.

We followed a few carrying some trays of strange smelling meat and entered the most prominent house in the middle of the compound. I held the door for one of the food carriers and noticed that the pungent food had a ring of parsley on top of it. Within moments, Garrott and his fellow cultist were introducing us to Tookus the Bigg.

The immensely overweight ogre had converted the living room into his private bedchambers. It was obvious he was too large to go up the stairs to the bedrooms, anymore. As a matter of fact, I doubted he could fit through the double doors leading outside, anymore either! Kellepto held her nose at the smell in the room, and Footpalm just stood there wide-eyed, as the giant creature quickly slurped down the contents of one of the heaping trays.

After a long belch, the creature used a hoist system of pulleys and rope to help him sit up. "Welcome to paradise, friends," he began. "I assume you're here to seek a new path. One with a glorious destination!"

One of the ogre's fat rolls shifted, and a human hand fell out onto the floor with a splat. "Oh," he exclaimed, "Come here, you little tidbit!"

He quickly picked it up and stuffed it into his mouth. "Oh, that's good," was all he could say, as he slowly chewed with a smile on his face.

"Did he just eat a human hand?!" Aiden shouted, turning to Garrot, who stood there with his mouth open.

"Of course not," Garrot stuttered, "Tookus is all-wise and kind; he would never do that…"

Tookus belched again, after a big swallow. "Oh, yes I did! Hey recruit, can you come give me a hand?"

Garrot's face turned red, as we all stared at him. It was at this point he understood that he had been duped. "But they said I could end up in the Belly of Para….oh. Never mind."

He then turned to his cultist friend. "When you said Tookus was eating all his profits, I thought you meant something else, entirely!"

"Hey, big fella," Tookus interrupted, looking at me. "Wanna join the group?"

"Ummm, no thanks," I politely declined. "It already looks like you have enough on your plate!"

The ogre didn't reply; he just turned to the next plate and started gorging himself. "You are not allowed to leave the Blankmind Prophets," Garrot's orange-robed friend stated, arrogantly. "We serve a higher cause!"

Garrot turned to the man and punched him in the face. His eyes rolled back and he crumpled to the floor. Garrot turned around and began to apologize. "I'm sorry, gang, I really thought I found something here."

"Don't worry about it; this kind of thing happens to everyone once-in-a-while," I said, consoling him. "C'mon, I'm getting a little hungry, I'll treat you to lunch."

As we all left, we could hear the ogre. "Hey, pass me that unconscious prophet….and the salt!"

Entry 13

Playing by the rules isn't always the easiest thing to do. Yet, as a paladin, I've sworn to uphold the law and do my best to make sure justice is served, but sometimes, the system can be corrupted by unscrupulous attorneys who'll do anything to make a few more coins, even if they have to use slimy tactics to do it.

For instance, there was this one time my party and I were sought out by a small-town sheriff. He wanted us to handle a situation where an ogre named Organmash the Jolly was coming into his village and pounding its occupants into jerky, before gobbling them up. His evil sidekick, a gnoll horseman named Cowling, would rob the people as the ogre made a quick lunch of them.

After disguising a very angry Footpalm as a child, we had Kellepto disguise herself in a drab farmhand outfit. "Why do I have to be the child?" the dwarf pouted. "I have a beard!"

"Maybe you're very childish," Kellepto commented, intending to poke fun.

The red-faced dwarf waved his finger in her face, growling "No, you are!" he yelled, before crossing his arms and kicking some dirt.

Aiden, Garrot, and I hid in a small hut, ready to jump out and apprehend the giant creature. It didn't take long before we heard the trotting of a horse. It was Cowling, riding a white bronco. Footpalm and Kellepto kept their backs to him, pretending to work in a garden, so our targets wouldn't get suspicious. "Excuse me," Cowling began. "My friend and I are famished."

"Famished," repeated a deeper voice.

Kellepto and Footpalm turned around, revealing who they were. "Whoa," Cowling remarked. "That's one ugly kid!"

Footpalm shouted, "Hey!" before Kellepto whipped out her crossbow and fired at Organmash as he began to stride forward.

He didn't even pay attention to the rest of us, as we rushed out from the hut, ready to fight! The ogre was bigger than described and wore a bloodied scalemail gauntlet on his right hand. The bolt from the crossbow stuck in Organmash's thigh, and he paused for a moment to try to pull it out. I was able to clothesline Cowling off his horse, before he even realized we had snuck up on him. He hit the ground hard, getting the wind knocked from him.

The angry ogre punched Aiden, and then kicked Garrot, before they could get any spells off. I socked the monster in the face; which, caught him off guard. Footpalm followed up with a few punches using his Bracers of Strength, while Kellepto reloaded her crossbow. The ogre knew he was in trouble when Cowling jumped on his bronco and started riding the white horse in retreat! Organmash tried jumping on the horse, also, but was too large and ended up crushing both it, and its rider.

With a badly swelling eye, the ogre looked up at us from the ground, first at me, then at Footpalm. "Ugly kid," was all he managed to mutter, before the infuriated dwarf punched him again, knocking him out cold.

Later, in the courtroom, we all sat watching as a silver Dragonborn named Silvertongue argued before the jury, defending Organmash the Jolly. "If the gauntlet doesn't fit, we must acquit!" he emphatically stated.

The pesky Dragborn smiled, as the ogre awkwardly tried misplacing the gauntlet over his hand, before shrugging and smirking at the jury. Silvertongue worked for Boldfibb, Pinchpurse, & Stretchlaw, a legal firm that specialized in getting criminals off the hook.

"He was trying to eat us!" yelled Footpalm from the audience.

"My client was there only looking for food," Silvertongue hissed. "Your group was hired by the sheriff to investigate the situation, not become vigilantes!"

"Me was hungry," Organmash said, innocently, with his eyes lowered to the jury. "Me lowly orphan."

Murmuring erupted in the jury box, before most of them turned to look at us with disapproving faces. I just shook my head in disbelief. By the end of the trial, Organmash the Jolly had been set free! To make things worse, the judge fined my party for taking the law into our own hands. He also remarked that Footpalm was behaving childishly. "I am not!" demanded the dwarf before running out of the courtroom, smashing his fist in the wall.

Later on, as we had lunch at a tavern a few blocks away, the bailiff burst through the doors, telling us that the judge was demanding to see us. Apparently, Organmash had decided to celebrate his victory by eating some of the jury and other employees at the courthouse, before taking off. Footpalm said he'd talk to the magistrate on our behalf.

When the curmudgeonly dwarf came back an hour later, he was all smiles. "Well, how did it go?" I asked.

The monk smiled and cracked his knuckles. "Everything is just fine," he began. "I just had to lay down the law!"

Entry 14

There's almost nothing worse than sleeping in your party's campsite and being woken by the alarm from whoever was on watch, especially if you were having a good dream about breakfast! I remember this one time where it happened, it was on our way to Omer, in the Province of Far-long. By the time I hopped to my feet, I could hear the not-so-friendly growl of a creature most of us all knew and feared...a troll!

Everyone knows that trolls are tough to kill because they regenerate so fast. Plus, it's hard to dodge around those razor-sharp claws! If it wasn't for their absolute fear of fire, I think we'd have all been killed. All of my party, except Garrot, grabbed a burning log from the fire and held the creature at bay, so the wizard could prepare his Ball of Fire spell.

"Do you have to dance around like a monkey?!" Footpalm said, exasperated. "Just cast the spell!"

"Are you a spellcaster?" Garrot shot back as he flopped his arms about flinging bits of spell components everywhere.

I have to admit; Garrot was the only wizard I knew who seemed to exaggerate his motions in his spellcasting. I didn't know if it was a cry for attention or if sorcery made him extremely itchy. Finally, the fiery ball shot from the wizard's hands and hit the troll square in the chest with a loud "foomphf."

The troll screamed for a minute before stopping, dropping, and rolling on the ground. After getting the flames to die out, the beast stood back up, howling in rage. "Do you smell that?" Aiden said. "Something smells delicious!"

Footpalm agreed by nodding his head. "Yeah, yeah, that's amazing!"

Kellepto sat down her bow. "Wait a minute," she said, quickly reaching into her pack.

She pulled out a Manual of Monsters book she kept and flipped through the pages, while we kept the smoldering monster at bay. "Aha," she stated, wavering a finger in the air. "This isn't a normal troll. It's a Rosemary Troll."

"What kind of troll is that?!" Aiden asked.

"It says here, that when cooked, they smell of the Rosemary spice," she began. "It also says they go well with a side of applesauce and some bread stuffing."

We all started drooling and licking our lips. The troll lowered its claws, slowly, and backed up a step. "Um," it growled in a coarse, guttural voice, "Me forgot to lock door on cave…"

It did manage to get away, but not before a long chase. Footpalm was disappointed, he had wondered if the troll tasted anything like a basilisk, one of his personal favorites.

<hr>

Entry 15

My party and I had seen a lot in our adventures, but hadn't seen it all, until the time we were in the Realm of Gaspenfall, traveling just north of the Barrendry desert. The area was lush and perfect for vegetation, so it had become a place with a large number of farms. The people of the area were usually peaceful, but when we had stopped in a village called Forkroad to figure out which direction to take, an angry group of its farmers approached us.

Once they saw that I was a paladin, they surrounded us, immediately demanding justice for something. By the time my party and I got them to calm down, one volunteered to be their spokesman. "Our crops aren't growing," the farmer complained. "I can't prove it, but we all think a dirt rustler is stealing our precious manure."

"Maybe it's just a bad year," I offered. "I don't know much about farming, but I know there are off years."

The farmers shook their heads. "That's not it at all," the spokesman explained. "There's a certain wizard who moved here last year. His name is El Chia, and we think he's the culprit!"

Yells of agreement filled the air, along with some hisses at the mention of the name. They weren't happy when Footpalm told them the idea of a dirt rustler was the dumbest thing he had ever heard. Farmers weren't much of a threat, but they were holding sharp-looking pitchforks; which, are something I don't want to experience because of the loudmouth dwarf!

"What can we do to help?" I quickly cut in, stepping in front of the feisty monk, hoping they wouldn't mob us in their frustration.

Their spokesman, a dwarf named Gourdan, asked us to stand guard over his freshly manured field for a few nights to see if anything unusual happened. We agreed and followed the farmer back to his place. My party did not mind helping, all except for Footpalm. "Something about this manure doesn't smell right," he kept mumbling.

The first night at the farm went without incident. We slept in shifts, while two stayed awake for a couple of hours, patrolling the freshly laid fields. Sure, the strong odors were hard to deal with, but the farmer's wife, Fertrude, had a large meal waiting for us the next morning that was always fresh and steaming.

Gourdan loved to talk about fertilization techniques; he claimed to be a real entremaneur. He could use any animal dropping you could think of to grow great tasting vegetables. All the talk of manure made Aiden set down a carrot he was about to eat. This gesture made the farmer laugh. "Hey," he said jovially, animal business is big business around these parts!"

Gourdan explained to us that all their trouble began when El Chia moved into the area the previous year to join the Forkroad farming community. "The old guy seemed likable enough, so we gave him pointers," the farmer stated, while chewing on a biscuit. "The mistake was telling him that proper manure mixing is the secret to successful farming. Each farmer in Forkroad has a secret formula. Mine works best for squashes and pumpkins. "

"I thought everyone knew that," Kellepto commented.

"Not him," the farmer's wife cut in. "He spent his whole life casting spells and developing all sorts of powerful magic. When he retired to his new farm, he was a fish out of water."

"He had no cows," Gourdan chimed in. "And he still doesn't. That's why everyone's suspicious of his large fields covered with fresh manure. He says he's using some kind of manure magic; which, would be fine, but everyone else's keeps disappearing!"

"No, crap," Footpalm stated.

We didn't know if the monk was stunned or stating the obvious. "How in the realms could an old wizard like that be stealing manure?" Footpalm asked. "That's an awful lot of work."

"That's what you're here to find out," the farmer stated. "He's up to something, that's for sure. I know because whenever anyone sees him, there's not one speck of dirt under his fingernails!"

The tale had us curious, now, so we all decided to stay here until we could solve the dirt rustling mystery. Besides, the home-cooked meals sat very well! I enjoyed Fertrude's vegetable juice she called Squashies; which, was three types of squash she blended with some goats milk. The second night went without incident. But, when it came down to the third, something surprising happened. Aiden woke me from a deep slumber and pointed to the field. "Look," he whispered.

A magical blue haze covered the ground and began to pulsate. We woke the rest of the party and watched as all the manure of the field started to congeal itself together, forming into dozens of golems! "Nightmairds," Kellepto stated, "That's what I'm going to call them, quickly sketching their likeness in her Manual of Monsters.

The creatures started marching off Gourdan's farm and onto the dirt road, right in the direction of El Chia's. "Well," I said. "Let's go stop them!"

"Hold on," Garrot stated. "I think I have a cunning plan."

The wizard pointed at me, while whispering into Kellepto's ear, and a crooked grin grew on her face as she looked at me. "I'm beginning to have a bad feeling about this," I mumbled.

Garrot flailed around for a minute like he had ants in his pants, chanting something, then raised an arm with his hand open, aiming in the direction of the last Nightmaird in line. With a vein in his forehead pulsing, he slowly squeezed his hand shut. His targeted creature froze in place. Its arms and legs crushed up into itself, and then it crumbled into a manurery pile. Relieved, Garrot wiped some sweat from his forehead.

"Great job," Aiden stated, patting the mage on the back. "But, there's still over two dozen left."

"That's okay," Garrot stated. "I only needed to squeeze out one big one!"

He then whispered something to Aiden, who turned to me with a big smile. I did not like the vibe I was getting, one bit. I soon found out what all the grins were about. "I don't see why I have to be the one going in undercover," I complained, as I stripped down to my underpants.

"Because you're the only one as big as them," Footpalm said, grabbing two fistfuls of manure and slathering me with it."

"This is awful," I complained, "The smell is burning my nose!"

"Get his nose," Kellepto said, a little too gleefully.

Within fifteen minutes, I was covered head-to-toe and gracefully catching up to the other Nightmairds. I hoped this ruse worked. We had to know if El Chia was the culprit behind all this! It didn't take long until all our suspicions were confirmed. After a half-hour of walking, the horde approached El Chia's farmhouse, I could see the mage in some overalls, rising from a rocking chair on his porch. "Welcome home, my pets," El Chia said, happily.

Walking off the porch, he grabbed a basket of corn seeds and approached the waiting formation of manure men. He addressed his new troops, while throwing the corn seeds at them, where they would sink in. "When you are fully seeded," he began, "I'll need you to lie down in the open field to our north."

He stopped when he got to me. "Hey," he said, slowly. "You're kind of a puny one. I better use better spell components next time."

"You shouldn't take other's crap," I said as I grabbed him, placing him in a chokehold.

The stunned wizard didn't know what to do and only flailed about for a minute, before finally realizing he couldn't break my hold. "My work here is not complete," he groaned.

"Well, it's time to pinch this little scam off," I warned. "Or my arm might pinch a little tighter!"

I could feel El Chia give up his fight against me, and he slowly mumbled a few words. All around me, hundreds of Nightmairds rose from the ground. Some were covered in half-grown plants. "My pets," the thieving wizard gasped. "You've soiled my plans!"

The Nightmairds were ordered to return to the farms from which they came. I ended up using a bit of rope from the farm to tie El Chia's hands. Gourdan, Fertrude, and my party were very happy to see me, as I brought the wizard forward through all the Nightmaids who were now finding their old spot and lying down.

"I hate to admit it, Garrot," I said, "but it was a good plan."

"It was more than a good plan," Gourdan stated, scooping a sprouting seed of corn from my shoulder. "It's good business!"

Entry 16

People often ask my party and me why we don't travel with a ranger. Our united response is always "Jengars!"

Jengars was a gangly elf who traveled with us for a bit. He was always nervous about something or another and tended to fall apart whenever a thing happened. Piece by piece, his nerves would build up, until he finally collapsed. Then he'd disappear for a while, until he got himself together, again. I don't blame the poor guy too much, though; there was a reason for his tension.

Early on in his adventuring career, Jengars found an Orbiting Stone; which, is a small, pebble-sized magical item that floats around the owner's head. It grants the owner a magical ability, depending on the kind of stone it is. Garrot warned me never to use Orbiting Stones. I guess back in his Wizarding Guild days, some classmates found some and were always using them after class. They would pressure him to try one, but he just said no. Garrot referred to these Orbiting Stone users as "Rock Heads" because they became too addicted to the stones' magic.

Each Orbiting Stone has a unique power, and unfortunately for Jengars, his first stone's only ability was an addiction to finding even lousier Orbiting Stones. The one he found after that made him attractive to bees; which, was inconvenient, to say the least. Next, Jengars got one that's only power was to change color with his moods. Then, there was the Blame Stone. Its power caused him to blame others when he would break wind. I always wondered if this was the power of the stone or not, because he tended to do that before he found this particular little floating pebble.

The one that got on Footpalm's nerves was the Orbiting Stone of Grand Entrances. I don't know how many surprise attacks were ruined when Jengar would, all of a sudden, jump out from our hiding place and shout, "Ta-da!" This type of behavior became even worse when he found a Jazz Hands Stone.

By the time Jengars was asked to leave our party, he had over fifty of these annoying stones orbiting his head at all times. It always looked as if he had a beehive hairdo. We all felt bad, except for Footpalm the Elflinger, about asking him to leave, but his useless orbiting stones were driving us crazy. Footpalm volunteered for the job of firing the poor sap and met with him privately to discuss the situation. When Footpalm returned, he had a great big smile on his face. "How did it go?" I asked.

"Everything is cool. Jengars took it well and understood," the dwarf explained, while cracking his knuckles. "If we ever need him, he'll be just a stone's throw away!"

Entry 17

One of the most exciting things about being a paladin is that you'll eventually meet all the crazies who populate the realms. There was a time in Neverspring when my friend, an overweight Half-orc name Dunlapp, asked me to fill in for him at his job. He had just become sheriff and had to leave town for the night for some business.

He knew I was a former Redeye Knight and didn't have a problem staying up all night and through the morning. "Be prepared," he warned. "This is when all the weirdos come out. Just last week, some fool rogue must have snuck in a mattress gremlin. It tore up the whole department!"

I reassured him that it would be fine, and he left, wishing me luck. Everything was going great, until about halfway through my shift when a group of deputies brought in three individuals, who had been fighting at a local tavern. As I walked over to inspect them, one of the constables explained. "They're all Rhuddist Monks, and they're pretty much regulars here."

All three grinned and nodded at me through swollen lips. "The first one's name is Rook," the constable explained, while the silent monk raised his fist to acknowledge it. "He started the fight by punching Draper."

The second monk nodded an affirmative and held up a flat open palm to me. "Who is the third one?" I asked.

"He is called Incisors," the constable explained, "and although he claims to be peaceful, he bites a lot."

The monk held up two fingers showing me a peace sign. Before I could nod and acknowledge the peaceful gesture, Incisors quickly lifted his leg, kicking Draper in the face. Before we broke up the scuffle, Inscissors beat Draper, Draper beat Rook, and Rook beat Incisors. "This always happens," one of the worn-out constables explained, holding back

Draper. "This is going to be a long night!"

By the time I got them registered and placed in three separate cells, they had two more skirmishes. What was fun to them was a whole lot of paperwork for me. That's when an idea hit me. I could make their squabbles into a game! I quickly stood up and rushed to where they were being kept. They listened intently, as I showed them the game.

For Rook, I held up a fist. For Draper, I held out my flat open palm, and for Incisors, I did the peace sign. I showed them on the count of three to do their hand sign. Rooks would beat Incisors, Incisors beating Draper, and Draper's beating Rook's. I told them they didn't have to use their own hand sign, and it was all a game of elimination. As ultraviolent Rhuddist Monks, they found this quite fun.

By the time that Dunlapp returned in the morning, the three monks were discharged without further incident. The sheriff was impressed and asked how I did it. "Oh, it was nothing," I replied. "They just needed a hand and to calmly count to three."

Entry 18

One of my favorite times as a kid was when Winterfest rolled around. After a bedtime story, our father would send us three kids to bed with promises of gifts and cookies in the morning. I could hardly wait because I could smell my mother baking them in the kitchen.

Then, one year, I woke up in the middle of the night on the kitchen floor, with crumbs all over my face. When my father heard the noise, he came in to investigate. "This must be the work of Buddy Olchum, the notorious cookie thief," he told me.

This was the first time I had heard of this culprit; I needed to know more! According to Father, Buddy would fill his pockets with goodies, just like I had, to sneak back to his hideout and distribute them amongst all the other Elflings who were craving sweets. I was shocked. And although my tummy ached, I felt it was my duty to stop this treat thief!

My father tossled my hair, sent me back to bed, and told me to quit sleepwalking. I couldn't sleep the rest of the night, it seemed, knowing that Buddy Olchum was out there somewhere, nabbing baked goodies from all around the realms.

Now that I was older, I swore an oath to bring this neer-do-well to justice. The first time I came close was when I was in Hollowood during the Winterfest activities. I knew sugary treats were a weakness for the rogue, so I convinced my party to pay a visit to Footpalm the Elflinger's older brother, Gobstop the Jawbreaker because he owned a sweet shop. "I can't wait to fling a 'ling," the feisty dwarf euphorically dreamed out loud, "...If Buddy Olchum is real."

"I'll prove he really exists, tonight," I told Footpalm, raising a fist triumphantly in the air. "Or my name isn't Nimbus 'Stormcloud' Slumberdim!"

I waited for a group cheer, but everyone just stood around looking at me. After Kellepto yawned, I lowered my fist and muttered as we entered Gobstop's store. The two brothers were happy to see each other and embraced in a big hug. Then, we each shook Gobstop's oversized hand. I noticed the dwarf had an iron grip, as well. "Why do you think they call me the "Jawbreaker," he said happily, lightly punching his right fist into his left palm.

After explaining our plan, Gobstop was on board. "I don't know if he's real or not, but if he's a stealer of treats, that's bad business for me!"

That night, we sat out a plate of freshly baked chocolate chip cookies, one of my favorites, in the middle of the shop. Then, we waited and waited. I kept smelling the cookies as the night wore on- so fresh! I knew they'd be soft still, so I thought, what could it hurt if I just sampled one? I snuck out into the shop, laid a silver coin on the counter, grabbed a cookie, and tasted it. It was absolutely the best cookie I'd eaten in a long time. Before I knew it, I had cleared the plate and was picking crumbs from my beard.

"Ha, ha, ha," came a laugh from outside the large glass window in the front of the shop.

I quickly spun around on my heel, with my hand on my claymore's handle. It was Buddy Olchum! I could see his silhouette in the moonlight, pointing at me and doing his famous laugh. A handful of elflings were peering in, as well, with their smiling faces pressed up against the glass. "Buddy Olchum!" I yelled, "It's Buddy Olchum!"

I heard a commotion in the back, so I turned around to see my party and Gobstop running from where they had been sleeping. They had their weapons ready, but were still rubbing the sleep from their eyes. I pointed to the window and shouted: "There he is; it's Buddy Olchum!"

Aiden, the cleric, clutching Pepper, his mace, peered out the window. "I don't see anyone."

"It's true," I claimed. "Buddy was really here, and I saw the elflings, too!"

I could see the excitement drain from their faces, as they looked at me more closely, noticing the crumbs in my beard. "And I suppose he ate the cookies, too?" Kellepto said, frowning.

Blushing, I turned to Footpalm and Gobstop. "Yes, yes, I ate the cookies. But you have to believe me," I said, frustrated. "Perhaps we could set another trap, and bring him back!"

"Maybe set out more treats," Garrot said, rolling his eyes and adjusting the sleeping cap on his head. "Perhaps this Buddy of yours would like some milk, too?"

"Yes, yes, that's good, that's great!" I replied, before realizing that they didn't believe me.

In the end, they all groaned and went back to bed. I couldn't, though. I couldn't sleep knowing that the infamous rogue was still out there. I knew he was real, and that someday I would bring him to justice! Plus, I wanted more cookies.

Entry 19

Once my party and I decided to eat at Auntie Omerta's Tavern in Omer. Garrot had noticed the sign out front and thought it looked pretty good. The painted image showed a chubby, dark-haired gnomish woman holding a dish of pasta and smiling.

After being seated, we were given menus and left alone. There were a couple of other patrons, but they sat in the back in a dark corner. It seemed strange that such a lovely place would be so empty during lunch hours. After a short bit, a gnome with dark, greased back hair came over to take our order. "My name is Gratzy," he began. "I take da orders, eh?"

"Where's all the other customers?" Kellepto asked. "It seems like such a nice place."

The gnome lowered his quill for a moment and looked over his shoulder, before whispering, "There wasa the incident," he began. "Inna booth three."

We looked over and saw a bunch of crossbow bolt holes in the wood of the bench and table. "It wasa some kinda accident. A local fooda critic, he'a dint lika da last dish."

I leaned forward, lowering my menu. "So, what happened?"

"I doan know the details, budda wagon drove by, and before we know, badda boom, this guy's bleeding all over my clean floors," he explained. "We doan like to talka bout it, you know?"

I believe he would have told us more, but I noticed Auntie Omerta glaring at the waiter from the kitchen window. Her thick eyebrows furrowed. Gratzy quickly stuttered, "I take-a your order now, see?"

We placed our order according to our budget. "Now, that shouldn't be more than two gold coins and a silver," I told Garrot, who was writing down all the costs in his notebook.

The wizard seemed impressed. "The prices here seem reasonable," he said, pointing out the appetizers to Footpalm.

The miserly spellcaster kept track of all of our adventuring expenses, so he could write it off at the end of the year on our taxes. "Dona forget da safety fee," Gratzy stated, watching the mage.

"Safety fee," Aiden stated. "What is that?"

"Cooking and waiting is dangerous," the gnome stated. "Who knows what could happen to youra poor innocent fooda on the way out, eh?"

I didn't like the sound of this, but my stomach was growling due to the smells emanating from the kitchen. "Just pay whatever it is," I said. "I'm starving!"

Garrot was not happy about the hidden fee, but we went ahead and placed the order. After a short bit, the food came out, and it was delicious! Auntie Omerta even came out, herself, and kept putting more food on my plate. "Eat! Eat! You are a bigga boy!"

After the feast, Gratzy brought out the bill, and Garrot threw a fit. "Eighteen gold! I can't believe it! Look at all these added on fees!"

Gratzy shot a look at Auntie Omerta, and her smile suddenly became dark. "What's a 'bedda fee'?" the old wizard griped.

"It means you 'bedda' pay up," the little gnome stated, giving each of us a quick glare.

"This doesn't seem right," I said, standing up, waving a half-eaten loaf of bread at the smirking waiter.

"Yeah," Garrot stated. "Especially since my dish didn't have nearly enough pesto sauce!"

Auntie Omerta's face turned beet red at the comment, and she grabbed Gratzy by the arm, hauling him back to the kitchen. "Let's just not pay," Kellepto said. "They are a bunch of thieves!"

"No, no," I said. "Let's just pay what the menu said and a few more gold, that way everyone's happy."

As I said those words, a wagon pulled up just outside of our window, and a bunch of crossbow bolts burst through. None of us ducked, because Garrot, knowing the possibility of what could happen, had told all of us he was placing a Shield Spell just on the inside of the glass. The bolts all seemed to stick in place in mid-air before falling to the inside of the windowpane.

We drew our weapons and turned to face Gratzy, who was standing about fifteen feet away. He was as pale as a ghost, and water began to drip from his pant leg. "Itza on da house, youza lovely customerz!"

At that moment, Auntie Omerta came around the corner, not knowing we were standing there. "Call your cousin Matzy to clean up the bod…"

It was the last thing she said before freezing in her tracks after seeing us standing there. She fainted on the spot. Gratzy rushed over and caught her, slowly lowering her to the floor, where he began waving a handkerchief in her face.

I almost felt bad turning them into the local authorities, because the food was so good. "Why does everything I like to eat have to be so bad!" I lamented.

"Fuggedaboudit," Kellepto said, trying to comfort me as we left the jailhouse. "I'll buy you some dessert to take your mind off of this. Earlier today, I saw a place called Fat Tony's Bakery just down the road."

Entry 20

After finishing a nice meal at the Drooling Tuna Tavern in Port Laudervale, my group was approached by an oddly dressed human who claimed to be a cleric. It looked like he had piece-mealed together his armor from plate, scale, and leather. He stated that his name was Ploy, and he was looking to hire a team of adventurers to solve a local mystery.

"I don't trust him," Kellepto whispered in my ear. "He doesn't seem very cleric-y."

Ploy explained that workers were missing from the docks down at the Snagginhook Piers. Snagginhook was a fishing company that was notorious in Port Laudervale for its run-ins with the D&R, which is short for the Docks & Rivers, a local law enforcement group. "It's killing all the business," he stated with a concerned look. "Can you help us? Port Laudervale would surely be in your debt."

We excused ourselves, momentarily, and formed a huddle. Everyone agreed it was worth looking into, except Kellepto. "I'm getting a bad vibe off him," she said, tucking a stray piece of her long dark hair behind a pointy ear. "But as usual, it looks like I'm going to be out-voted!"

I gave her one of my best grins, and she reluctantly placed her hand out into the middle of our circle. The rest of us followed suit, before returning to our table and letting Ploy know that we accepted the challenge. Ploy grinned and gave us the address. The cleric said it was best to wait until sundown because that's when most of the others had begun to vanish.

Later, as the sun had lowered in the sky, we began to patrol the pier, looking for clues. "Do you see anything unusual?" I asked Aiden, who was kneeling at the end of one of the docks.

"I'm no ranger," he began, "but even I can see that this is a clue!"

I bent down and noticed that all over the wood was a dried bit of slime that was in a swirling pattern. Garrot came over and looked at it, too. "It looks like an octopus tentacle slid across here. A giant one!"

"Either that or its one of Footpalm's bad attempts at art," Aiden whispered.

"I heard that!" the dwarf shouted from the next pier.

Aiden couldn't resist pushing the dwarf's buttons. "I'm not saying your paintings are bad, but that last one looked as if a plumberhulk snorted up all of your paint and then sneezed on a canvas," Aiden laughed, loudly.

"How did you know how I did that?!" the dwarf shouted back in surprise. "Listen here, cleric. You need to keep your big nose out of my studio, and furthermore…."

Before the dwarf could say another word, a giant black tentacle rose from the dark water and wrapped itself around Aiden's waist! Garrot and I couldn't even grab our weapons, because we felt the firm grip of other tentacles wrapping themselves around us! "Help!" Garrot cried out to Kellepto and Footpalm, who were looking at us with mouths agape. "We're being suctioned off!"

"Hold on!" Kellepto cried out, shaking off the shock and pulling Footpalm by his tunic. "We're coming!"

I managed to activate Sparky, my Powerglove, to shock the thing, but it only loosened it just a little. As I tried again, the creature's head rose from beneath the water. The octopus's eyes were black and unblinking. I used the fear that I felt at that moment to fuel my rage, and with that, I was able to push out of its grasp, and I fell about ten feet into the water. As I was falling, I noticed that Aiden had passed out and was limply dangling in the grip of the giant creature.

The water was cold and dark, but it only took a moment before I was able to raise my head above it to see what was going on. The first thing I noticed was Kellepto on the dock with Footpalm. She was pointing at the creature.

"There's someone invisible on top it's head!" Kellepto cried out while reaching for us. "I can see their body shape with my infravision!"

When I looked up, I witnessed Ploy the Cleric become visible, as he released his spell. He was riding on top of the creature's head! On one of his fingers was a glowing ring. It was now evident that he was magically controlling the gigantic sea creature with it!

"Wave goodbye to your friends, rubes!" Ploy shouted, gleefully, as he commanded the octopus to kill us. "I can't wait to pawn your stuff at the nearest Flip-N-Wink! Perhaps, if you survive, we can go out for a fling, eh elf?"

"Sure thing," Kellepto replied. "But why wait?"

Kellepto turned to Footpalm and said, "You know what to do, Elflinger!"

Footpalm's smile was from ear-to-ear. "I've been waiting a long time for this, lassy!"

The elf rolled her eyes and held her dagger close as the monk grabbed her, spun around a few times, and launched her from the dock, straight at Ploy, who couldn't believe what he was seeing!

The elf plunged her dagger deep into the octojockey's leg, and he screamed out in shock and pain. Both he and Kellepto tumbled off the giant creature and splashed down into the water. The octopus then dove under the water and disappeared, along with Garrot and Aiden.

"Destroy his ring!" Footpalm shouted from the dock. "Before the mage and cleric drown!"

I immediately swam over to Ploy and quickly removed the ring from his finger and tossed it up to Footpalm, who set it down and smashed it with his powerful staff. With a small crackle and a puff of green smoke, the ring now laid smoldering and broken at the dwarf's feet.

With a splash and a few coughs, we could see Garrot rise from the water, holding a still unconscious Aiden. I swam over to help while Kellepto hauled Ploy to the land. When we all got there, it took a few moments to catch our breath. Kellepto had bound the deceitful cleric and had bandaged his leg by the time Aiden came around.

"You had quite a deadly scam going on, cleric!" I stated. "But, your ring is no more!"

"I'm not a cleric, you dolt," Ploy growled. "I'm a rogue!"

I started to gasp in shock at the revelation, but I realized from the look on everyone else's faces that they never believed he was a cleric in the first place. "So, you're not a master of disguise?"

"I'm terrible at disguises," Ploy stated, bluntly.

"No kidding," Aiden said, groggily. "We might have fallen for your dock scam, but none of here actually thought you were a cleric. I mean, your outfit looks like it was pieced together at a local Copperstop store!"

"That's because it was!" he admitted. "You'd have to be blind not to see that!"

Kellepto looked at me with a big grin. "Not a word," was all I managed to say, throwing the injured rogue over my shoulder.

"His name is Ploy," she said, walking behind me and giggling. "I mean, hello!"

I hoped the reward for this rogue would help my party forget this small bit of embarrassment. I was wrong. The real reward, as least to them, was bringing up this faux pas every chance they could.

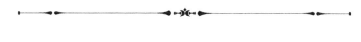

Entry 21

Before Aiden joined my party, I would have to pop into local clerical establishments for healings. Sometimes, I'd go just to tithe; which, lets me demonstrate thankfulness and keeps me grounded in whichever community I'm serving as a paladin. On one of these occasions, while in the city of Tidepool, I decided to drop off a few gold coins before meeting my party at a local tavern.

A local woman wearing a banana bandaged on her head pointed me to the cleric's office just two blocks over from the tavern. I asked if I could help the ailing lady, and she said "no, thank you" because she had just left the clerics office and was already undergoing treatment. I shrugged and said "thank you" before finding my way to the small office she described. It was easy to spot because outside the place was a gnome in a mailman's uniform standing on his head, shouting, "Fresh horses! Fresh horses!"

On the other side of the front door was a skinny man dressed as a farmer with a wooden bucket on his head. He would jump up and down, hitting the bucket with a small metal spoon. The sign above the doorway read "Khandria's Cures". I was starting to think this place was a little strange.

When I opened the door, I walked into a nearly empty waiting room. There was only a little old lady sitting in a corner with small carrots inserted into her ears and one up her left nostril. "How are you?" I asked.

"I've been better," she nasally honked back a little loudly. "My hearing isn't what it used to be!"

"That's because you have carrots in your ears," I politely shouted, before commenting, "Carrots are good for your eyes, not your ears."

"I'm not sticking carrots into my eyes," she replied with a look of disdain. "Are you daft?!"

"The cleric will see you now," the assistant behind the desk cut in. "Just come through the door."

"Gladly," I responded, hoping to get away from the strange old woman in the waiting room.

The clerical assistant led me to a small room and told me the cleric would be in to see me, shortly. Around the room were all sorts of knick-knacks and whatnot. It had everything from fruit & vegetables to baskets full of whistles, colorful string, feathers, and even a jar full of glowing leeches. I reached out and was going to tap the glass, but pulled my hand back when the door opened. Khandria, the Cleric, walked in holding a small chart and a quill.

The little halfling gal had long brown hair; which, she wore in about 50 knots on the top of her head. It appeared as though the knots were trying to contain a small pie plate turned upside down. It was hard to notice her bright blue eyes because her face was covered in all kinds of scribbles made with black ash. Her one eyebrow was shaved, and she was wearing a potato sack that had been dyed purple. She looked me up and down for a moment and declared. "Don't tell me what's wrong, I already know!"

As she went for the jar of leeches, I stood up and said: "Whoa, whoa, I'm only here about donating!"

She stopped and turned around with her only eyebrow raised. "Really? Are you sure? You look terrible!"

"No, no," I replied. "I'm feeling great."

I handed her the sack of coins and gave her a big smile. I knew I had better get out of there quickly. But, before I could make it out the door, she handed me a small piece of broccoli tied at the end of a long colorful string. "Take this, just in case," Khandria said, looking concerned. "Do you know what to do with this?"

"I'm afraid to ask," I replied, working my way around her, slowly. I was hoping to make a hasty exit.

"Tie it between your boots," Khandria explained. "It will help rid you of any current pain."

With a sigh, I did what she suggested and shuffled out of her office. Once out of there, I did begin to feel better. It was as if the pain in my backside was gone after leaving Khandria's. With my mission complete, I untied the string with the broccoli and threw it in a nearby trash can.

When I got to the tavern, the rest of my party was already there finishing a meal. I sat down and told them of the silly things that Khandria did, instead of healing anybody of anything. We all shared a laugh, except for Garrot, who sat in awe, then asked if I thought she had anything for indigestion. I told him not to bother, but somehow I knew that he would. On our next dungeon excursion, he spent most of it with peach pits stuck in each armpit and every pocket packed with noodles.

Entry 22

"How come Clerics can heal gaping wounds and wizards can perform world bending magic," Kellepto complained, "yet no one has invented rope that doesn't get tangled the minute you set it down! It's like it ties itself in knots!"

She muttered this while hurriedly trying to untangle the jumbled mess her rope had become. The worst part was that she needed to do it quickly because we were escaping the cave of a giant two-headed Crettin! The creature, whose names were Scarph & Gobble, had captured a local constable's daughter. I managed to free her, throw her over my shoulder, and run!

Sneaking in the place was easy, because of a secret door, but it had become blocked by the Crettin when he discovered us trying to rescue the girl. Scaling the side of Sheercliff was our only choice for escape, so we decided to give it a try. Little did we know that luck was not going to be on our side.

"I knew I should have memorized my Untangle spell this morning!" Garrot stated, while quickly flipping through his spellbook.

"If you don't hurry, Garrot," Kellepto stated, "we're going to need an Unmangle spell!"

By the time the rogue had managed to undo a second knot, Scarph & Gobble emerged from the large cave door; the fearsome creature was holding two giant spiked clubs. "What have we here?" Scarph asked his other head.

"It look like dinner be trying to steal lunch," Gobble laughed, even though he never cracked a smile. "Me can't wait to bite head off juicy looking dwarf!"

"No, me get dwarf," Scarph corrected him. "You got dwarf last time, and don't say you didn't, me still see parts of beard in your teeth!"

"Dwarves are a delicacy," Gobble shot back. "You'd probably cook him in fire, raw dwarf is best."

"That disgusting," Scarph said, rolling his eyes. "You get diseases that way."

Footpalm had heard enough. "Listen, you two. If anybody is going to eat my guts, you better do it right! Can you tell me, do you have any spices in the cave?"

We all caught on that the monk was stalling for time and also providing a distraction. "Do bugs count?" Scarph asked. "Oh, and pebbles. We use those for crunch."

"We also have vat of halfling fat, for greasing pan," Gobble added, "and some paprika."

"That just might work," Footpalm stated. "If you want the ultimate dwarven feast. But if not, go ahead and eat me raw."

Scarph and Gobble started whispering to each other; both were drooling. "Go ahead, show us recipe."

"Nimbus," Footpalm waved at me, while giving me a subtle wink. "Can you give me a hand?"

When I walked up to Footpalm, he started digging around in his backpack. He pulled out a small piece of charcoal. "First," he said while removing his tunic, exposing his chest. "Is you have to know which cut of meat works best with the spices you have. Nimbus, can you mark me up?"

I started drawing patterns on the dwarf's chest. I had no idea what I was doing, but I noticed this utterly enchanted the Crettin. So much so, that Aiden, Kellepto, Garrot, and the girl slowly snuck around the creature without it noticing and ran back into their cave where they could easily make their way back to the secret door exit. The Crettin crouched down to study the made-up pattern.

"Can you guys roast me at an even temperature?" Footpalm asked. "Because you do want a little pink in the middle, and then slightly crisp my outsides. That will give you the ultimate flavor!"

"Me think so," Gobble replied. "When do we sprinkle on dead bugs?"

While the dwarf explained the proper portions for the spices, I slowly backed off and grabbed our rope. "I hope you remember all this," Scarph said, "because he can't repeat it after we kill him!"

"Me mind is like steel trap," Gobble responded. "Nothing get by me!"

That's when I got by him and grabbed Kellepto's rope that she had left and tossed it over the top of them. "What is this?" they both said at once.

Footpalm grabbed two handfuls of his belly fat and said, "Take a look, boys, cuz' that's all your gonna get!"

The dwarf and I then made for the cave opening as fast as we could. "Come back here!" Gobble yelled while the Crettin stood up.

When it started to run, its legs became tangled up in the knotty mess. "What in the realms?!" Scarph said, as he tripped and collapsed onto the ground. "Come back," he yelled. "We didn't order our food to go!"

Entry 23

One of the responsibilities I have as a leader is trying to solve problems between people in my party. I remember one argument between Aiden and Garrot that got especially heated. Aiden had purchased some land to help build a small temple in Achincorn. The wizard, a real pennypincher, as most of them are, was wondering what he had spent.

"Hey, Garrot," Aiden began. "I just purchased a lot."

"I thought you were going to buy something small," the wizard replied.

"I did," the cleric stated. "A lot."

"Humpf," Garrot stated, then leaned over to me, whispering, "Sounds like he spent a fortune."

I just smiled and shrugged.

"It was a lot, wasn't it?" the wizard said, frowning and crossing his arms.

"Didn't you hear me the first time?!" Aiden said, getting frustrated. "That's what I just said!"

"How are you going to start a temple if you spent all the gold?" Garrot said, tersely.

"It's just a lot, so there's plenty left!" the cleric stated, looking at me like, duh…

I knew they were not on the same page, but I didn't care, I found it all quite amusing. I turned in for the night and found them still arguing when I woke up. "I can't believe you two are still arguing about a lot!" I said, shaking my head.

"We quit that fight hours ago," Garrot replied. "Once I found out that he bought the land from a traitor!"

"Nimbus, tell this goofy wizard that all purchases are made through a trader," Aiden said, "I don't think he gets anything I say!"

"Ugh," I said, frustrated. "Can't you just leave Aiden alone?"

"What!?" Garrot said, looking indignant, "I'm not loaning him any money if he can't control his spending!"

Entry 24

I enjoy helping others, but sometimes, even I have my limits. I remember one time I was on my to Dociletoff to meet the rest of my party when I spotted a small campfire burning in the twilight. I could hear the sound of human laughter, so I thought I would ask whoever it was if they wouldn't mind me joining up with them for the night; after all, I explained to them, there was safety in numbers.

"He said numbers," the dark-haired fighter, laughed. "Did you hear that, Beakus?"

"Yeah, yeah, Burkhead," the blonde-haired one dressed as a cleric replied, giggling. "Numbers. Like two."

They both giggled for a while, while I set up just around the perimeter of the fire. "My name is Nimbus Slumberdim, and I'm meeting some friends in Dociletoff. I plan on leaving at the first crack of dawn."

"Crack," Burkhead repeated, before laughing again. "Hey, Beakus, show him your crack of dawn."

Just as Beakus stood up, I waved my hand, "No thanks, guys. I'm good."

I watched the two for a while and wondered how these two survived out in the Unremembered Realms, at all. At one point, a wandering bard strolled by and asked to join us. I enjoyed a few songs by the fellow, but Beakus and Burkhead just made fun of him until the musician finally got fed up and left.

I would have stayed longer, myself, but the two started pulling a stunt I couldn't bear to watch anymore. It all began when Burkhead seemed to get an idea. "Hey, Beakus. You're a cleric, right?"

"Yeah," Beakus replied. "Curing is my middle name."

"I thought Elizabeth was," Burkhead laughed.

"Shut up, Burkhead," Beakus laughed in response, sounding peeved. "Why do you ask. Are you ill?"

"No," the fighter said. "But, your healing powers are magic, right?"

"Ya yuh," Beakus replied, trying to sound suave, "that's right."

"So, if I stuck my hand in the fire, you could heal me?" Burkhead asked with a smile.

The mention of the word "fire," seemed to get the scrawny cleric excited. "Fire!" he repeated with a wide-eyed expression. "Fi-yur!"

Without hesitation, Burkhead stuck his right hand in the fire, grabbing a burning ember. "Ow!" he hollered out, with a pain-filled giggle.

"Whoa!" Beakus laughed. "That was cool!"

"What in the name of a bugbears rump are you doing?!" I said in frustration. "Are you crazy?"

"Watch this," Burkhead laughed as he held his hand out to Beakus, who quickly cast a cure spell. Within moments, the fighter's hand appeared to be back to normal. Although, I don't think that phrase could be used whenever describing anything else about these looneys.

The two couldn't seem to get enough of this and did it over and over again, laughing and giggling the entire time. That is, until Burkhead pulled his hand out one last time, and Beakus stated, "Um, heh heh, huh, huh, I guess I'm all out of my daily allotment of healing spells…"

"Uh…this burns," Burkhead said, wincing in pain while turning to me. "You don't have any healing potions on ya, do you?"

"Ugh," replied, "Why did you keep doing that in the first place?" I said, pulling out Abbott, my cleric soul-possessed claymore sword from its sheath. "My sword has one heal spell left."

A light blue glow emanated from the blade, and when I touched it to his hand, it healed immediately. "So cool," Beakus said in awe.

After this last burn, I had had enough and decided to walk to Dociletoff in the dark. The two seemed innocent enough, but their foolish actions helped me decide it would probably be better if they were left to their own devices. "I have to go, guys," I explained. "I wish you two well."

"He said, go," Burkhead laughed.

"Pththth," Beakus replied, making the raspberry noise, then laughing.

As I walked off in the dark, shaking my head, I swore I could have heard Burkhead shout, "Ow, that burns."

Entry 25

Picking a path is never an easy choice. Do you take the left, center, or right door? If one is locked without some kind of trap, it's probably the wrong choice. So, you must pick the door with the most dangerous and challenging trap, unless, of course, they were using reverse thinking techniques, and you should have stuck with the first one!

"Just make a decision," Aiden said, pressing his knees together. "I really have to use the bathroom!"

"I'm trying, I'm trying," I replied, "Just be grateful that dying orc even pointed out where the restrooms were, at all!"

We had been hired by locals to go into the dungeon of a mage named Nostrildommus, who had a nice sized reward on his head. He had been raiding the local villages and killing anyone in his quest for power. He was known to be a bit of a cruel prankster, too. We found this out the hard way when we discovered that this insane spellcaster thought it was funny to boobytrap all the latrine doors.

His weird sense of humor wasn't so funny to someone like Aiden, who had been cursed with a small bladder, literally! We tried to get the curse removed, but we could never find a cleric powerful enough to do it! I wish someone would explain to me why a powerful wizard would make a Small Bladder Ring in the first place, that's just weird!

"Each door has a trap," Kellepto said, after investigating. "See the carved wooden faces rising out from the doors?"

"Yes," Footpalm replied, approaching one of the faces, "these have bigger noses than Aiden!"

Aiden gave the dwarf a look of disapproval, then Kellepto explained, "That's where the trap mechanisms are located. It looks like one of us will have to pick a nose and see what comes out as a result!"

We all stood staring at Kellepto, who immediately became defensive. "Listen, fellas, I know I'm a rogue, but I'm not sticking my fingers up any of these noses. I am still a lady, after all. Aiden can wet himself, first!"

Rolling his eyes, Garrot marched forward to the door on the left. "Stand aside," he stated. "I'm going to try the one with the biggest nose. It has the biggest nostrils, and it should be easy."

The wizard stuck his hand in the carved head's left nostril up to his wrist and starting digging around, looking for a switch. "is this what it's like for you, Aiden?"

"Very funny," the cleric stated, still sweating in restraint. "Just hurry, please."

The mage chuckled to himself, before letting out a scream, "Aahh!"

When he pulled his hand out, it was covered in a green slime. "Get it off me!" he hollered.

I immediately withdrew Abbott from its sheath and held it over my head. "Not with a sword, Nimbus!" he shouted at me. "You'll cut my hand off!"

Aiden ran by me to cast a cold spell, and the green slime began to gel up. Garrot immediately walked to a nearby wall and wiped the darkening creature on it. "Do you have to wipe it on the wall, Garrot?" Kellepto commented. "That's so gross."

"What else am I supposed to do with it?!" he replied in frustration. "Do you have a Bottomless Box of Tissues?!"

"You know, I sold that two weeks ago," Kellepto replied, "Now, I'm beginning to regret it!"

"Spread out. Let an expert nose picker get this job done," Footpalm said, cracking his knuckles. "I'm the most qualified here for choosing the right door in this dungeon. I am a dwarf, after all. I recognize fine craftsmanship when I see it."

The dwarf went up to the smallest face carving and then reached into his backpack. "Be careful with those nostrils," I warned him. "Big traps can be in the smallest places. So don't blow it."

Footpalm pulled out a small bag of dark powder with a wick hanging out of it. "That, my friend, is exactly what I plan on doing! A little bit of exploding snuff will get this baby open!"

After stuffing each nostril, the dwarf uncoiled the wick a bit and ran it down to the floor. "Is that good wick?" Kellepto asked. "It looks stringy."

"Just cover your pointy ears, elf!" was all he replied before lighting it.

With a quick hiss, the flame shot quickly up the wick and into the nose. The explosion wasn't huge, but it did blow the nose off the carved face, leaving a hole in the door. "Well, what do you know," Footpalm said, walking up to it. "It was a fake door! There's just a wall behind it!"

"That's right, adventurers!" a high-pitched voice spoke from the dark corridor that led us to this area. "And thanks for letting me know where you were. I have so much fun toying with my prey!"

I could see Nostrildommuses's hands light up with an icy blue glow. My party and I took our fighting positions, ready to hold our ground. "You picked the wrong group this time, mage," I said to him.

That's also when I noticed that Aiden was missing. In the end, it didn't matter where he went, though, because when the crazy wizard took a step forward while casting his spell, he slipped and fell on his back! His ice spell was released, hit the ceiling, and ricocheted back down on top of him! He froze himself solid. Garrot walked up to him and tapped him with his foot. "I bet you didn't predict that Nostrildommus!" our wizard laughed.

"I'm glad it worked out," I said, picking up the frozen mage and carrying him over my shoulder. "But we better get this madman to the authorities; it feels like he's already starting to melt!"

"That's not water," Aiden appeared from a dark corner near the corridor entrance. "The room must be off level."

"Are you saying he slipped in a puddle of your…" Kellepto stated, leaving out the last word.

"I had to go," Aiden said. "It's his fault for setting the traps!"

Garrott and Footpalm burst out laughing when they saw the shocked look of disgust on my face. Upon realizing what the wetness was, I shouted, "Eeew!" and dropped the frozen wizard.

Nostrildommus shattered into a few dozen pieces. We all just stood there. "Oops," I muttered before they all turned to me, frowning.

"There goes our reward, Nimbus!" Kellepto growled. "I was going to treat myself to a spa!"

"Sorry," I told her. "But at least we can all be relieved that this threat is over."

Entry 26

The question I am most often asked is why I left the Order of the Redeye Knights and became a paladin. The truth is, I wasn't given a choice. My desire to be helpful can sometimes get the better of me. I loved the city of Lhentil Keep in Dragonshelm, and fought hard as one of its most ardent protectors.

My last day as a Redeye Knight was on a Tuesday. I remember it well because it was trash day. I had just passed my fifth anniversary of being on the force when my partner, Toody, and I got the news that we were supposed to be a color guard at the funeral for the recently deceased city Mayor, Tipton Dover.

Mayor Dover was a jovial little halfling who enjoyed good food, gambling, and dating unattractive humanoid women. Halflings were such weird little creatures that nobody ever gave it a second thought. Tipton died in middle age, so rumors were flying everywhere. Was it a spurned loved interest with poison? Or maybe the mob, settling a score because of his gambling debts? It didn't matter. The public adored him, and our job was to help make sure he was sent off in style.

Toody and I were given our assignment early by Chief Vanetemple, who always seemed to have a headache or bad stomach acid. I think the funeral was getting on the chief's nerves, so we didn't bother to ask any questions about the assignment. We just headed over to Undersod's Cemetery & Funeral Home. We knew we'd be there early, but we wanted to make sure things went extra well being that this was such a high-profile funeral.

A scrawny, pale, and well-dressed elf met us at the door and let us in early, before leaving us to wander while he went to his office. "I need to use the outhouse, Nimbus," Toody mentioned to me while pointing to the door. "You take a look around, and I'll be right back."

After he left, I wandered into a large parlor filled with flowers. "They mustn't have had time to set these up yet," I spoke softly to myself.

I didn't see any casket either, so I assumed they hadn't wheeled Mayor Dover out yet. That's when I heard a tiny buzzing noise. I immediately stiffened up. I had an allergy to bees and got very nervous whenever they were around. Then, I felt it, a small bit of wind passed my face. I panicked, ducking, and bobbling to try to get away, and I accidentally knocked over two flower pots. I grabbed a rolled up piece of paper that I found and was able to shoo the pest out of a nearby open window.

I was quite satisfied with myself until I turned around and saw the mess on the floor that I had created. I didn't think much of the one vase, I just put the flowers back in and tipped it back up. But the other vase didn't have flowers in it at all. It was filled with dust. I assumed the janitor must have left it amongst the other flowers by mistake. Luckily, I found a broom nearby and managed to get almost all of the dust back in. I heard a wagon pulling up out front so, while still carrying the vase, I walked over to the window to see who it was. I was happy to see the trash collectors outside beginning to load their wagon.

"What luck!" I thought to myself, before bolting outside.

I dumped the dust into the back of the wagon and gave the trashman a big thumbs up. I figured the janitor would appreciate me helping out like this. I chatted with the driver for a few minutes while his partner finished loading then waved goodbye as they left. That's when I decided to head back in and maybe help with the flowers. When I stepped inside, though, it was a panic!

The funeral director was running around, shouting while Toody was searching the place, frantically. "The mayor, the mayor. Where is the mayor?" the elf shouted.

"Hopefully at the pearly gates," I said, trying to calm him down.

Toody and the elf both stopped then looked at me. Both were wide-eyed, but then, when they saw I was holding the vase look relieved. "There he is!" the elf almost sobbed. "We thought we lost him!"

Suddenly I realized what I was holding and the blood drained from my face. I looked down into the empty vase and said, "Mayor?"

The elf ran up to me, grabbed the "urn," and began shouting. "Mayor Dover! Mayor Dover! Argh!"

Toody had grown pale too. "Nimbus! Where's the Mayor!"

"I…uh…think he's taking a ride to the dump…" I said, stuttering.

The funeral director fainted, almost falling on his face. Luckily I caught him and lowered the elf to the ground. "I can't believe you emptied Mayor Dover in the trash!" Toody lamented. "What are we going to do?!"

"We got to tell the chief, maybe he can postpone the funeral until we can track down those ashes," I suggested.

"We can't do that!" the funeral director yelled, shooting straight up. "My funeral home will be a laughing stock when the reason for the delay comes out! People were dying to get in here! Thanks to you, they'll be dying to leave!"

"Don't you need a cleric for that?" Toody chimed in.

The director was just about to respond then he jumped up to his feet excitedly. "I've got it! There's is a campsite not too far from here. It's always being used so, if you head down there, you could refill the Mayor's urn from the ashes from one of their campfires!"

"I don't know about that," I said, holding my hands up. "That's not honest."

The director got real close and looked up at me. "Listen, Redeye Knight, this is your fault to begin with!"

"It was an honest mistake," Toody responded. "Nimbus was just trying to help."

"Then he can get the urn filled," the elf said harshly. "We just need it for the funeral. After that, we can track down the real ashes and put them back in. It will all work out, I promise!"

The look on my face told the director I wasn't liking his plan. "Listen, we don't want the Mayors wife to be even more upset, do we? She's already been through enough," the elf added. "So listen. We have thirty minutes, so we have to make a decision right now!"

I reluctantly agreed and ran out the door, looking for the campsite. The thought of the poor widow lady was too much, and I felt it probably would be better for now, and then explain things later to the chief. I ran as quickly as I could over to the campsite that the director had told me about. Lucky for me, it was still early, and all the adventurers were still asleep. Carefully, I removed their pots and pans away from the pit and started scooping up the ashes into the urn as quickly as I could. "Mmm… something smells good," I mumbled.

I made it back to the funeral home just in time, I could see the attendees queuing up outside the funeral homes front door. Toody was helping the director set up the flowers when I ran over and handed the director the urn. The elf lifted the lid slightly and breathed a sigh of relief. "This should get us by for now."

Toody and I both gave each other a nod while the director placed the urn on a small dais in the center of the floral arrangement. Before we knew it, the funeral home was packed with hundreds of mourners. Many people were sad, but I swear there were a few people who didn't seem mournful at all, they just looked at the urn and smiled. I thought things were going well until the Mayor's dog came sniffing around the urn. "Scram, mutt…" Toody whispered, trying to shoo the dog away with his leg.

"Look," said a lady in black sitting next to the Mayor's widow. "Moprag misses his master!"

The crowd all stopped talking and let out a collective "awwww."

Then, before we could react, Moprag turned around, jumped at the dais, and knocked the urn over onto the ground. There was a collective gasp from the audience and a few screams, but that wasn't the worst part. The dog shoved it's nose into the ashes and pulled out a half-eaten sausage! No wonder they had smelled so good!

The widow's wife fainted into the arms of someone revealing Chief Vanetemple, who was sitting right behind her. From the look on his face,

I could tell this was not going to go well for Toody and me. Who would have thought a funeral could be so life-changing? Later, after Toody and I received a severe chewing out back at the Redeye Temple, I decided to turn in my badge and weapons and retire. Everyone was sad to see me go, even the chief. The incident was a faux pas that had blackened the proverbial eye on the Redeyes. I made a public statement saying it was my fault before leaving the force. I didn't know what to do next so I spent a few nights looking for work as a hired sword.

Before I knew it, I was running down an alley on the seedier side of Lhentil Keep following the sound of screaming! Justice was in my blood, and Redeye or not, I was ready to protect the people of Lhentil Keep! Then I finally saw what was going on; it was at a cleric's temple. Two rogues, one skinny and one large were trying to rob an old cleric and a mage. The mage was magically choking the larger rogue with some kind of choking spell.

The cleric was not faring so well and was knocked backward by the smaller human rogue. When the rogue turned around, I could see he was holding some kind of donation box. Luckily for me, he didn't see me emerging from the alley. He was knocked end over end by my clothesline maneuver and crashed into a large pile of trash. The box came crashing down by my feet.

Distracted by my presence, the wizard let go of the larger rogue who ran over and grabbed his unconscious friend. "Elfalfuh is going to hear about this! We'll be back!" was all he managed to yell out through his sore throat.

The wizard and cleric walked up and shook my hand. "Thank you!" the cleric stated as I handed him the box. "Wow. You're quite the large fellow!"

I laughed and smiled, glad that I could still do some good. "Are you a paladin?" the wizard asked. "Cuz, you're not dressed like one."

"No, no," I stated. "Me a paladin? That would be something!"

"Are you looking for work, mister?" the cleric looked at me, with a sparkle shining in his eye. "Because this place needs a paladin. I could give you the blessings of my temple."

"I could take you adventuring!" said the wizard, happily, "You're like a wall of muscle, with red hair and a beard! We should form an adventuring party!"

"You two would make a great team, Garrot," said the cleric, who waved to me to step into the temple. "Are you willing to sign up?"

I didn't hesitate, "I'm in!" I declared boldly.

I didn't regret it either. Not only did I just meet Garrot, one of my best friends in life, but the old cleric gave me what was left of his old plate mail armor. I was now a paladin and eager to bring justice in a whole new way!

Entry 27

I have to admit that, once in a while, things can go a smidge off track when doing a job. That's why I like to follow the orders that I'm given, do my best, and let the chips fall where they may. Like the time when I was in Hollowood. Footpalm the Elflinger and I were hired by a well-to-do couple, named the Goldburys, to take them east to the city of Dockport for some personal business they did not disclose.

They were impressed with my size and had heard of my reputation for honesty and heroic bravery. Not only was I hired as the couple's guard, but I was also to chauffer them in their fancy carriage. I don't think they were too fond of Footpalm, though, especially with the way he stared at them. I thought it was kind of them when they paid me up front, but after the first hour on the trail, I was starting to understand why they did so; they enjoyed pushing people's buttons. Even though they were inside the carriage, there was a small window behind Footpalm and me so they could see us.

"Do you have to drive in the center?" Mrs. Goldbury would complain, in a disdainful voice, "You're going to get us all killed!"

"I'm on the correct side, ma'am," I'd reply, smiling at the older elf gal.

"Humpf!" was all I could hear from behind me.

"Can you believe they let that illusionist couple in our club?" she'd whine to her husband. "They're so fake!"

The old elf shook his head a little and sniffed, "How gauche, Penelope," before returning to his news scroll.

I'd like to say that her husband, Richman, was better, but he too seemed to hold himself in higher esteem than others. I was used to elves being a little on the snobby side, but these two took the cake, literally! When they attended an associate's wedding, they were scolded for taking a slice of the wedding cake, before the bride and groom! "I don't know what the problem was," I heard her comment, "that nouveau-riche couple should have been thankful we attended in the first place!"

Once-in-a-while, I'd look over at Footpalm sitting next to me; his face would get beet red as his blood pressure rose. The complaining was getting on his nerves. "Remember the gold," I said, calming him down.

When the couple grew bored of insulting their friends, they turned their attention to us. "Paladin," the old elf huffed, "can't you make this ride less bumpy?!"

"I can't control the shape of the ground," I patiently replied.

"Do you horrid dwarves ever bathe?" she asked Footpalm, who nearly drew blood biting his tongue.

The insults and questioning of our intelligence or wealth went on for about an hour. Then, we came to the small village of Convenience, which is halfway between Hollowood and Dockport. There wasn't much there, except a small temple, a tavern, and a general store with a built-in hay station for the horses. "Dimbus," Mrs. Goldbury began, "stop at that store; I want you to buy me a refreshment."

"It's Nimbus, ma'am," I corrected her, but she acted like I had never spoken.

"Dimbus, fetch me a kale-turnip latte with a twist of kettlefluff," she replied.

"And make sure it has frothing cream on top that tickles my perfect elven nose."

"In the Convenience store?" I asked. "I doubt they have any of that fancy stuff."

"You were paid to follow my orders exactly!" she huffed. "You'll do as you are told, and nothing more!"

"C'mon Dimbus!" Footpalm whispered, with a small grin. "Let me fling these two! Or at least her!"

I just rolled my eyes before guiding the wagon into the Convenience store parking lot. "Did you hear me, plebian?" Mrs. Goldbury asked.

"Yes, ma'am," I nodded, hoping to avoid more conversation with the annoying elf.

I had worked for her type before, so I just smiled and shook my head. Dealing with demanding customers didn't bother me that much. People are people, and I try to see the best in them. It was Footpalm that I was worried about. If I didn't keep him calm, these two would end up flung up into a tree or a pile of ogre dung.

After tying the horses to a post with a water trough, Footpalm and I jumped down and walked in. Footpalm grabbed the outhouse key from the halfling working behind the counter. It was typical dwarven bowel trouble; I was surprised he rode this far without having to hunker down behind some tree along the trail. I approached the halfling right after that hoping he could help.

His name tag read 'Yokle.' "Excuse me, sir," I stated. "I'm looking for fancy coffee, do you carry anything like that?"

The halfling pointed to an old dirty coffee pot that had steam coming out of it. "That's as fancy as we git round' here," Yokle stated. "But be careful, it's probably stronger than you, big guy!"

I guessed it would have to do, so I threw some coins on the counter and started to reach for a 'To go' cup. When I grabbed it, I noticed a couple of rogues coming into the store. They quickly disappeared a few aisles down from me. As I poured, I could hear them arguing over something. By the time I was placing the lid on, they had begun to approach me.

"Excuse us, mister paladin," one said, approaching me from around the corner. "Can you answer a quick question?"

"Sure," I replied with a smile. "Anything to help."

"Which type of rope would you recommend; cotton or hemp?" one smiled, showing two missing teeth.

"For climbing and such," the other one continued with a giggle, before getting elbowed in the ribs.

"If you're going to be outside a lot," I started. "I'd recommend hemp; cotton will get wet and shrink."

They both nodded their thanks and ran off. It felt good to get a smile of appreciation. If only my current employers were so nice. After helping the two rogues, I went and knocked on the outhouse door. "Hold your horses, Nimbus! Can't a monk get some tranquility?!"

"Not with those two waiting outside," I reminded him. "Remember, we're only halfway there."

"Me too," he shouted, "I'll be out in a minute."

I paced the store for five minutes until Footpalm came out grinning. "That's a load off my mind!"

I hurried the monk out, and we jumped into our seats after untying the horses. "Can you give Mrs. Goldbury her coffee?" I asked the now frowning dwarf.

After a long sigh, he grabbed the cup and looked into the window. "Hey, Nimbus, they are all tied up! I think they've been robbed!"

Stunned, I stopped the carriage and jumped out before running back and throwing the side door open. It was true; the elves had been tied up…with hemp rope! Mrs. Goldbury could only respond with grunts and growls. "Hey," I said, noticing the ropes. "These look just like the ropes that I recommended to the two rogues inside the….oh."

Both of them were now looking at me with one eyebrow cocked. "Um…nevermind, here, let me untie you…"

"Hold on there, Nimbus," Footpalm cut in. "She told us to get her drink and do nothing else. We've got to obey orders!"

I don't know what they were now trying to shout through their gags, but I'm pretty sure they were affirming what the dwarf was saying. I wasn't about to get an earful from her, again! "Thanks, Footpalm," I said. "That was a close one!"

Footpalm seemed especially cheerful for the rest of the ride; he even took the reins for a bit, so he could take us down a shortcut he recommended called Pothole Path. I don't why he looked so happy, it didn't seem any shorter to me!

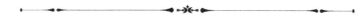

Entry 28

I love camping out while on the road. The stars at night, the breeze, scary tales told around the roaring campfire, and best of all- the food. Of course, trying to sleep under the stars doesn't always go well. I remember one time when my party and I were traveling through the Province of Rippenwind and were on the outskirts of Bogmarsh when we encountered a bit of unpleasantness.

There was a full, bright moon, and the campfire was nice and big. That's when we all started to notice the campfire glow reflecting in little eyes that surrounded us. We could hear the buzzing of whispers as we quieted down. Then, from a light flicker, we spotted the small shape of a humanoid run from one bush to another. "Oh brother," Kellepto stated. "vampire halflings…"

Everyone in the camp groaned. We all knew the little pests, called Vamplings, would try to be all over us all night. It was tough to sleep with a bunch of these monsters buzzing around. "Did anyone pack the spray?" Aiden asked, while rifling through his backpack, "because I can't find my turn symbol."

"Even if you could find it, it's probably out of fluid," Garrot grumpily stated, while searching through his gear. "You're always leaving your turn symbol on, cleric!"

"Humpf," was all Aiden said back, not willing to argue about it.

The wizard was right. Aiden had a habit of leaving it on, sometimes for miles before remembering to turn it off. Then, he would always forget to buy more of the fluid that kept it energized when he needed it. A lousy memory was just one of his quirks. "Just stay close to the fire," I reminded everyone. "They don't like fire; besides, when the sun comes up, they'll disappear."

"Not before we run out of firewood," Footpalm stated, pointing to the now dwindling flames. "We didn't collect all that much, to begin with!"

The dwarf was right; we had built a fire quickly and hadn't had the chance to collect more. "I'm never going to sleep with all these buggers circling us!" Kellepto complained. "Just the thought of their bites makes me all itchy!"

Footpalm circled the fire while looking at the red glow from the vamplings eyes as they moved about the outer rim of the light. "We're going to have to make a break for it."

As the fire died down, we gathered our gear and got ready to run. "On the count of three," I whispered to them.

But, it was already too late; they had all taken off, not even bothering to wait for my countdown! One of the pale little creatures ran up and tried biting my leg. With a quick kick, it hissed off into the air and landed on a couple more, knocking them into the dirt. Without hesitation, I ran at full stride, trying to catch up with the others. "Thanks, guys!" I shouted ahead. I swear I could hear Footpalm laughing.

Luckily, we came upon an abandoned cabin in the woods and ran inside, slamming the door behind us. We heard multiple thumps as the small creatures smacked against the wood. Garrot did a light cantrip, and the place became fully illuminated. The others scurried about the room closing and covering windows and searching for any items that could help us at the moment. I held the door until the thumping stopped. We all looked at each other, still catching our breaths. That's when I heard a small knock.

"Who is it?" I said through the door.

A small, tinny voice replied, "um…uhhh…delivery!"

"We didn't order anything," I shot back. "Now, buzz off!"

We could hear some whispering outside the door, then what sounded like a bunch of feet scrambling. Then a voice, which seemed like it was deliberately trying to be lower, said, "This is the Rippenwind Publishing House, an um, certain person here has won. Open the door, and we'll give them the grand prize!"

Garrot's eyes grew big. "That's me! I may be a winner! I got a letter a few months back saying just that!"

Footpalm and Aiden held the hopeful wizard down in a chair, keeping him from running to any of the doors. "It's a trick, you fool!" Footpalm yelled. "Don't be daft!"

Garrot struggled anyway, screaming, "This could be my chance!"

"Whose name, is it?" I yelled through the door, trying to outsmart the Vamplings.

After a few seconds of whispering, the voice spoke, "Gerald!"

"Nope," I shot back.

"Dave?" came the voice, again.

"Dave's not here," Kellepto chimed in, smugly.

"Blood feast?" the voice shouted out.

"No, no, no," a whispering voice said to the one speaking. "That's what we call our victims!"

"Sorry," came the gruffer voice again, "Kevin?"

"Too late, Vampling," I replied. "You've already given away the trick. I don't know what major vampire controls you, but you minions are not getting through this door!"

When I said that, Garrot finally got himself free. "But what if we won!" he screamed, while making for the door.

Garrot was a great wizard and good friend, but sometimes he could be a touch on the gullible side. "I have to know! Please back away from the door!" Garrot had a wild look in his eyes, so I knew I'd have to talk him down.

"I will if you tell me what you plan on doing with all those riches," I said, trying to stall.

Garrot's expression changed, and he started imagining having that much in gold. He removed his pointy hat and slowly crumpled it between his fingers as he joyfully listed off some items he'd been dreaming about.

"Oh, I'd like a nice wagon, to start. Then, I'd head to a lairport and ride a red dragon first class to…", Garrot went on and on for what seemed like forever.

Even the poor vamplings started to get impatient. I could hear them outside the door, complaining. "Would you shut yer' pie hole Garrot?!" Footpalm yelled out from a corner. "Some of us are trying to sleep here!"

The blood-drinking halflings took advantage of hearing his name and started pounding on the door again and yelling out, "It's Garrot! We're here to give Garrot all the prize winnings!"

The wizard couldn't take anymore and ran over to a window, unlocked the panels, tore them open, and dove out of it! We heard a rustle out front, and the sound of Garrot's voice cry out in great pain! "That fool!" Kellepto yelled out in frustration. "Stormcloud, grab your claymore, and open the door!"

I nodded, grabbed Abbott by the hilt, and swung the door open to the deep cries of Garrot, who was kneeling by the front door with his head in his hands, sobbing. It was now full sunlight, and black dust swirled all around him! "My one chance to win big!" he cried. "Gone!"

I felt sorry for the wizard and even bought him breakfast that morning when we reached a small diner in a village by Two Snake Lake. When he sat his spellbook on the table next to his plate, Kellepto noticed an envelope that fell out onto the floor. "What's this?" she asked, picking it up.

"Well, what do you know!" Garrot stated, grabbing it from her. "It's my entry letter to the Rippenwind Publishing House! I forgot to mail it!"

Everyone stopped in place, frowning at the smiling wizard. "That means I could still win!"

When he ran out to mail the letter, we all sat quietly, looking at each other for a moment. "Who gets to strangle him first?" Footpalm grumbled.

Kellepto immediately held out a fistful of straws. I have to admit the temptation to move forward with the plan was great, but eventually, I managed to calm them all down. After all, what if he did win?

Entry 29

One of the greatest dangers in the Unremembered Realms is not dragons, orc armies, or even the undead, it's teenage girls. Sure, they look innocent, but never let that fool you! They'll tear a man limb-from-limb if they are determined enough. For example, my team and I got hired to do security for the famous entertainer, Elfis. His manager, Colonel Crom Parker, had booked him for a show at Candlewick Park in Dankpond. We were hired as security for the famous singer, while he rested at the Hearthbreak Hotel.

I have to admit that it was a little exciting. I also enjoyed the aging bard's music. I didn't mind that the pompadoured elf had gotten on the heavy side over the years; after all, he could still sing like nobody's business. Because of my size, my job was to guard the entrance. Footpalm and Kellepto were to roam the crowds of teenage fans looking to weed out the nosy paparazzi and take away their sketchpads. You never knew when they might draw the popular elf in an unflattering pose.

Aiden and Garrot were errand boys, going out and fetching whatever it was that Elfis demanded. The worst item, they told me, was from an obscure deli from across town called Greaseland. Apparently, Elfis had a craving for fried peanut butter and jellied fish sandwiches. He would consume these with wild abandon, even gobbling down a few on stage during his act.

I don't know how many teenage elflings I had to carry out of the concert spattered with peanutty fish innards that Elfis would toss down from the stage. They would swoon and collapse, so it was my job to carry them off to safety before they were trampled. I had to hold them above my head because the elvish herd would stampede at me to get a bit of the weird food concoction the girl was covered with.

I never understood the girl's fascination with the overweight, out-of-shape, and aging elf. Maybe it was just the power of music, I guess. You'd think they'd be grossed out by the time he made his now-famous Moonwalker move. That's when he got too tired to stand, and a roadie would wheel out a walker with a built-in chair. When the blubbery crooner sat down on it to catch his breath, it would expose part of his backside, hence the name.

Facing the hordes of screaming fans was tough, we'd leave with bruises, scratches, and be half deaf from the joyous shrieks. But, it was always worth it, though. Elfis was quite generous. We left with pockets of gold, autographed sketches, and even a few customized Elfis tunics from the merch table.

Entry 30

One time, while making our way out of the Province of Darkenbleak, we stopped in the town of Horkenspit to relax. We had barely gotten into a meal at the Dubbledover Tavern when we were approached by another patron, who introduced himself as Shoddenfroy. "You want some advice, adventurers?" he began, rolling out a map on our table between our plates. "I'd leave this town before it's wiped off the map!"

"Sorry," I said, using a napkin, "I must have spilled some sauce."

"Not literally!" he said, looking frustrated at the smear. "I meant that there is danger!"

"You want my advice?" Kellepto said, leaning over the table. "Don't get between the large man and his food."

It was good advice. I do tend to like food and have been known to lose control of my manners around the table. It's a vice I've yet to conquer. It's hard when you're my size, though. Not only that, but why do they have to make food so delicious? Cooked at the right temperature and with a combination of spices, I swear almost anything is edible. I can't count how many times Kellepto has caught me eating garnish, potpourri, or an occasional decorative candle.

"There are a dozen or so orcs, just over the ridge to the south," Shoddenfroy said, looking frustrated. "They've been raiding this place almost every day. Everyone in Horkenspit will soon be broke, starved, or dead. You're eating the last of this tavern's food!"

"What!" I shouted. "No seconds?!"

Kellepto tried me calm me down, but now things had gotten personal. "This town needs justice! And dessert!" I said, staring off as in a dream. "Preferably two…"

"Here we go," Aiden said, rolling his eyes.

"So you'll help us?" Shoddenfroy said happily. "Because it won't be easy. They are led by a powerful orc bard named Hikoo, son of Jax."

"How many have this creep and his gang killed?" Aiden asked.

"None so far," Shoddenfroy replied. "But the bard shows up every day at the same time, with a few empty wagons. Hikoo uses strange magic; it has an effect on us. It makes us give him all our goods. It's like we're robbing ourselves!"

"Why is everyone so scared?" Footpalm stated, before letting out a deep, low belch. "It's just a small group of orcs! Just kill the fool, the rest will run!"

"We've tried dozens of times," Shoddenfroy lamented. "But the Bard uses his weird spellcasting style to mind control us. His unique voice is his instrument."

Footpalm was going to say something else, but we heard some commotion outside. "That's him! He's here!" Shoddenfroy yelled. "Please help us!"

My party sprang up from our seats and ran out the front door to see three wagons full of orcs pull up in the parking lot. Leading them on a large white horse was their leader, Hikoo. He was a thin pale orc, with slicked-back hair. He wore black leather armor and wore a sequined war gauntlet on his left hand. The most bizarre part about him was his nose.

"It's a human nose he had a cleric Mend Spell onto him," Shoddenfroy said, noticing the look of bewilderment on my face. "He's quite the odd fellow."

Hikoo raised a fist in the air and yelled, "Heyyyooo!"

All the orcs in the wagons jumped out simultaneously and walked over on either side of the whacko, awaiting their orders. A bunch of town folk, along with Shoddenfroy, screamed and fell to the ground, shivering. The odd-looking orc leaped from his horse, looking at us with a curious smirk. Hikoo raised his gauntleted hand in the air and snapped his fingers, shouting "Shamoan!" and then "Eehee!"

Two large orcs appeared on either side of him. They both had clubs with bloodied, razor-sharp spikes sticking out of all sides. "I don't know who you are," I said to the bard, while drawing my magic sword, Abbott, from its sheath. "But do us all a favor and turn yourself in!"

The orcs gathered on either side of Hikoo and then mimicked him as he strode forward one step, stopped, and started waving his arms around. He then made some herky-jerky dance moves that they copied, while he rattled off some weird kind of poetry.

"Your defense is weak/My force is way much stronger/You fight no longer" is what he rattled off.

At these words, a magical mist seems to appear in the air. I could feel a strong pull on my will, but I was able to resist it. Garrot couldn't, though. Like a lot of the townsfolk, he stepped out and began mimicking the dance moves of this peculiar bard. "That boy can't dance," Kellepto said, watching our wizard make a fool of himself.

"Resist not weak ones/You will fall to my command/Dance until your end," Hikoo added while making this weird side-to-side head motion.

The magic got thicker, at this point, and dancing maneuvers started swimming in my head. I gripped Abbott's hilt even harder, trying to resist. The soul of the cleric trapped inside of my trusty blade must have awoken, because a green glow came from the blade and worked it's way over me, releasing any pull from the bard's magical influence. That's when I realized that the rest of my party was all dancing to Hikoo's charm spell. Even poor Kellepto. I grinned, knowing that I'd never let her live this down.

"To the houses now rob/Take the loot and fill wagons/Obey my will minions," he shouted to the crowd.

He then tilted his head down and spun around on his heel. With that, the people under his spell ran off to rob and plunder, except me. I did a half spin and shuffled my feet backward, sliding up close to him. "Whoa," he stated out of rhyme. "I like that move!"

Within a few seconds, I was close enough to face him, so I punched him in the jaw with the hilt of Abbott. "Shamoan!" he cried out after the first punch and then "Eehee!" after the second.

But, it was too late. Hikoo fell to the ground, unconscious. This result seemed to break everyone from the bard's spell. Within a short period, we rounded up the rest of his gang and put them in the wagons; which, we would use to take them to the town's jail. Hikoo was gagged, so he couldn't pull any more stunts with his weird sing-song poetry.

"He was smooth," Kellepto said, feeling a bit awkward that she was swept away by his magic.

"I'll say," I agreed. "It's just weird that Hikoo is the one going to jail when it was your dance moves that were truly criminal!"

The elf chased me around for ten minutes, before giving up. I sure was glad that the red-faced elf had already been worn out from all that dancing!

Entry 31

Sometimes as a paladin, you have to find peaceful resolutions to squabbles. I've settled a fair number of them in my lifetime, but one that sticks out to me was when visiting the city of Tidepool. My party and I happened to be hungry, so we tried to get into a booming tavern named Malarian's.

"From our bowl to yours," Aiden said, reading the taverns slogan under their sign. "Sounds good to me."

"I don't know," I responded. "It looks dirty in there; we should eat at the other place just across the street."

"I want to try the food here," Garrot said, "I've just got a good feeling about it."

Not one of us trusted the wizard's judgment, especially when it came to food. But then, as we were about to leave, a half-orc came out and introduced himself. "Come right this way, folks, my name is Malarian. I'm the owner and cook at this fine establishment."

Garrot started to follow him, but the rest of us headed back down the steps. "Hey," he yelled out. "Where are you going?"

"Across the street," I replied.

"Sam and Ella's?" Malarian scoffed. "Good luck with that!"

None of us paid any heed to the competitive tavern owner. We got across the street and were warmly greeted by the Skawurtz family, Sam, and Ella, who seemed nice. They complained that their traitorous son opened Malarian's just the day before, and they were mad at him.

"The boy never listened," Sam, the balding, overweight human sighed. "I tried teaching him everything, but the hotshot just had to try things his way!"

Ella, his surprisingly non-ugly orc wife, just patted him on the back, shaking her head. We were seated at the best table in the house and were soon digging into the daily special of Phishy Fish; which, they caught fresh from the pond out behind their establishment. Footpalm ate rabbit they said came from the Ecolian Islands. By the time we finished our food, we had begun to feel a little funny. Kellepto excused herself and ran out the back door.

"How's the bread, Nimbus?" Aiden asked after a deep guttural belch. The cleric appeared a little off-color and was starting to sweat.

"Doughy and undercooked," I replied before optimistically stating, "But it does make it easier to chew."

By now, all of our stomachs were flip-flopping, and we all got up to run for the outhouse. Footpalm quickly dashed there first and started pounding on the door. "Let me in, Kellepto! Please hurry!"

Kellepto shouted back, "I'm powdering my nose, now beat it, ya' scruff!"

"I've got gold!" the Elflinger begged, "I promise not to talk about flinging you into the woods anymore!"

I could hear the elf make a raspberry noise back at the dwarf, well, I hoped that's what it was. But I wasn't about to stick around to find out. "There's another outhouse at the tavern across the street," Aiden shouted as he began to run. Suddenly, he clutched his bottom with both hands and ran straight for the woods. "No time!" he cried out before scuttling off, while reciting some prayers.

Because of my iron stomach, I was able to fight back some of the intense pressure, so I hot-footed it around the side of the building and took the front corner at full speed. Being distracted by the off-smelling chicken leg I was still eating; I wasn't watching where I was running. With a crunch, I collided with Garrot, and we both fell to the ground with a thud. "Watch where you're going, Nimbus!" he said while rubbing his head, "I was heading for your outhouse!"

"I was heading to yours!" I said back, flustered.

"What's that smell?" Garrot asked, sniffing with a big smile.

"Look!" I stated, noticing that my chicken leg had landed in his jellied swill. "Your swill is all over my chicken!"

"No," Garrot replied, "Your chicken is in my swill!"

The owners of both restaurants rushed out to see what the ruckus was about. They watched in awe as we both took a bite of the mixed food. "Whoa," Garrot stated. "These are two great tastes!"

"That go together!" I continued.

Sam, Ella, and Malarian ran down and tried a taste too. "Amazing!" they all said together.

It wasn't long before the parents were hugging on their son and talking about sharing the new recipe. I would have felt much better about such a great family moment, but Garrot and I made a break for the woods. I went one way, and he went the other. I found a big Wanderoot tree that had some big soft leaves. Garrot, on the other hand, concealed himself behind a nice bush.

By the time we got back, I was ready for dessert. The others started throwing things at me until Garrot emerged from the woods holding a small plant with some berries. "These are great little plants," he stated. "They are soft, absorbent, and have a good fragrance if you pop the berries. Hey Aiden, you know a little bit of botany. Do you think these plants berries would make good tea?"

"Not really," the cleric said, chuckling. "That's poison ivy!"

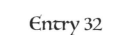

Entry 32

As the leader of my party, it's my responsibility to keep up morale. One way I do that is by keeping track of everyone's birthdays. It's not easy, though. You have to keep their likes in mind and carry little notes around with you for months.

One weird birthday moment that sticks out in my mind was when Garrot had shown interest in getting a familiar; which, is a magical little animal that is a sidekick for mages. I knew that he had seen a mini-griffon and thought it was cool, so I thought I'd swing by Pallid's Familiar Shop in Omer and see if they had one. After a misleading purchase, I decided to return the present and make a complaint.

Pallid, the store's owner, was polishing the counter as I walked in holding the cage. "Can I help you, sir?" Pallid asked, pretending not to recognize me.

"Why, yes," I began, setting the cage on the counter. "You, sir, have sold me a dead mini-griffon."

"No, no, no," he began. "Griffons are just heavy sleepers."

"Heavy sleepers? Really? I don't think so," I replied. "This toy-sized beastie is dead!"

"I think you're wrong," he said, glancing around nervously, then shot his finger through the cage poking the corpse. "See! It just moved!"

"No, it didn't," I replied, rolling my eyes, "You poked it!"

"That's just silly," Pallid said indignantly. "I would never touch a dead animal. I'd be too afraid of catching a horrible disease. I swear on my mother's grave, wherever that is, that this mini-griffon is alive and just resting."

I removed the creature from the cage and could feel its body was stiff as a board. I tapped on the counter with its head to prove how stiff it was. "See! Rigormortis must have set in at least a few days ago!"

I dropped the creature on the counter with a dull thud and watched Pallid wipe a bit of sweat off his brow. "It's faking it," he commented. "I saw it's chest move!"

"Listen, buddy," I said, getting even more frustrated. "This beast is dead, gone, finito, kaput, given up the ghost, taken the rainbow bridge. It's pushing up the daisies, snuffed the candle, cashed in its chips; it's gone to Smallhalla!"

"Hmmm," Pallid sighed, reluctantly. "There are no refunds, but I will do an exchange."

A week after the birthday party and a brief hiatus, my party got back together to do some more adventuring. That's when I noticed Garrot didn't have his familiar that I worked so hard to get him. "Where's your new pet?" I asked.

"I killed him," Garrot replied, looking at me like I shouldn't be so surprised. "He kept biting me. I mean, he was a mosquito after all."

"But he was extra large, the size of a toad!" I said, feeling disappointed.

"Exactly," the wizard complained, "It was leaving me weak!"

"But not too weak to squish it, apparently," Footpalm laughed while pointing to the stain on Garrot's shoulder."

"You could pay for my dry cleaning," Garrot suggested. "That would be a great birthday gift! My robes have needed a good washing, anyway."

I felt terrible. After all that trouble, the familiar had turned out to be just a pain in the neck. I swore never to go back to Pallid's Familiar Shop again. Luckily, Pallid's twin brother owned a pawn shop and dry cleaners right next door, or Garrot's birthday would have been a complete mess.

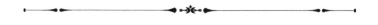

Entry 33

Before I left the Order of the RedEye Knights, I had dreamed of reaching one of their highest levels. It was in the air division called the Fly By Knights. Only twenty-five knights at a time were ever in this elite troop. Once in, you were given a magical Gold Wings of Flight Pin and trained in the ways of air combat. I always dreamed of seeing the look on a dragon's ugly mug when coming face-to-face with a band of these heroes of the air!

The Fly Bys didn't always have magical pins, though. Legend has it that they had started by using catapults to launch themselves at flying enemies. This technique didn't work so well. Their second attempt at flight wasn't much better. The RedEye Auxillary Balloon Corps didn't exactly strike fear into the hearts of flying monsters. Their official battle cry of "Wait Up!" was usually followed by another cry of "Aaaaaahhhh!!!!" as they fell from the sky as a dragon would turn around and pop the balloon or breathe fire on it.

Fortunately for the RedEye's, one of their balloons, named the Tinderberg, crashed into the shop of an elderly sorceress named Fairheart. This Sorceress, out of a desire for revenge against the dragons, spent the rest of her life building twenty-five Golden Wing of Flight pins, which she graciously donated to the order.

Entry 34

One time, while searching through the Googlebing Forest on the south end of Thunderfuss, my party and I spotted a tall tower that rose through the trees. Footpalm led the way as we maneuvered through the thick brush overgrowing the path leading to the structure. We came upon a small wall surrounding the place and followed it to a small iron gate; which, had rusted so badly that it fell off.

After reaching the base of the tower, we could see it was covered by rose bushes that had grown wild and out of control. When we discovered the thick, oversized wooden front door, Footpalm noticed an orc skull lying off to one side. "Well," I said, nudging it with my foot, "maybe they are good guys."

I knocked once or twice, and we patiently waited. Not a peep could be heard from within. "I don't think anyone's home," I commented, after turning to face my party.

Then, before I could react, Kellepto raced around me and opened the door, using the black iron handle that pulled downward. "I thought I heard something," she said. "I'd hate to miss a golden opportunity…"

I started to protest this bit of rudeness, but the whole party brushed past me to get in. I wish they wouldn't do that; it was getting to be a bad habit for them. I followed behind them, quickly. I was expecting darkness, cobwebs, and maybe some mold, but what I saw completely caught me off guard. The room we stood in was beautiful!

The insides were lit by what seemed to be magical lanterns. Bookcases were filled with what looked like brand new books. Antique chairs, tables, and few couches were placed here and there in this stately room. A polished oak banister swirled up a long stairwell leading to upper levels. The smell was of fresh roses and some kind of spice that made me a little hungry.

"Wow," Kellepto said, wandering about as she inspected the items in the room. "Everything is so nice, and I'm not detecting any traps."

"Not every place is filled with traps," Garrot told her. "You're too paranoid."

"This whole place is a trap!" a gruff voice came from behind a bookcase in the middle of the room.

We all jumped back, pulling out our weapons. We breathed a sigh of relief when an elderly, furry humanoid appeared as if out of nowhere. It looked like it might have been my size once, but was now hunched over and shriveled. "No one leaves here alive," the creature said, sadly. "Ever since 'she' went insane."

I sheathed Abbott and took a few steps forward. "Who is she?" I asked.

"I cannot say her name," the furry man said, fearfully, "but if I ring one of these, she'll come."

He pointed to a bell on a small table next to him. "She was my wife. We fell in love when we were young and beautiful. We've lived here for about eighty years or so. Over time, she slowly gained weight. I didn't care much, but she started trying every diet plan she could find. Every book you see here is some diet plan; which, has ended up failing."

He tapped a shelf where there was an open space; it was obvious that a book was missing. "Things have gone south ever since she started

70

reading this one. It's called the You See Diet," he explained. "Everything that you see…."

"You eat," Aiden finished the sentence for the beast-like creature.

"I think the book is cursed," the elderly creature continued. "Not only did it drive my wife insane, but it taught her how to wield powerful magic for catching her prey! She's been chasing me around this castle for over seven years!"

"Why not just leave?" I asked.

"The magic she uses has turned this place into a trap. Once you enter into this castle, you can never leave!" the beastman responded.

Everyone in my party began running to doors and windows. "I can't get the main door open," I shouted.

"The windows have some kind of magic force field over the top of them," Garrot shouted back.

"Quit shouting," the beastman said, trying to shush us.

Then, with a sudden shudder of fear, the gray beast stuck his nose quickly in the air. "Hide me!" he said shakily, ducking behind a bookcase, once again.

"Where's the beast?!" came the creepy shrill voice of an old woman.

We all looked and saw a wrinkled, plump, elderly woman hobble around the spiral staircase and into our view. She slowly descended the stairs using a knobby little cane that I could swear was stained with blood. "Where's the beast?!" she repeated.

She did not appear to be a threat, so we slowly approached her, meeting her at the bottom of the stairwell. She was holding the missing diet book in one hand and was wearing a bloodied apron. She looked around my party, then arched her neck with a big rotten toothed grin and looked up at me. "We're just passing through, ma'am," I said, looking into her glossed over black eyes. "Would you mind opening the front door?"

"Where's the beast?!" she demanded, more than asked.

She looked us over, once again, and began to lick her lips. "It's the You See Diet," Kellepto shouted out. "Everything you see, you can eat!"

The old woman suddenly raised her arm, holding the cursed book. A massive surge of energy burst out from it, knocking the entire party into the air and into furniture, walls, and me across the highly polished chamber floor. I tried to stand up, but the old woman had cast another spell at me. I was magically covered head-to-toe with some kind of peppery herbs that burned my skin, while at the same time, made me smell delicious.

Garrot had been thrown over a table and had gotten up to cast one of his well-known asphyxiation spells. The old crone grasped at her throat, barely choking out the words, "Where's the beathht!"

But, before Garrot could do any damage, the woman waved her knobby cane, and all the furniture in the room came to life and started to attack the party. Kellepto fought with an animated candelabra, Aiden fought with a small clock, Footpalm tried stomping on an elusive teacup with a small chip in it, and an angry teapot assaulted Garrot. I was attacked by a psychotic feather duster that made me sneeze, over and over again.

The insane old hag then waved her hands around, and a secret door opened on the floor. A large group of skeletons rose out of a pile of bones that had been stored there. As they began to overwhelm us, I noticed bite marks in their bones. It was the crazed woman's past victims! "Where's the beast?!" she cried out happily, before giving me a hungry wink.

While I smashed through some skeletons with my claymore, I heard Kellepto shout out, "Nimbus! By the wall, in the shadows!"

I would have missed it completely. Between all my swordplay and sneezing, I spotted the elderly beast trying to shadow crawl out an exit. "Footpalm!" I cried out. "Don't let him escape!"

I have no idea whether the bald dwarf meant to do this or not, but luck was actually on our side, because he slapped the teacup out of his way, leaped over an elven skeleton, and did a cartwheel all the way to the old woman. She was so stunned by his tumbling skills she didn't have time to blink before the dwarven acrobat kicked the book from her hand, sending it sailing at the beast just as he was about to exit. There were two thuds. The book hitting him on the head, and him hitting the floor! "There's the beast!" the old woman shouted.

The second that the book left her hand, all the skeletons collapsed to the floor with all the animated cookery. She seemed dazed like she just woke from a dream. "Where am I?" she muttered.

"Good work, Footpalm," I said, slapping him on the back. "That was some good thinking! I would have never thought of getting the cursed object away from her!"

"Me neither…oh, why yes, of course, I did," the dwarf bragged.

Even the old woman was impressed. "Where did you learn moves like that? A temple?" she asked, shaking the cobwebs away from her mind.

"Not exactly," he responded. "It was by a temple. I lived in a wagon, close by it, down by a river. Let me tell you all about it…"

Before he could bust into one of his long stories, the old lady hobbled over to where the gray-furred creature lay on the floor, all splayed out. "Oh husband," she said, smoothing the hair covering his forehead.

"He'll be alright," Aiden said, quickly muttering a few words and placing a glowing blue hand on him.

Within moments, the beast was blinking again and looking up at his wife. "Is it over?" he asked. "Has the curse been lifted?"

"Not really," came Garrot's voice.

When we looked up, the wizard was holding the cursed book. "Where's the feast?!"

Footpalm wasted no time kicking the book from his hands and sending it flying in my direction. I was ready for it, though. With one good cleave of Abbott, the book was sliced in half in midair. A strange bit of magical lightning burst forth when I hit it, sending red and black streaks of light into the air around it.

Everyone sighed with relief. "You tried to eat me, you old battleax!" the beast said, slowly standing back up.

"It's a good thing I didn't; you would have given me gas!" she responded.

"That would be an improvement around here," he snorted. "I swear you never clean!"

"Why should I," she spat back, "You still leave hair all over my furniture!"

After watching the two for a moment, we all snuck out. Apparently, the couple was back to the routine they had before this curse had begun. We never went back to that place after that, but from what I hear, the two lovebirds lived crabbily ever after.

Entry 35

One thing I've never been able to figure out is the odd relationship between Footpalm the Dwarf, and Kellepto the Elf. One minute they are fighting side-by-side, and the next they are squabbling over the silliest of things.

"Why do you chew your food with your mouth open, dwarf?" Kellepto complained, obviously disgusted by his actions. "Half your food ends up in your beard!"

"Mmmm," Footpalm replied, closing his eyes while lifting his beard and smelling it. "Beard pickens…you never know what you're going to get!"

The elf rolled her eyes while the rest of us just enjoyed the show. "That's so disgusting. How do you know bugs aren't living in that matted mess?"

"As long as their juicy, I don't mind," the monk laughed. "Although they do tend to itch."

"Can you believe him, Nimbus?" Kellepto said to me. "We should use your water pail as a dunk bucket, for his head!"

The others laughed, but not me. I pulled my water pail closer. I didn't want the elf trying to do what she was thinking. Footpalm taunted her by taking a big bite of a turkey leg, letting it's juice drip down into his beard. "You didn't even swallow your last bite!" Kellepto growled. "You shouldn't eat with your mouth full!"

"And you shouldn't talk with your mouth open!" Footpalm shouted back, with bits of food shooting out of his mouth.

You'd think they'd get along better, since they were still partially spattered with orc blood from the dungeon we left only hours before. They had saved each other's lives dozens of times on this very adventure. I'll never understand it. I guess it's just and elfy-dwarfy thing.

* * *

Entry 36

While on our way to the city of Bellowmoan in the Province of Winterspring, we were lucky enough to come across an abandoned cabin in the woods. It was getting dark, and we were all tired and hungry. We decided to camp inside the creepy little place for the night. Footpalm had opted not to sleep inside with us, on account that someone had scratched the word "Haunted" on the front door.

"The place is probably loaded with floaters," he said, setting up his hammock between a couple of trees. "If Aiden wasn't off helping with his temple's bake sale and bingo, I'd be with you in a heartbeat."

"Fine," I said. "But you don't know what's creeping around out here, either."

"No," he replied. "But I know what's floating around in there!"

There was no arguing with the monk, once his mind was made up, so Kellepto, Garrot, and I walked up to the porch and opened the front door. It felt cold and smelled of dampness, but the worst part was the pitch blackness. Someone had boarded up the windows for some reason. I sat down my gear and dug out my lantern; which, I lit as quickly as possible.

To our surprise, the place was well furnished. I had expected worn-out furniture or none at all. But, the room had a stuffed couch, chair, and a beautiful looking kitchen area. "Nice," Kellepto said with a big smirk. "I'm going to light a fire."

Within an hour, we were warm, cozy, and just finishing our meal; which was placed on plates left in the cupboard. I took Footpalm his plate of food; which, he ate quickly before wrapping himself in his warm blanket. "Just come inside, there aren't any ghosts."

"Nope, nada, negatory, ixnay on the loaterfay," he said, stubbornly. "I don't need some ethereal nitwit ripping my soul from my chest!"

I gave up and left him out in the cooling night air. When I got inside, I saw Garrot heading into a room holding a towel and a small toy duck. "The place has an inside lavatory?!" I asked.

"With a full-size bathtub," Garrot stated happily, giving the toy duck a squeak before closing the door.

"It also has a bedroom," Kellepto grinned, now dressed in her traveling pajamas. "Looks like you and Garrot can fight over the couch and chair."

I immediately jumped on the couch, and within a few moments, started dozing off. I hadn't been asleep very long when I heard a scream coming from the bathroom! I heard a loud crash and jumped up, running for the bathroom door. When I flung open the door, I saw a terrified Garrot as he cast a flame spell directly into his underpants; which, were floating in the air just in from of him!

"Betrayed by my underwear!" he screamed.

The fiery y-fronts flew about the room, still trying to attack us. I wasn't as scared of the flames as I was the burning smell. It was awful! Just then, Kellepto burst into the room, holding her crossbow. "What's going on!" she yelled.

"We've been attacked by Garrot's underpants!" I yelled, dodging another dive bomb by the flaming bit of clothing.

"I'm surprised this has never happened before," she said, aiming her crossbow. "I told you to wash them, mage!"

With a thunk and a shriek, the flaming skivvies were impaled to the wall. They continued to burn for a few more seconds before the ashes fell to the floor with a simple "foof."

"The sign on the door was right," the mage said, still in shock.

"Footpalm is right, Nimbus, this place is haunted," Kellepto said. "Garrot's socks could be attacking us next!"

"That would be deadly," I replied, looking at the two gaudily stained pig blankets piled on the floor next to the tub.

"Very funny. Now would you two skedaddle? I'm stuck in the tub, and this water's getting cold!" Garrot complained, still sitting in the tub while holding a towel up to his chin.

Kellepto and I both left and stood in the main living area of the cabin, trying to figure things out. "Hey, why don't we do some of that mumbo jumbo that Aiden does to turn the undead?"

"We're not clerics, and we don't have turning symbols," the elf said, pacing back and forth. "But maybe you could emulate some of his exorcism moves."

"I guess," I said with a frown. "I'm not good at that stuff."

Kellepto crossed her arms and gave me "the look." I knew better than to argue, so I started flopping around awkwardly and began chanting, "Ohh, toe, tee, ta, toe!"

The elf waved her hands in the air, "Oh, please stop! Please, that's terrible!"

Red-faced, I looked at her and said, "Okay, hotshot, let's see you do any better!"

After a couple of stretches and a quick crack of her knuckles, she started waving her arms about and doing this weird looking shuffle. It took all I had not to laugh at this, and my eyes were welling up with tears of laughter. That's when I heard Garrot's voice yell out, "They've got her! They've possessed her!"

With that, the wizard, wearing his bathrobe, jumped across the couch, tackling the poor rogue and trying to hold her flailing body. "I got her, I got her!" he yelled.

I quickly started pulling him off of Kellepto as she yelled, "I'm not possessed you dolt! I'm not possessed!"

"Get out," came a ghostly voice from around us. "Or become one of us…"

"That's our cue to leave," Garrot said, while grabbing his pack.

We all grabbed our gear and made a break for the door. It was at that same moment that Footpalm opened the door and slammed it shut behind him! "Stay inside!" he yelled.

"Get out of the way, you crazy dwarf!" Kellepto yelled back, trying to grab the handle behind him.

"Why does it smell like burnt underpants in here?" he said, slapping all our hands away repeatedly as we hurriedly tried to grab the door handle.

"Stop! There's a goth giant outside!" Footpalm exclaimed loudly, "and he doesn't look happy!"

The dwarf cracked open the door so that we could see. He was right. Standing by what was left of the dwarf's hammock was a fourteen-foot tall goth giant. His jet black hair was combed over to one side, and he had large bags under his eyes. "That dwarf snores louder than a bone saw! Me not sleep with that racket going on! Stay in cabin or I pound you all!"

"I'll take my chances with the floaters," Footpalm said, turning around, wiping the sweat from his forehead, and closing the door. "So, has anyone claimed the bed?"

"Does it matter?" Kellepto said in frustration. "This place is haunted, and our cleric's off shouting bingo numbers to a bunch of old people! Could things get any worse?!"

Just as she said that, a ghoulish apparition phased through the bathroom door, the ghost's long ghostly hair swirled around her eyeless sockets. Then, with an echoing voice, slowly asked, "Who clogged the latrine?"

We all turned to Garrot, who just grinned nervously, "I had a big lunch," he muttered.

Without hesitation, the ghost flew at the mage, grabbing him by the face. Garrot's eyes turned white, and his hair stood on end! "She's devouring his soul!" Kellepto shouted.

"I think that's just his bathroom face," Footpalm noted. "I've seen it before."

True or not, I decided to try hitting it with Abbot, I figured maybe it could harm the undead soul devourer, since it was possessed with the soul of a cleric. Unfortunately, it had no effect, but on the other hand, it did miss Garrot and hit the front door, sending pieces all over the porch.

It was at this moment that the goth giant saw the ghost and vice versa. They both froze in place. I'd like to say their eyes met, but the one didn't have any. Smiles crossed their faces as they approached each other, and then he said, "You can haunt my place anytime, me dig the whole unliving vibe."

The ghost giggled and started saying something back, but we didn't stick around to find out what; this had gotten too weird for us, so we took off as fast as we could.

When we finally arrived at Bellowmoan, I met up with Aiden at Druthers Tavern. I was surprised to see that he was sporting a black eye that was nearly swollen shut. "What happened to you?" I asked.

"Old ladies," Aiden said, over his plate of food. "I called out the wrong number at bingo, and I swear I was nearly beaten to death! You wouldn't believe how fast they can be using magically enhanced walkers. I was lucky to get out of there alive. Just be glad your trip didn't get all weird. Hey, where is everyone else?"

"They went underwear shopping. Now they are at the local temple having them blessed," I replied.

"Garrot, again?" he asked, already knowing the answer.

<hr>

Entry 37

Sometimes I think my party is out to drive me crazy. While trying to clear out a small dungeon near Watercliff, I noticed that Aiden had started renaming his potions. Restorpitulan was the name he assigned to healing potions, and he refused to hand them out unless we used the new names. "That's just silly," I told him. "Why can't we just use easy to re-member names?"

Aiden crossed his arms and looked at Garrot, who just rolled his eyes. "He's just mad because my spell components all have unique names. I can't help it that my spell crafting is more legit than his!"

"And just what exactly is Rodentical Audicoleen Mallaborus?" Aiden asked the mage.

"Ahem, " Garrot replied. "It's one of the main components for the majority of fire spells. I don't want to get too technical; Nimbus probably wouldn't understand the complexities of this rare substance…"

"It's a bat's ear wax," Aiden said, cutting him off. "And it's gross."

"Oh, yeah," the wizard replied. "and what are you calling that in-grown toenail cure you've been working on? Innie Ouchy Foot Owie?"

"Don't be silly," Aiden replied. "It's called Pustulux Wobblewalkus. Hey, that's not any worse than your name for dried fly brains?"

"Miniscopulon Noodilicus?! How dare you insinuate that is not an accurate representation in the vernacular!" Garrot retorted.

The two kept this up for an hour until we encountered the Plot-filler, the chief orc of the dungeon. He earned the name because he had a reputation for filling cemeteries with dead heroes. We fought Plotfiller and a group of his finest troops in the lowest level of the place. At first, they hit us with crossbows; then, his orc shaman covered Aiden and Garrot with a Webbing spell. "Dispel this web," Aiden cried out.

"Only if you heal my shoulder with a healing potion," the wizard said, pulling a crossbow bolt from his shoulder.

"Call it by its real name," the cleric replied, haughtily. "This must be done properly!"

"Then you call my Dispel Magic spell by its name, Dilutimagifaux Dismissiquivitus!"

"You just made that up!" Aiden yelled, while pulling his hand off the stickiness of the web.

Plotfiller must have overheard the argument during his one-on-one swordplay with me and asked, "Whut is Dilutomax Dismissgiviss?"

"It's pronounced Dilutimagifaux Dismissiquivitus!" both Aiden and Garrot shouted at the same time.

I just rolled my eyes and ducked a sword blow. "Oi," Plotfiller re-marked. "How do youse put up wit deez two?"

"It's not easy," I remarked, before kicking him in the chest with a boot, knocking him backward into three of his guards.

I whirled around and slashed the fourth guard, sending him crash-ing into the web. "He's bleeding on me," Garrot cried out. "It's grossing me out!"

The wizard finally cast his Doofrificus or whatever he called it and got rid of the web. "Fine, fine, fine," he snarled. "It's Dispel Magicks!"

Aiden smiled and tossed him a blue, glowing vial. "Here's your potion of healing," he smirked.

After a few more minutes of battling, we had slain half of the orc horde, and Plotfiller managed to reach a secret door and escape. I had a feeling it wouldn't be the last time Plotfiller would appear in my journals.

After taking a moment to catch our breath, we started sorting through all of the leftover loot. "You know, it's a shame it took a repulsive orc like Plotfiller to see the error of our ways," Aiden stated.

"I agree," I told them, while Kellepto picked up random coins scattered about the floor. "You could both use a little more humility."

"Let's take an oath never to argue or annoy each other ever again!" Garrot stated, proudly.

"Hear! Hear!" Footpalm stated, while going through the dead orc's food rations. "I'm all for that!"

Aiden and Garrot shook hands and started sifting through bits of treasure. "Hey Aiden, could you hand me that circlometer of guardolical?"Garrot asked, pointing to a magic Protection Ring; which, was resting in the treasure pile.

"That didn't take long," Footpalm laughed, watching Aiden chase the wizard around the room with his mace.

———————————•◦✳◦•———————————

€ntry 38

Word around Hollowood was that there was a group of unscrupulous characters who found it amusing to go into theaters and wait until the show began, before robbing the place. To add insult to injury, they would not even pay for whatever play they were going to see. I thought this was silly, I mean, why not pay if you're going to steal it back, anyway?

The leader was an elven rogue named Twicks and was known to be a sweet talker. The mage in his group was named Twizlar Redvane, a young human wizard who would threaten his enemies with a spell he called the Astromic Fireball. Last, but not least, was a deeply tanned halfling archer named Snowcap. He was the easiest of the three to spot because of his pure white hair that he wore in a bowl cut.

We had heard from locals that a fighter named Reece had attempted to capture them in the act, but the trio had torn Reece's group to pieces, leaving them lying on the theater floor. The trio would not hesitate to kill again, so we knew we had to wrap this up quickly. The rumor was that Twicks and his band were planning a raid at the Goodritz Theater, so we showed up to stop them.

"Maybe we can dip into a show when we're done," Garrot said, hopefully. "That would be fun."

"Yeah," Footpalm added. "Let's hit the concession stand and get some goodies; that would be sweet."

I shook my head. "Not till we've ended this spree, we need to get paid. Besides that, why fill up on candy when you could eat some juicy fruit? That's much better for you."

The party snickered at me, but I ignored them. I just wanted to get to the theater and do what we did best, bring bad guys to justice.

After speaking to the theater owner, a nervous human named Mr. Gudenplent, we decided to take our positions in the lobby, disguised as vendor staff. The uniform I was given was a bit tight, even after cutting off the shirts sleeves. "Just act natural," Kellepto said, adjusting my top. "And don't pop any buttons. I don't want to lose an eye!"

It wasn't long before the theater's doors opened, and hundreds of people started pouring in. Kellepto and I worked concessions; Aiden sold tickets at a booth in front of us, and Footpalm and Garrot took the tickets at the stairwell leading up to the main seating area of the stage. It wasn't long before Aiden gave me a wave, signaling that he had spotted the suspicious trio who had snuck past him, trying to blend in with the crowd.

They were disguised as farmers, but we could see the flaw in their costumes because they didn't have any dirt under their nails. They giggled amongst each other as they walked past me, but I wasn't about to let these jovial ranchers get away with their crimes today.

"Today's our big payday," was what I lipread from Twicks as he passed by, talking to Twizlar.

As I repeated the words to Kellepto, Twizlar jumped up on my counter and pulled out a Boomstick; which, is a magical wand that fires a powerful magic force ball that loudly explodes, sending shockwaves out around it. He yelled, "Everybody on the floor now, and nobody gets hurt!"

While the crowd quickly began laying on the floor, Kellepto wasted no time in grabbing the pan of hot butter by the popcorn kettle and threw it in the wizard's face! "Aaagghh!" he screamed, before clutching his face, slipping in butter, and falling off the counter.

"Grab the archer," I yelled over to Aiden, who stood just behind the white-haired bandit.

Our cleric quickly grabbed Snowcap from behind before the halfling could notch an arrow. The surprised little criminal flailed around while Aiden yelled, "I got him!"

Twicks, seeing the bad situation he was in, pulled out a dagger with a curved blade, and jumped at me. The evil rogue's speed was incredible! Before I had time to respond, he was right in front of me. He grabbed my shirt and pulled back his weapon, ready to sink it into my unarmored chest! It was at that moment that one of the the buttons of my tightly fitting shirt finally gave way!

"Ow!" Twicks hollered, as one of them hit him in an eye.

The elf dropped his dagger and staggered back, in total shock. I stepped forward, ready to grab the pointy-eared thug, but he held up his hand, and said, "Did you think we didn't have a backup plan?"

With that said, he put two fingers in his mouth and let out a loud whistle. A few of the quivering patrons got up from the floor, and a dozen more came running through the front doors of the Goodritz. Twicks rubbed his red eye and said. "These hirelings are from the trail park just outside of Hollowood, named Guberton. These Gubers are kind of nutty, but they work cheap, and believe me, they are not afraid to take care of business!"

Twizlar was being held at bay by Kellepto, but Aiden had dropped Snowcap, who bit his hand and rolled to the floor, before grabbing his short bow, getting ready to fight.

Twicks laughed, menacingly, while backing up away from me as the Gubers surrounded me. Unfortunately for Twicks, he didn't realize he was backing up to Footpalm the Elflinger, who hadn't revealed himself, yet. Because I stood much taller than the band of Gubers, I got a good glimpse of the smile on the feisty dwarven monk's face; I swear he was nearly drooling at the thought of what he was about to do!

Twicks lost his smile when he felt a hand go around his ankle, then one on his wrist. Within the blink of an eye, he was screaming as he was whirled about in a circular motion. He was then flung into the air and sent crashing into a mural of an elderly lady drinking tea. Twicks hit the wall hard. The crunch of breaking bones was heard throughout the lobby. That's when the chaos began!

Snowcap shot an arrow at me, but I blocked it by picking up a Guber, using him as a shield. Then I hurled him into two others as they tried to advance. Once they hit the floor, six others jumped on me, biting, punching, and pulling at my beard. I would have ripped them off me easily, but I was holding off two that had swords drawn, and I had managed to grab both their wrists.

Kellepto, in the meantime, had put Twizlar in a sleeper hold, and the wizard was struggling to stay conscious. Aiden started fighting with Snowcap, who deftly dodged the blows from Pepper, his magical mace. More Gubers poured in the front door at this point, and I began to lose hope. That's when a thundering boom came from what seemed like nowhere, knocking everyone off their feet! Standing in the middle of the room was Garrot, holding Twizlar's Boomstick wand!

"Whoa," he said, looking around.

A bunch of the Gubers, not knowing what just happened, fled the scene. "Wow, that was amazing!" I said to the wizard, who just stood there, sniffing the wand.

"Can you smell what Garrot is cooking?!" he yelled out, holding the wand into the air. "Wooooo!"

After helping patrons to their feet, we loaded up a few dazed Gubers, Twizlar, and the heavily injured Twicks into our wagon. We couldn't find Snowcap; it seems he managed to escape with many of the Gubers. Mr. Gudenplent couldn't thank us enough. "Anything you want, you name it," he declared.

I thought about it for a moment, then said, "How about a few things from the snack bar? A bucket of popcorn sounds delicious."

The older man looked sullen. "Have you seen the prices of the snacks here? I'd rather give you gold!"

In the end, Gudenplent relented, and when we came back after dropping off the criminals at the local jail, he let us raid the snack bar and watch the play. The popcorn was good, and there was plenty of it. Kellepto said I'd have a jelly belly if I kept going back for refills. She kept shushing Footpalm and me for chuckling out loud at certain moments of the play. Apparently, it wasn't supposed to be a comedy, but the acting was so bad you really couldn't tell. Kellepto was a sucker for anything with romance, so the rest of us just tolerated the cornball acting, even though we all thought it was a dud.

Entry 39

We had been staying at the Splinterstep Inn on the outskirts of Thudbunker for about a week when we caught news of a powerful Illusionist attacking people's homes in the area. His name was Selson Van Druff and would use his magic to manipulate people and take all their gold. The word around town was that he was head and shoulders above many other illusionists, so we'd have to be extra careful. I was very excited at the thought of getting out there and bringing this villain to Justice, because we had come to Thudbunker for the Fallfest celebrations and had nothing to do since the festival ended.

Garrot didn't mind the downtime, but I get antsy, and for a good reason. The mage usually ended up being my roommate, so I had to endure every one of his oddball life theories, at least three or four times. Plus, the nights typically end with me unhappily watching him bite at his crusty toenails. "Isn't there a cantrip or something you do?" I'd ask.

"Yup," he always replies, while sniffing his big toe with a frown. "But where's the fun in that?"

After learning of Selson, we went to the shops to restock our supplies. I couldn't wait to start the hunt for him first thing in the morning, renewed and refreshed. I like to be prepared. I even bought Garrot a nail file, but he just used it to clean his ears, before nibbling on a hangnail on his pinky toe.

When sunlight finally shot a ray through our window that morning, I jumped out of bed and ran over to Garrot's. He was snoring loudly and drooling. "Wakey, wakey, eggs, and bakey!" I shouted, shaking him by the shoulder.

He blinked and groaned, then pulled a pillow over his head. That's when I heard a knock on our door. "Nimbus, Garrot, are you two awake?" came Aiden's voice.

I opened the door, and he walked right past me and threw open the shutters on our window. A cold gust came in and gave us a chill. Aiden turned to us and smiled, "It snowed last night!"

I ran over to the window with the bleary-eyed wizard right behind me. "Well, I'll be," I muttered, "I've never seen it snow this early in the year."

"There must be three feet on the ground," Aiden said, "You know what that means?"

"Snow day!" Garrot shouted with Aiden simultaneously.

The cleric ran out, and the wizard immediately started rifling through his gear, looking for his warm clothes. "I'm going to build a snow golem!"

"Are you kidding me?" I asked. "We've got a mission, remember? We're supposed to stop Van Druff!"

"Pish posh," Garrot said. "If we're snowed in, then so is he, let's have some fun."

I couldn't argue with his logic, but that didn't make me any less annoyed. Even though the thought of hot cocoa by the fire of the Inn sounded great, I knew that I had to endure one more night of Garrot's bad habits. With a sigh, I reluctantly went to my pack and started looking for my warm leggings. I preferred to wear my kilt, but I didn't want to catch a cold and be stuck in the room for yet another week.

After dressing, I stepped out in the hall and banged on Kellepto's door. "Get your curlers out and come join the fun. Whoever makes the worst snowman has to buy breakfast!"

Her door opened quickly, and an already dressed Kellepto quickly strode past me. "I hope you have some gold left, Slumberdim. Cause there's no way you're topping what I'm going to make!"

Whenever she used my last name, I knew that it was on. I was just about to respond, but Footpalm blew past me, as well. "Morning, Nimbus," he said without turning around. "I'm gonna build me a snowman with elf ears to fling!"

That morning, we goofed around in the snow, having a good time and building multiple snow creatures. By the time we finished, we had a dragon, a golem, some sloppy looking elves, and even a snow clam. We took a break and decided it was time to determine who would buy breakfast. "My snow dragon can't be beaten," Kellepto said, packing a last bit of snow around its tail.

Garrot shook his head, determined that his golem would be voted best. "Hmmph!" he muttered. "There are no surprises here. My snow golem is the real head turner!"

With that said, the frozen creature came to life, turned its head and slapped the mage upside the noggin', sending him tumbling into a snowbank! Before we could react, Kellepto's snow dragon launched itself into the air and started using a snowy breath weapon at Aiden, who fell backward and was quickly covered in snow. The three crude snowmen with elf ears that Footpalm made became animated and grabbed Kellepto's limbs and tried to pull her apart! "Footpalm!" she screamed out, "Fling these snow elves!"

The monk, with a huge toothy grin, replied, "Yessss!"

Within moments, he had flung two of the creatures away, before getting hit with the snow breath of the dragon. The dwarf was quickly buried up to his neck. Meanwhile, Kellepto had begun punching the last snow elf in the guts, before biting its ear. "Ow!" she yelled, tumbling backward, "Brain freeze!"

It was a good thing for my party that the creature I had made, the snow clam, didn't pose much of a threat. It just snapped at me without moving. They may have laughed at me earlier for building it, but they weren't anymore! I saw the dragon circling for another go at us. Luckily, I was in a hurry for breakfast and didn't want to roll a proper snowball for the pearl I place in the clam. I had used a nice sized rock instead, lightly packing snow around it.

"Do you think you can beat the army you created?" asked a robed man as he appeared as if out of nowhere.

"Who are you?" I asked, slowly turning around.

"Why, I'm unstoppable," the tall, gangly human replied. "Muwah ha ha! That's all you need to know!"

Without hesitation, I spun around and grabbed the stone from the biting clam's mouth just before it snapped shut again. The dragon had swooped down in front of the man and began breathing its snow weapon at me. But it was too late, because I launched the stone! The rock sailed between the creature's legs as it ducked! For a moment, I started to feel the coldness of the snow cover my body, and then I heard a crunch and a sharp moan. In the blink of an eye, all the snowy creatures, along with the snow itself, had disappeared!

I rubbed my eyes and blinked. The rest of my party was taken aback, as well. "It was all an illusion," Kellepto said, looking around. "Hey, that's

Selson Van Druff! What an illusionary genius!"

"I wouldn't say that, anymore," Footpalm stated. "It looks like he has rocks for brains!"

The dwarf stood over the crumpled form of Selson Van Druff. The large stone that I threw, nailed him in the head! "He must have thought the snowball I through was part of his illusionary magic," I realized, "so he never ducked!"

Aiden tried patching him up the best he could, but it was apparent the illusionist was never going to be the same. Which, in our opinion, wasn't such a bad thing. "Well, he should look on the bright side," Garrot stated. "The bump on his head will make it a lot harder for his pointy spellcaster's cap to fall off!"

We turned over the bewildered and babbling fool to Thudbunker authorities, and collected a nice little reward. My party still made me buy breakfast for them, even though my snow clam idea had saved the day.

◆——◆——◆ ◆◈◆ ◆——◆——◆

Entry 40

Sometimes an adventure ends before it even has a chance to begin. My party and I were sitting at the Blue Light Tavern in Horkenspit when the door flew open, and an excited looking elf ranger ran in the room holding a scroll. He surveyed the room quickly, then noticed how big I was and immediately came over. "Are you for hire?" he asked.

"Maybe," I answered. "It all depends on what the job is."

"Perfect," the elf smiled, setting a sack of coins on the table. "My name is Tagtow, and boy, do I have a job for you!"

Garrot's eyes twinkled as he reached out to touch the bag, but Kellepto gave his hand a quick slap. "Just what is the job?" I asked.

"Ever hear of Castle Trapadore?" he asked, watching the reaction on our faces.

We were interested, now. "You mean the place loaded with countless deadly traps?" Kellepto stated, more than asked. "Rumored to be hidden somewhere in the Ruins of Rippenwind?"

Tagtow nodded. "I found what I believe to be a map to its very location!"

"Whoa," Aiden said. "How in the realms did you find that?"

The elf looked around, then sat the scroll on the table. I didn't know what it was about, this particular piece of parchment, but my whole party scooted our chairs back, it just reeked of evil. "I found it amongst the bodies of a dead party not far from here. I figure some random monsters must have ambushed them. This scroll is all that was left, treasure wise."

"How do you know it's to Trapadore?" Footpalm asked.

"It's written right here on the outside corner," Tagtow stated, pointing to a bit of script.

"I don't know," Kellepto said. "Castle Trapadore is supposed to be cursed!"

"If it's loaded with treasure," Tagtow state. "Who cares?!"

With that said, he broke open the seal on the scroll, and we all instinctively leaned back a bit. "See," he said. "Nothing to fear!"

He rolled the scroll out on the table and blew some dust off, some of which went around his face. With a thud, he immediately collapsed on the table, turned into a dried husk, then slid down to the ground, stone dead. The scroll on the table slowly rolled itself shut and magically resealed itself!

The whole tavern was utterly silent and looking directly at us. "Clean up at table seven!" Garrot blurted out, while I grabbed the scroll and walked out. "You still want to go?" Kellepto asked, amazed that I grabbed the scroll.

"I took an oath to save lives," I replied. "The treasure sounds nice, but I don't like the price."

We found a nice place out in the forest, and we buried the scroll. To this day, I think it may still be there. The mysteries of Castle Trapadore are still unexplored, but I'm not curious. Besides, we still ended up with a sack of gold.

Entry 41

One day, while in the city of Port Laudervale, we had decided to take a break from adventuring to enjoy a few days off with some of our newly earned riches. Garrot begged us to give him our gold to take to Laudervale Trust, our preferred bank in the city. We were all sitting in the Four Shadow Tavern when he finally returned, smiling and holding a scroll.

"Did you make the deposit?" I asked, taking a bite of a buttered roll.

"Yes," he started. "But not at the bank."

Everyone quit eating as the wizard, fighting back a huge grin, pulled the string from around his scroll and rolled it on the middle of the table. "I have invested in the future!"

"What?!" Kellepto growled. "You know you're not supposed to do that without consulting us!"

"Can I strangle him, Nimbus?" Footpalm declared, angrily. "I promise to make it quick!"

Aiden just laid his forehead on the table and sighed. I glared at Garrot, but he ignored me and happily started to explain what was on the scroll. "I bumped into Captain William Gull by the docks while on my way to Laudervale Trust," the wizard explained. "Do you remember him?"

"You mean old Gully Bill?" Footpalm groaned, slapping his hands over his face. "The halfling bard who has tricked you at least a half dozen times in the past?"

"Yeah, that's him," Garrot said, happily. "But this time, it's the real deal!"

Aiden groaned again with his head still on the table. "We are now one of many proud owners of a luxurious delivery ship called Gitanic!"

None of us were happy about this, but, as usual, Garrot was completely sold on this investment. "Let's head down to the docks; they are going to christen it today!"

I figured old Gully Bill would be long gone by now, so we had better find out where all our money had been spent. As we walked through the city toward the bay, we could see the top of the ship in the distance. It really was huge! I was beginning to think maybe Garrot had done well this time and invested in something worthwhile! By the time we reached the colossal boat, we saw a crowd had gathered in front of a small, cobbled together platform that had a podium on it. The Mayor of Port Laudervale stood in front of it, waving at people. He had just finished his speech and was now taking questions, like how fast it will go and will it survive pirate attacks.

Word around Port Laudervale was that a local pirate, known as Moldywart the Unpleasant, had a secret base on Warmwater Island and would occasionally attack delivery ships coming in from Seabay. Mayor Udderglove seemed pleased as punch about the new ship and stated he invested a large portion of the city's tax dollars into the project. "Who built this?" Footpalm shouted his question.

"Dworcs from the Island of Hemridge," the Mayor answered. "Using the affordable lumber of the Balsadoom Forest."

"Why didn't you hire gnomes?" Kellepto asked. "That would seem to make the most sense."

"Dworcs are very underrated," the Mayor explained. "Besides, they are much cheaper, and just as short!"

Murmurs of agreement went throughout the crowd. I have to admit; there was logic to that statement. I was very tall, and I never invented anything. "If there are no other questions," Mayor Udderglove stated. "Let's christen the ship!"

On a fancy pillow on a table next to the Mayor was a bottle decorated with lots of ribbons. We lightly applauded as he held it up, then walked out on a walkway specially built to reach the front of the boat. "I christen thee, the Gitanic!"

With a swing, he smashed the bottle on the front, and the audience started applauding wildly. It didn't die down until large cracking noises began. That's when we noticed some cracks expanding out from where the bottle had hit! Within seconds, the cracks doubled in size, before a huge chunk of the front end fell apart, sending pieces down into the water. People started to run as the Gitanic began taking on water.

From the shore, hundreds of people watched in sadness as their investment slowly sank to the bottom of the bay. Garrot turned around and asked, "Do you think it's repairable?"

We all looked over the edge of the pier, watching it sink. "Maybe there's still hope," I said, unconfidently.

Just then, we could see it start separating into various pieces under the water. "Maybe some magic glue could get those back together," Aiden remarked.

It was that moment that it caught fire...underwater! "Wow," Footpalm stated. "I haven't seen anything like that before!"

"Well," Garrot said quickly, clapping his hands together and rubbing them. "That's that. But don't fret, Gully Bill told me of another opportunity. It's a large balloon that uses fiery gas to fly people around. It's called the Tinderberg, and Gully says it's a sure-fire winner!"

Sometimes I wonder about our mage; he's gullible, hard-headed, and easily duped. But the one thing I learned that day is that he runs fast!

Entry 42

A common sight you see in many dungeon entrances of the Unremembered Realms is vending contraptions that have cheap toys or candies. Although beings of pure evil run the dungeons, they can't resist making a few extra coins off adventurers. These little machines were usually sold to them by gnomes from the vast city of Omer from the province of Winterspring.

These "vending contraptions" are quite ingenious. They have a solid wooden frame with glass boxes showing you the goodies inside.

They also have a slot in the front where you'd stick a copper coin or two. Below that is usually some small crank you turn after inserting the coin. With a few turns, you'd have your bauble or treat and be on your way.

I always liked these, because even if you failed in your quest to clear a dungeon, you wouldn't always have to leave empty-handed. I preferred the candy, but Garrot and Footpalm would fight over whatever cheap toy the contraptions happened to have in stock at the time. "They're collectible!" would always be their answer when I questioned them.

The dungeon delve I remember vividly was when we found a hidden set of double doors at the base of one of the Hoktu Mountains. My party paused and immediately made a bee-line for the machines. "Let's just hit them on the way out," I said. "Let's stomp some monster backsides first."

As usual, they ignored my command and lined up at the vending machines. I rolled my eyes, muttering about Omerians, and started looking at the door. It was no use; I was terrible at spotting traps. "Kellepto," I said. "I could really use your skills here."

"Hold on," she answered. "I'm just going to get a piece of gum."

"Well, hurry up," I replied.

After a few minutes, I could hear her grumbling, so I walked over to see what the fuss was about. Kellepto was pulling on the crank and yelling at the vending contraptions. "This thing stole my money!" she complained. "It's not giving me my gum either. It's a piece of junk!"

"That's because you tried using a button, not a copper," Garrot said, squealing on her.

Red-faced, the elf stood back and kicked the machine. To everyone's surprise, the contraptions transformed into a living creature with large teeth and flailing wooden arms! "It's a Gimmic!" Kellepto cried out as it bit down on her leg.

The whole party immediately responded. I withdrew Abbott from its sheath and chopped at one of its arms, breaking it off. The Gimmic howled out in pain, letting Kellepto go. Aiden cast a Ring O' Fire spell, and within moments, the magically transformed creature was engulfed in flames and howling! "The toys!" Garrot and Footpalm cried out, "You're burning the toys!"

"They weren't real, you dolts!" Aiden said, backing away as the creature fell forward into a pile of flaming goo. "And there goes my best fire spell that I'm only allowed to use once-a-day."

"What about my lucky button?" Kellepto said, holding her bleeding leg.

The wound didn't look that bad, so I used the small healing spell from my clerical magic sword, Abbott, to heal her. I'd like to say that everyone learned their lesson that day, but that would be wrong. A few months later, I lost my coin inside a nacho vending contraption and burned my hand with hot cheese when reaching in for it.

⸻

Entry 43

You never really know someone until you travel with them. For instance, my party became lost in the Tanglewood Forest because Footpalm never told us he was a terrible scout. We all stood around in silence for a moment, wondering where we were. We could hear the familiar growl of bugbears moving around, so we had to be quiet. "Why did you ignore all the trail signs?" I asked the dwarf in a whisper tone. "Can't you read?"

"Of course I can read," replied the dwarf, through clenched teeth. "I just can't read symbols!"

"Shhh!" Kellepto interrupted, trying to keep us from being detected.

"Everybody can read symbols," Garrot whispered. "You just look at the shapes!"

Footpalm just shook his head from side to side. "It all looks like nonsense to me. I can't tell you how many times I've stumbled into the wrong bathroom by mistake." He said, rubbing his face, "and I have plenty of slap bruising to prove it!"

"Shapes are so easy," Aiden stated. "I find this difficult to believe."

"Hey," the dwarf replied. "It's all elven to me!"

We heard a bugbear growl, so we ducked down. After a few moments, it passed. "What's the deal with bugbears, anyway," Garrot whispered. "How come there's no buggoats, bugllamas, or bugpossum?"

"What about a bugbunny?" I chimed in, "I'd rather face a bugbunny than a bugtiger or whatever."

"Let's not get sidetracked, here," Aiden said. "How do you even function in life not being able to figure out symbols, I mean, what's up with that?!"

"How do you function having a deathly fear of raw potatoes?" Footpalm shot back.

Aiden's face turned bright red as we all turned to face him. "You see," Footpalm said, "I'm not the only one with secrets around here!"

"I was told of the Legend of the Werespud when I was a kid," the cleric stated, angrily. "It scared the socks off me! And besides that, anything with more than two eyes is just creepy!"

"That's hilarious," Kellepto laughed. "I'm enjoying myself now! Werespud? Symbolitterate? These two take the cake!"

"You shouldn't talk, Kellepto," Aiden retorted, "Should you?"

"What's that supposed to mean?" the elven rogue replied, as her laughter quickly diminished.

"It means I wouldn't be making fun of the dwarf for not understanding types of languages, if I was you," Aiden stated. "Like Elvish…"

"Huh?!" everyone said at the same time, turning to the elf.

"You can't speak elven?" I asked Kellepto, who was shooting severe eye daggers at the cleric. "but you are an elf!"

"It's not as easy as common is!" Kellepto explained. "Phylubtervall or whatever is a word for fish, I guess, why not just say fish?! C'mon! It all sounds like gibberish! Plus, it's hard to write with all the big frilly loops. Elves even have three silent letters in our alphabet….three!"

Garrot couldn't handle it. He was laughing so hard he fell to the ground. "An elf who can't speak elven! That's so rich!" he began. "I think I'm going to bust a gut!"

"Is that why you wear a girdle?" Kellepto said, crossing her arms. "To not bust a gut?"

The mage was no longer laughing. "That was our secret!" Garrot said, standing back up and wagging his finger at the elf. "You promised not to tell!"

"You told me you did sit-ups every day," Footpalm laughed.

"Only when the dinner bell rings," Aiden said, joining in on the fun.

The wizard took off his pointy hat and threw it on the ground. "Calm down Garrot, don't pop a button!" I said, teasing him lightly.

"You should talk, Nimbus," Garrot said. "Aren't you the one who stuffs cabbage in his socks to cover the smell?"

I grimaced at that, hoping that would be the end of the embarrassing reveal. It wasn't. "Yeah," Kellepto said. "Weren't you the one who hid the last piece of Footpalm and Garrot's one thousand piece puzzle?"

"What!?" they both shouted. "That was you!"

"I just did it as a joke, at first," I explained. "But you two got so mad it made me afraid to say anything. I thought the revenge pranks would never end, so I threw it into my backpack and forgot about it."

The look on the mages face made me feel terrible; then, he started pointing at me. The rest of the party did, too. "You don't have to all point at me," I said. "It was just a prank!"

Then, I realized they weren't pointing at me at all. I slowly turned around and saw three extremely large bugbears standing right behind me. We had been louder than we thought. We fought hard and barely escaped the creatures. It was embarrassing to be caught off guard like that, so we vowed never to speak of it again. It did make us get over our anger of the revealing of each other's secrets, though. It's amazing what life or death combat can do to help us forgive one another.

"I'm glad we can overcome petty nonsense," I told them all around the campfire that night. "Now, let's make some dinner."

"As long as you're not making us cabbage soup!" Footpalm declared, while the rest of them laughed.

Entry 44

Sometimes when adventuring, things don't always go as planned. For instance, my party and I met with a rogue promising us big treasure. "My evil cousin, Chincey Bindelver, runs a dungeon, and it's loaded with riches!" Tillman the Rogue, explained. "I just need a band of heroes brave enough to help me take him down. Then, we can split the profits 60/40."

"As long as the 60 part is us," Kellepto snapped in quickly, while crossing her arms and leaning back in her chair.

I was a bit hesitant about this venture. Tillman, with his crooked smile, and nervous gestures, did not seem like the kind of person that I would usually align myself with. Unfortunately, the rest of the party had been swept away by the promise of treasure, and I had a feeling my vote wouldn't count. "How hard will it be to get into your evil cousin's dungeon? What will we be looking at there, fight-wise?"

"Oh, you know, the usual. Some orcs, kobolds, maybe a few slob-goblins, nothing big," Tillman explained. "We'll zip in and bada boom bada bing we're out of there!"

Before I knew it, we were walking down a trail in the Allahoy Forest in the Province of Rustwood. It was lightly raining, but everyone seemed cheerful. They chatted back and forth about what they would do with their share of the treasure. "I think after a big haul like this," Footpalm stated. "I'll just buy me a little island, marry a pretty monkette, and then fill the place with monklings! I'll probably have enough change left over to buy a few elves to fling around!"

Kellepto playfully flicked the top of the dwarves' head, and he laughed, but something told me he wasn't joking. "What about you, rogue?" Footpalm asked the elf.

"That's easy," she replied. "I'd hire a small group of bards to travel the realms and sing my praises. I'd name the group The Kellepto Maniacs, and they would help me be known as the most famous rogue of all!"

Tillman chuckled as he kept leading us down the trail. We hid for a moment to let a wandering Crettin stroll by, then continued forward again.

"What are your dreams, Aiden?" Kellepto asked.

"Oh, I don't know," he began. "Maybe I'll try to find a cure for everything; that would be nice."

"We already have potions and spells for curing ailments," Footpalm stated. "What's left? A cure for boring us to death?"

"How about a cure for death?" Aiden shot back.

"In theory, that's fine," the dwarf harrumphed. "But if you did that, the Unremembered Realms population would be out of control. What a lousy idea!"

"I never said I'd cure you," the cleric stated.

The rest of us laughed at Footpalm's expression. He certainly wasn't expecting that answer.

"You want to know what I'd do?" Garrot chimed in. "I'd buy a walrus."

The rest of the party stopped and turned toward the mage. "What?" Garrot said. "Don't tell me I'm the only one!"

"Besides eating walrus burgers, what in the realms would you do with one of those?!" Footpalm stated, both hands in the air.

It was at that moment that an arrow flew between his wrists, before flying off into the woods.

I ducked just as I felt a singe of pain as an arrow sliced across my ear. "Where are they coming from?" I yelled to Kellepto.

The elf had incredible hearing. I could see the rogue's ear twitch as she moved a dark braid away from it. Kellepto pointed to the west as a volley of new arrows hit the trees around us. One even went through Garrot's hat and stuck it into the trunk of a nearby tree. He did not look happy as he leaped up, holding his Boomstick Wand and pulled back its middle section, or "racking it" as he called it. Then, he released a massive shockwave that made a loud boom!

Three orcs flew from the woods high in the air, bows and arrows flying in every direction! Six large orcs with swords charged us from their hiding places and attacked us, immediately. I didn't have time to draw Abbott out, as I dodged a swing and punched one out cold. This move gave me time to drop kick another one in the chest; which, completely winded him.

Before I could do anything else, Tillman was on top of the orc and stabbing him through the visor of his crude leather helmet. When I turned around, I could see the rest of my party had gotten the better of the rest of the orcs. That was too bad. My adrenaline was up, and I was hoping for a little more fun! "We must be close to the entrance," Tillman explained. "My cousin hires a lot of orcs; they work cheap."

Aiden quickly rushed over to tend to my ear; which, was almost sliced off. He held it back into place and said a few words. Within seconds, it almost felt like nothing had happened. "It'll still be a little sore," Aiden stated, patting me on the shoulder.

"Why didn't you hear them sneaking up on us, Kellepto?" I asked.

"You can usually hear a pin drop a mile off."

"How could I with everybody jabbering?" she replied. "Especially, when it's about walruses. That's the dumbest bling I've ever heard!"

Garrot stuck his tongue out at the elf, and before she could reply, we heard groans coming from one of the orcs. I quickly grabbed him and tied him to a tree. "Do you speak common?" Tillman asked the creature.

It nodded back at him, "Yeah."

"Where's the entrance to the dungeon," Tillman asked.

"Our treasure," he replied wobbly, through his fat lip. "Be not yours. It be ours. Me never tell."

I walked over and held my fist close enough to his face that his eyes crossed when looking at it. "Up 50 yards, take right, on side hill, behind fake boulder," he muttered.

It wasn't long, and we were pushing the surprisingly light boulder away from the entrance to the dungeon. We filed our way into a poorly lit waiting room with a few beat-up old couches, tables, and chairs. It was obvious this was where the guards hung out when not on duty. There was even a teenage orc still asleep on one of the couches. Tillman withdrew his dagger and started moving toward him, but I grabbed his shoulder. "That's not a fair fight," I said, pushing him out of the way.

I walked over and gave the orc a nudge. He blurrily blinked up at me a couple of times before his eyes grew large. "Scram, kid," I said, before he leaped up and ran out the door.

Tillman just shook his head. "He'll just come back and try to kill us later," the rogue said, unhappily.

"Not before he changes his pants," I replied, waving my hand around. "I think I may have scared him."

"Hey, Tillman," Footpalm said, while looking around. "This place is kind of dumpy. I thought you said your cousin was rich?"

"This is just a guard room," the rogue explained confidently. "It will get much nicer… I hope."

Sadly, the next room wasn't much better; it was just the sleeping quarters of the same orcs. All we could find were some filthy clothes, some flea-ridden mattresses, and a scroll. Garrot was excited, at first, thinking it could be valuable. "Ugh," he said, after unrolling it. "It's just a drawing of one of their mother's. You know, you'd think the artist wouldn't draw his mother with crossed eyes and drooling."

A couple of rooms later, we found a secret door. Usually, this would be exciting, but it had been left half-open. On the floor in front of it was a half-assembled trap that had been abandoned. "I wonder why they quit," I said to Kellepto.

The elf poked through the pieces. "Some of these pieces aren't the right size, and it's missing a few screws."

"She'd know," Footpalm whispered to Aiden, who began chuckling.

"I heard that," she stated, glaring at the duo, before returning to her inspection.

"Aha!" she said suddenly, holding up a slip of paper. "No wonder they gave up. This trap was made on the Island of Taiwan."

The next room we came to was large and filled with lots of boxes stacked up one upon the other. I pried open the wood on one of them and sorted through the contents. "It's just a bunch of dried rations," I said to everyone else.

It turned out that most of the boxes had precisely the same thing. "Maybe there was some kind of deal or something," Tillman stated. "I've heard that my cousin Chincey loves a bargain."

"Yep," Aiden said, reading a marking on one of the sides. "They are a month past their 'sell-by' date."

"I bet he saved a fortune," Tillman said with a big grin. "I have a good feeling about this…"

"Hold on a moment," Kellepto interrupted, her ears twitching. "I hear a rat."

"I'm not a rat," Tillman stated, sounding insulted. "What makes you think…"

He never got to finish the sentence, because a giant rat leaped from behind a stack of boxes and tackled him. Others appeared as well, and a battle commenced rather quickly. By the time the fight ended, Aiden had to cast a few healing spells on Footpalm, Garrot, and then himself. Poor Tillman was beyond help, so we gathered up his body and laid him out on some boxes. "Poor Tillman," Kellepto stated in a brief eulogy. "At least he checked out like a good rogue, trying to rob his own family."

We left the room and found a stairwell at the end of a hallway that led downward. Cautiously, we descended and gathered in front of an open doorway. We could see in the room; which, was fifty feet long and about twenty-five wide. Carved out of each side along the walls were water fountains, three on the left, and the same on the right. The room had a green glow about it. There were magical lights that emitted from the eyes of lions heads; which, had been carved into the rock at the top of each fountain.

"That's a little eery," Aiden said, walking into the room. "I wonder if the water is drinkable?"

I nodded to Kellepto, and she went to the closest fountain to inspect the water for poisons. Footpalm went to another with a different thought in mind. "I don't care if it is, I've got to wash this rat blood out of my beard. I can't impress the ladies smelling like a rotting rodent!"

"So, what's new?" Kellepto cracked wise, as she stuck a fingertip into the water.

It was at that moment a watery skeletal hand grasped onto her wrist! Footpalm yelled out in shock when one rose from his fountain as well, grabbed his beard, and pulled his whole head under the water. Footpalm clung to the edge of the fountain's stone rim.

From the remaining fountains, four skeletal shaped figures arose. "Water Skelementals!" Garrot shouted, "Wow! That's some high-quality magical H2O!"

I left the others to take on the liquid monsters, while I ran to Footpalm, grabbed him by the feet, and pulled him away from the skelemental's grasp. "Aaahhh!" the dwarf screamed. "It's pulling my beard!"

I ran up to the creature as it jumped out of the fountain and I cleaved off its skull with my magic sword. When it hit the floor, it splashed into a puddle, before quickly moving back into the body. Much to our dismay, the skull reformed itself, once again. "Good grief," Footpalm stated. "That's a bit of a shock!"

Suddenly, an idea hit me. I activated Sparky, my magically enhanced gauntlet, and grabbed the skelemental as it kicked Footpalm over. The watery beast exploded all over the two of us, but this time the drops didn't reform! When I turned around to tell the others, I saw that Kellepto, now held by both wrists, was being dragged headfirst into a fountain. Aiden had been backed into a corner by two of the monsters. Garrot was blasting the other duo with some sort of flame spell that only left them steaming mad. "Use electricity!" Footpalm and I shouted at the same time.

Aiden nodded, folded his hands, whispered something, then shot two powerful electrical arcs that hit the two on him, instantly destroying them. Garrot, on the other hand, fumbled a spell component, dropping it to the floor. The two watery skeletons grabbed him just as he got his spell off. "Wait!" I cried out to the wizard. "They are too close! You're kneeling in a puddle of..."

There was a loud pop as the two skelementals exploded into a fine mist. Garrot just sat there on his knees with his hair on end and smoking. He blinked a few times, then fell backward. "That's no way to conduct yourself!" Aiden shouted, before running over to help the mage.

"Quit making jokes and help me!" Kellepto screamed at us, as her tormentor pushed her under the water in the fountain.

I ran up to the creature, as it held Kellepto under the water with one hand and swung at me with the other. I knew I couldn't use Sparky at this point, because the high voltage would hurt Kellepto, as well. I did keep punching its face; which, would disappear and reform. That's when I heard Aiden's voice yell, "Coming through!"

Not knowing what he was doing, I ducked out of the way and saw the cleric attack the skelemental with a pair of his underpants! He stretched them over the creature's head until they absorbed some water, then he did the same thing with a pair of socks, an undershirt, and finally his travel towel. He discarded each one to the floor after each use. "Absorb the foul thing until he lets her go!" Aiden shouted.

I quickly dropped my pack, took whatever spare clothing I had, and followed suit. I thought the cleric was on to something, because the creature had visibly grown smaller. After using every bit of cloth I had, I saw Footpalm running toward us, "Make way!" he shouted, while bounding into the air holding a pair of his skivvies.

Apparently, the monk hadn't washed his undergarments in a while, because of the look of horror on the creature's face. "Eat my shorts!" the dwarf yelled, as he stuffed them into the watery beast's jaws. It was at that moment the creature let go of our rogue and pulled the sopping underpants from its mouth. But, it was already too late; I used this moment to activate Sparky and make it disappear into a giant puff of steam. "My lucky drawers!" Footpalm shouted, racing over to pick up his bit of clothing.

"Look," he said, holding them up. "You've put holes in them, especially in the back!"

"I don't think that was Nimbus," Kellepto stated, crawling out of the fountain. "You can blame that on your poor diet!"

"Of all the terrible ways to die," Garrot said, stumbling over. "Being choked by Footpalm's horrid undershorts!"

"This has been a blessing in disguise," Footpalm dryly stated, while wringing out his underpants, "Look how clean these are!"

After taking a few moments to recover, we poked around the room for a bit, inspecting the fountains for secret switches or hidden underwater gold, but it was to no avail. All that was left was an unopened door at the end of the room. Kellepto checked it over for traps and couldn't find any. So, I tried to open it using the handle. But, it was locked. I jiggled it a couple more times, hoping for the best, but it was useless. "Go away," a voice came from the other side of the door, "We're closed. Come back on Monday!"

"We killed your minions with our underpants, Chincey," Aiden shouted. "Don't think it will go any better for you!"

We could hear a lot of scrambling in the room before it went silent again. With a few steps back, I launched myself at the wooden door and broke it off at its hinges. When I looked around, I was very excited to see large sacks neatly tied up and stacked along the walls. There was a bed, a small dresser, and a desk covered with scrolls, papers, and a pair of scissors.

After the rest of my party entered the room, a pair of human eyes peeked out from behind the desk, "Are you after my treasure?" Chincey sputtered.

"That was the plan," Kellepto said. "Thanks to your cousin, Tillman. RIP."

"That's just great," the wizard complained, rising from behind the desk. "All my years of hard work, ruined!"

"Crime doesn't pay," I reminded the wizard. "You should know that. Now you're going to return what you stole, and we'll be collecting some kind of reward."

"Stolen?" Chincey stated questioningly, "I haven't stolen anything."

"Ha!" Footpalm cut him off. "Your cousin Tillman spilled the beans!"

"Did you say beans?" Chincey stated, before quickly opening one of the sacks and muttering to himself.

I looked at the dwarf, who just shrugged back at me. "Aha!" the wizard said, running over with a slip of paper in his hand. "This is a coupon for two coppers off on some beans at the local food market. That is, if you use it on a Tuesday between, 5:15 am, and 5:25 am."

He handed me the coupon, so I looked up at the other curious faces. "Wait a minute," I said, suddenly realizing something.

I walked over to one of the sacks and opened it. It was filled with coupons! My heart sank, and I heard my party groan as I held up a fistful of the paper. "It's just coupons!" I told them.

The look on my party's faces was a mixture of surprise, anger, and sadness. "What do you mean, just coupons," Chincey stated indignantly. "These coupons are saving me a fortune! Do you know how much starting up dungeons cost nowadays?!"

Kellepto clenched her fists, placing her arms straight down and marched out the room, muttering under her breath. Aiden and Footpalm wasted no time in following her out the door. Feeling a bit perturbed myself, I sheathed Abbott and headed out the door, before pausing and looking back to see if Garrot was following. He was stuffing his pockets with some of the coupons. "Really?!" I said.

"We have to leave with something!" he replied, his hair still on end.

Entry 45

One time, my party and I heard about a team of gnome bandits who were planning a bank robbery in the city of "X" in the Province of Darkenbleak. The city had been built centuries before by pirates who used the place to bury all sorts of treasure. "X" had grown and was now a respectable town occupied with large communities of the Unremembered Realms elite.

The Gnoman bandits knew of this, so they hatched a plan to rob one of the city's many banks. They cleverly built a suped-up Boondoggle Enduro racecart to be used to getaway. We almost turned down the job of capturing them, because we thought we'd never be able to catch them. Lucky for us, Kellepto had caught wind of a used racecart for sale in Port Laudervale. The owner claimed that it once belonged to the famous Dragonborn racer Baron Tolaren, who was an occasional champion of the famous annual race.

The racecart was in pretty rough shape, but seemed to roll smoothly when I pushed it. It still even had a fading "94" painted on its side, Tolaren's famous race number. So, we haggled with the owner and took it off his hands for two hundred and fifty gold coins. It was expensive, but we figured the reward for bringing in these bandits would well pay for itself with plenty of extras. After inquiring about the compensation with the city's top constable, we hit the road driving around the banks, hoping to catch the gnomes in the act.

Aiden called down some lightning to power our wagon cart, and soon we were moving down the town's cobblestone roads at a pretty good clip. It didn't take long to find action, because as we pulled close to a nearby bank, we spotted an elf outside with an arrow in his shoulder.

"They robbed the bank," the elf panted. "You have to catch up with them, paladin!"

We were a little late, but I figured we could still get them. "Which way did they go?" I asked the elf.

"They went north on Bridgeover Street," he said, pointing. "It's a straight shot over the river and leads to the Vaygramble Forest."

The Vaygramble Forest was a great place to hide-Knee deep fog, a constant drone of frogs that made it hard to think, and Wanderoot Trees continually moving so you could never mark one effectively to remember your path. Luck was on our side, though, because one of the gnoman bandits had sprung a leak and barely had time to pull up his trousers and get back into their racecart when we spotted them.

Kellepto wasted no time and began shooting bolts at their wagon. Their mage quickly hit the propulsion gears with a lightning bolt, and the wagon swished from side-to-side as it peeled out. It left s-shaped skidmarks on the ground behind it. "Just get me close, Nimbus," Footpalm shouted at me through the wind. "I'll fling them all!"

I turned the steering hard to the right to avoid an old stump, and Kellepto nearly fell out. "Watch where you're going," she shouted.

"The fog is getting thicker," I shouted back, "it's hard to see the ground."

Aiden called more lightning down from the sky pumping up our wagon with a massive dose of power. Within seconds, we were within thirty feet of their wagon and were gaining fast! "More power Aiden," I yelled back to him while trying to steer, "just a little more!"

"I'm giving it all I've got, captain," he yelled back to me. "I doubt she can take much more!"

The cleric was right; I was starting to hear some cracking noises coming from underneath the steering column. "Garrot," I shouted. "Check the glove box and see if there's an owner's manual!"

The wizard wasted no time and opened the small wooden box, located on the front of the racecart. "There's no manual," he shouted. "But this thing has had a bunch of recalls. Something about falling apart under extreme duress!"

"Duck!" I shouted, as I ducked below the passing branch of one of the Wanderroot trees.

"I have an idea," shouted Garrot, as he headed to the back of the wagon, pulling out his Boomstick Wand. "Trust me!"

I cringed at those words every time the wizard used them, but he was the only one with any ideas, at the moment, and I didn't have any of my own. The wizard said something close to Footpalm's ear and then headed toward the back. Little did I know his plan would actually work!

Two days later, we walked in the jailhouse covered with scratches, bruises, and dirt. "Here are the bandits," I began, "and the loot!"

Footpalm shoved the grumbling gnomes forward, and they were led off by a couple of jailers. "Good work, gang," the constable said, opening a safe and handing us a decent sized sack of coins. "Here's your reward."

We didn't have to count it; we knew it was a decent haul. We thanked the constable and started to leave, but then he asked, "How in the realms did you catch up with them?"

I explained the story to him all the way up to the Boomstick Wand, when the rest of my party cut me off. "We were flying down the pathway," Aiden began.

"In ole 94," Kellepto said, "With Aiden calling his lightning."

"But we needed a little more," Garrot chimed in.

"But our wheels couldn't take it, and the doors flew apart," Footpalm cut in, "All because of Garrot's, Boomsticking from the cart!"

The constable's eyebrows were raised. "And then?"

"The force from the Boomstick propelled us forward, crashing into their racecart, smashing both of them to bits!" I said, resuming control of the story. "It took a while to recover the gold, as it was scattered all around, but not the gnomes, they were hanging from tree branches like some angry bearded fruit!"

I'm glad we got paid, but as far as I was concerned, my racing days were over. Especially, when I found out that Garrot forgot to get our vehicle insured and used the money on some fancy axle caps that he said were "Fly." They flew off all right, right into the fog!

Entry 46

Trouble had been stirring in the small town of Drywell. It was a growing town to the north of Lhentil Keep, just west of the city of Humderum. The place had finally grown enough that it caught the attention of the Pathfinders Union; which, had decided to build some roadways to make trading go smoother. Things had gone well for a few months, but then their workers had started to disappear.

A representative from the P.U. spotted us at the Fishudder Tavern and hired us to investigate an evil cleric from Drywell, named Gladman. The psychotic healer had sent him a note saying their plans with the city have now been hauled out to the road. Gladman was now claiming the town for himself.

We left the tavern in high spirits because we thought the job would be easy. Plus, it was only a day's travel on foot, and the weather was just about perfect. Little did we know how that would all change when we reached Drywell. "What's that smell?" Kellepto said, as we neared our location. "Garrot, did you forget to use your deodorant cantrip again?"

The wizard lifted an arm, gave his armpit a deep whiff, and smiled. "Nope. I'm good. Want to give it a try?"

Kellepto frowned and held up a hand. "No, thanks."

We found out what the problem was as we stepped into town. The streets were piled high with garbage! The closer we got, the stronger the odor had become. "This is strange," Aiden said, looking around. "One of the first things the Pathfinder's Union usually sets up is a garbage collection system."

"Maybe this Gladman character raised an army of undead," Aiden stated, "then trashed the place."

"You are very close, fellow cleric," a voice stated as, who we would assume could only be Gladman, appeared from behind a towering pillar of garbage.

The scrubby looking man wore disheveled plate armor. It wasn't real plate mail, but made from dinner plates! The dirty clothes underneath were stain covered, and a cloud of flies surrounded him. His whole ensemble was tied together with a drawstring around his waist. He was short, plump, and had an unkempt beard that had bits of old food in it. "I was once on the city planning board," he started to explain. "But they hated all my ideas, so I became depressed. My emotional state was in the dumps, you might say."

I thought I imagined things, but I swore I heard the big pile of garbage next to him shift around. My party and I instinctively adjusted ourselves into a battle-ready position. "You see, I had been working in the temple clinic for a few years," Gladman explained, while more piles of garbage shifted. "But I became disenchanted, so I ran for the head of the city garbage collection board set up by the P.U. That's when I finally got a taste of real power!"

The piles of garbage had now begun to take the shapes of men! Some short, some tall, and all of them very, very smelly! A dozen of the creatures started surrounding the cleric as he continued, "To earn a few bucks on the side, I began accepting kickbacks for dumping trash from Neverspring here. Elfalfuh, the most powerful elven crime lord there paid me quite handsomely. The problem was where to put it all."

"What does it have to do with these garbage golems?" I asked, pulling Abbott out of its sheath.

"I call them Binwraiths," the cleric stated smugly.

Aiden chimed in, "You couldn't call them wraiths unless these were undead of some sort…wait a minute. Did you do what I think you've done?"

Gladman let out an evil laugh. "That's right, fellow cleric, I started dumping all the garbage into the cemeteries! Then, I raised the undead, but not into flesh, into the garbage itself! You are now surrounded by the town's fallen elders and heroes! And they are fully under my control!"

"Your army stinks," Aiden stated bluntly, "and when we capture you and put you in the Humderum Prison house, you'll have to pay a hefty fine!"

"Enough of this trash talk," Footpalm yelled, flipping his lid. "Let's take these abominations to the curb!"

I would have liked to have written how this was just a throwaway battle, but the creatures got the best of us. It was nearly impossible to stand toe-to-toe when slipping on an old banana peel or getting pelted with dirty diapers. It only took about ten minutes before we were covered with goo, falling, or getting rotten cabbage punches to the face. We quickly retreated down the road and made the long smelly trek back to Humderum with a little bit of blood, bruising, and hurt egos.

To make things worse, the owner of the Fishudder Tavern made us sit outside when we stopped there for a much needed warm meal. "Those Binwraiths are tough!" Footpalm complained. "I still have bits of eggshells in my beard!"

"That was from yesterday's breakfast," Kellepto pointed out, prompting a scowl from the grumpy dwarf.

"We need a new strategy if we're going to stop Gladman and bring Drywell back to its former glory," I said sternly, tapping the table with my finger.

After lunch, I decided to break into one of my extra-long encouragement speeches. I was hardly ten minutes into it when some shouting came from down the road in front of the Humderum Barbershop. "Who is that, Kellepto? You got good sharp eyes and even better ears," I stated.

"Oh, brother," she said after walking out a bit on the road to get a better look. "It's a bunch of druids protesting out in front of the barbers. Something about headlice. One sign says "Bugs are People Too."

"Druids are funny," Aiden said, picking his teeth. "And speaking of druids, we all need to bathe."

All of a sudden, Garrot stuck his finger into the air and yelled, "Aha!"

He jumped from his seat, ran down the road, and started jumping up and down in front of all the protestors. Within five minutes, the twenty or so spellcasters ran by our table and took off down the trail we had come down earlier. "What was that all about?" I asked Garrot, who came back to our table, smiling.

"You'll see," he replied. "Let's wait a couple of hours and go see our ole buddy Gladman.

I didn't know what the wizard had said to the druids, but by the time we reached Drywell, all the garbage was gone, and Gladman sat in the town square in his boxer shorts. Cautiously, we approached the weeping cleric. "What happened here?!" I asked.

"A bunch of dumb druids came by and tore my army apart!" he yelled, before burying his face in his hands again. "They tore them to pieces like it was nothing!"

We all turned to Garrot, who stood there smiling with his arms crossed over his chest. "I told them there was a major recycling drive going on in Drywell. At first, they didn't believe me, but then they smelled me, and it was almost a stampede!"

The representative from the Pathfinder's Union was ecstatic to see us bringing in the renegade cleric and gave us a handsome reward. So, in the end, the P.U. was happy, the druids saved the day, and we were all able to get rooms at a charming inn where we got hot baths and tasty meals. It was only Gladman who was left feeling down in the dumps.

Entry 47

Orcs are not exactly the smartest creatures in the realms. For instance, one time, a dozen of them appeared at my party's campsite just outside of Watercliff when the sun was beginning to set. They came out of the thick brush after I had stepped out of the camp to answer nature's call. "You humanoids are dead meat," said one with a long sword.

Garrot, Footpalm, Aiden, and Kellepto formed a circle around the campfire and waited for the attack to begin. "We kill you slowly," one laughed, while dragging his green finger across his neck.

"I hope not," I said, stepping out of the woods and removing Abbott from its sheath. "We were just about to eat, and I never miss a meal!"

"Whoa, whoa, big guy," the leader said, looking a little surprised. "We not see you. That not fair."

"There's twelve of you and only five of us," Kellepto stated. "You think that's fair?"

"Fair enough," one stated. "We like those odds better."

"Would you mind sitting this one out, paladin?" the leader asked, while pointing to a fallen tree. "You could read book or eat sandwich."

"I don't think so," I said. "And watch you slaughter my friends, while I eat stale bread?"

"That be fair," an orc with a spiked club added. "Me like that plan."

"Sorry, fellows," I stated. "Not today."

"We thought paladins were supposed to be fair?"

He had me there; it took me a few seconds, then I turned to

Kellepto, who was now giving me the icy stare of death. "I don't think so. Let's get this over with."

The orcs took a step back and gasped as I stepped forward. "We have change of heart," the leader stated quickly. "We turn from wicked ways."

"Yeah, yeah," one of them hollered. "We good now."

"Don't listen to them, Nimbus," Footpalm yelled out. "They're lying!"

I lowered my sword. I couldn't harm someone who just turned good. That would've gone against my code. My party couldn't believe it when I sheathed my sword and held up my hands in a peaceful gesture. "You did it, boss," one with half its teeth missing proclaimed. "You tricked him good!"

"That right. I did!" the leader proclaimed, proudly. "Stupid humanoids! I uh…wait minute…uh oh."

The battle didn't take long, and we ended up killing all the orcs, except for the leader who had tried to run but tripped in the latrine hole I had dug earlier. We felt sorry for the poor guy, having to walk home with a smelly and swollen ankle!

<hr />

Entry 48

Bad habits can be hard to break, but you have to want to break them. Footpalm had been biting his fingernails for as long as I could remember, but on one particular day in a Neverspring inn, Kellepto approached him about it. He was playing cards with Aiden, Garrott, and me at a table in the small eatery of the establishment.

As usual, he was nibbling a cuticle, out of habit. This gesture was also the false clue he would use to bluff Garrot into thinking he had a good hand. The wizard would always double his ante and wink at me, before losing his tunic. It was on this particular day that Kellepto came up to the table with a spellcaster none of us had seen before. He wore a heavily sequined robe of red and yellow, had long brown hair, a handlebard mustache, and a protruding overbite.

"See," she told the man, pointing at Footpalm. "He's doing it right now!"

The man nodded and smiled, then began reaching into a side pouch that was slung over his shoulder. "Hey," Footpalm said, setting down his cards. "What are you up to? Who is this clown?!"

"This is Henning," Kellepto replied. "He's an Illusionist. I've just about had it with you biting your nails, so I hired him to hypnotize you and break you of your filthy habit!"

Aiden, Garrot, and I began to chuckle. I didn't know anything about hypnotism, but the thought of our stubborn headed dwarf being under anyone's control highly amused me. "Good luck with that," Footpalm said, crossing his arms and leaning back in his chair. "That malarkey only works on the weak and feeble-minded!"

Henning just grinned while pulling out a pendant on the end of a golden chain. "I've seen this work on one of the biggest brains in the Un-remembered Realms. As a matter of fact, it stopped the pinkish floating creature from attacking my party!"

"C'mon Footpalm," Garrot said. "I've always wanted to see someone hypnotized!"

The dwarf, whose face had gotten red, rolled his eyes. "Alright, al-right," he sighed. "But I have to tell you, nail nibbling has been in my clan for generations. The only way you're going to convince me about this is to have me think I'm a chicken or something!"

Henning asked the dwarf to pull out a chair at the head of the table and face him. Everyone was excited to see what was going to happen, and we watched as the illusionist waved the pendant in front of Footpalm's face. Henning's soothing voice had a relaxing tone; which, I found quite pleasant.

With the snap of a finger, I woke up inside of a broken henhouse with chickens and feathers flying all around me. I was sitting on a crushed pile of eggs. I blinked a couple of times and realized that the people sur-rounding me were laughing. There was Henning, Kellepto, Aiden, some angry looking farmer, and Footpalm, who was biting a nail on his thumb. "It didn't work," I said, as our cleric helped pull me out of the smashed eggs and hay.

"I wouldn't say that," Aiden said. "Well, at least not on the person we hoped."

"Are you saying I thought I was a chicken?!" I stated more than asked, looking at Henning, who just flashed a toothy grin at me.

"It was all just an illusion," he said. "Magic!"

"You should have seen yourself, Nimbus," Footpalm said, while scratching his feet on the ground and flapping his arms. "It was truly a sight to behold!"

Everyone was laughing except for the farmer, who was collecting some gold coins from Kellepto. "Sorry," I told the poor man. "I guess I got a little carried away. I hope we have enough gold to cover this damage."

Kellepto finished paying the farmer, then turned to me. "It's not just you, big guy."

It dawned on me that I had not seen Garrot. "We have just enough to cover his bail," she continued.

"His bail?!" I said, stunned. "How could he be in jail if he just thought he was a chicken?"

Footpalm could hardly suppress his laughter. "Let's just say he laid an egg…in the middle of town…in front of the Mayor and his family… who were having a picnic!"

Entry 49

When I was a teenager, I had dreamed of becoming a RedEye Knight, so I would do odd jobs here and there to save money up to pay my way into their guild. I remember my last summer job was entertaining children at birthday parties dressed up as a clown. Due to my bigger size, I called myself Thunder Britches the Clown.

Kids got a kick out of this character, as I would fight all sorts of comical monsters by crushing them by falling on my bottom. This antic always made them laugh. The job didn't pay much, but I love kids, and hearing them laugh made up for it. Everything changed for me one day while on my way to some small village. It was another birthday gig, so I had slathered on the colorful makeup ahead of time.

My costume always made for a fun walk on the way to the party. People would laugh and wave as I went along in my checkered trousers and large, floppy, red leather clown shoes. Much to my dismay, though, it had started to rain. The house I was to go to was about two miles from town, so I tried to run as fast as I could; which, wasn't easy with those shoes on. The clouds in the sky were darker now, and the rain started coming down even heavier.

When I found the house in the woods, I noticed that it was completely dark. I didn't want to get any wetter, so I ran to the door without knocking and flung it open. At that moment, a flash of lightning lit up the living room of the house. "Aaaahhh!!!" went a bunch of screams.

I thought I scared the children as I saw shadows scurrying all around the room in a panic. Then, out of nowhere, a small staff emitted a magical light that filled the room. It was a band of kobolds! They had taken the partygoers captive and had them tied up on one side of the room. The kobolds had hidden behind bits of furniture when they saw me.

I didn't think I was that scary; after all, I was just a larger-than-normal teenager. A kobold shaman who was holding the magically lit staff pointed to me, and shouted. "Warpaint! Run!"

Apparently, my facepaint had run down my face making me look like a wildman. The kobolds all screeched and panicked, literally running all around me, screaming like banshees. I danced around them, trying to keep upright, but my shoes were still wet, so I fell onto my backside, crushing the kobold shaman in the process! By this time, the remaining creatures dived out windows and ran out the now open door into the night.

I quickly stood up and freed the children and parents. Everyone burst out in applause and started chanting, "Thunder Britches! Thunder Britches! Thunder Britches!"

Word of my feat got around quickly, and the RedEye Knight Guild was so impressed that they waved my enrollment fee and let me join. To this day, I still hear stories about this. Humbly, I like to tell people, "Aw shucks, I was just clowning around!"

Entry 50

Once in a while, I visit the grave of a schoolmate I knew called Dimli. The impetuous boy couldn't wait to become an assassin. It was his life's dream, and he wouldn't stay quiet about it. As a matter of fact, he told everyone he knew that he would be the best backstabber the realms had ever seen. Because of this, it was tough for him to make a lot of friends. He was a friendly kid and honestly thought everyone would be happy about this dream of his. This honesty didn't help when he got older, especially when graduating from a secret guild known as the Hush.

"I can't wait to tell everyone I know that I'm going to be a member of the Hush and the best assassin ever!" he told me after a lunch meetup. "Now, if you'll excuse me, I'm going down to the local paper to make a public announcement!"

"Are you sure the Hush wouldn't mind you doing that?" I asked. "It seems like they wouldn't appreciate press coverage."

"Trust me," Dimli replied. "They have my back."

Entry 51

Sometimes, Garrot impresses me. Not only is he full of surprises, but he gets cool ideas, once in a while. It all started when we stopped at the Dice Tower Tavern in Miftenmad. We had gone in to pick up a new adventure supplement for the Adverts & Accountants Role-Playing Game we enjoyed playing. Garrot went in and came back out, smiling. "I can't wait to play it," Footpalm said, rubbing his hands together. "I can't take any more of Nimbus' stories around the campfire!"

I rolled my eyes as the dwarf gave me a wink. I knew he didn't mean it, I think. So, I made a mental note to drag out my next few stories even longer. "Let's see it," Kellepto said, grabbing at the bag.

Garrot quickly pulled it away. "Tut-tut," he said, slapping at her hand with his free one. "I want this to be a surprise tonight at the camp."

Later that night, we settled into our places around the fire. Garrot stood before us and slowly removed the box from his shopping sack. "Gammaland?!" we all said at once, shocked we didn't see what we had planned on.

"That's right," Garrot stated. "This game is the future, literally!"

"What is it about?" Kellepto said, suspiciously. "I wanted to be a low-level office worker at Nokatomo Industries like we planned."

"Yeah," said Aiden. "I wanted to be a pointy-haired executive!"

"Gammaland happens in space," Garrot explained, pointing at the sky. "Our characters fly around in armored space boats, and use cross-bow-like weapons to shoot energy lights at bad guys!"

The rest of us looked around at one another and shrugged. "I'm willing to give it a try," I said, "It sounds intriguing!"

We filled out our character sheets, and soon we were on our first adventure. My creation was a red-bearded, 7'2" tall, human who wore a green kilt. I named him Angus "Spacestorm" Amberslim, and he carried an energy sword named Energizor. He also had some sort of power pack on his back that allowed him to fly around. Everyone else said this character sounded familiar to them. I had no idea what they were talking about.

Kellepto's character was a slicer named Tinkhull. Slicers were a specialized class that allowed her to break into these light-up space machines that "calculate" all sorts of information.

Aiden played Coppertop, who was a Durocellian. This class carried specialized packs that had renewable energy. They were good at tapping into all sorts of resources to withdraw energy. It's not the most popular class, but Garrot told us you wouldn't want to have a campaign without one.

Footpalm chose a mechanical man called a Bicybormech; which, were like metal golems, except smarter. These man-like machines had the brains of living people stuck inside their metal domes. The dwarf named his character Shortfuse, because it was always angry about being trapped inside a Bicybormech body. Apparently, when he was still in real flesh, he was a rich and handsome space hero.

Garrot was the Game Master, of course, and he led us through a first-level adventure where we battled some floating space goo that liked to cling on to our ship. After overcoming that challenge, we fought a few spy fighters; which, were small ships that worked for the Space Union of Evil, or S.U.E., for short. "That's a girl's name!" Footpalm shouted as he rolled his dice, trying to hit their ships with our energy beams.

"Don't tell them that," Garrot said from behind his Gammaland Game Screen. "You see, they thought it would be funny, since their Imperial Leader was a former intergalactic space lawyer."

We were happily playing our game, then were rudely interrupted by a small band of kobolds who appeared from out of nowhere and started attacking us. The threat was quickly squashed with a few well-placed smashes, kicks, and stabs. Garrot finished off the last one with his Magic Arrow Wand.

"Too bad this wasn't a cool space weapon," the wizard said, blowing on the end of the wand and pretending to holster it in his waistband.

"I swear you live in a fantasy world," Aiden said, casting a small healing spell on a bite that Garrot received.

"I wish I did," Footpalm said, while chucking a kobold corpse into the woods, away from camp. "Then, I wouldn't have to fling dead kobolds into the woods to keep bugbears away from our camp!"

"Why can't we make it a cool weapon?" Kellepto asked everyone. "I know a couple of wizards in Neverspring who'd take a task like that as a challenge."

Everyone agreed and the next day we went to Neverspring and stepped into the Palm Eye Finger Magic Shop. The place was owned by two aging wizards name Bub and Lar. Their magic shop had been around for what seemed like forever, and they had a reputation for thinking out-side of the box. They specialized in customizing magic items to fit the needs of their owners.

"Are you sure you haven't seen him?" said one of two bounty hunters who were showing a wanted poster to the two wizards behind the counter.

I knew who these two were. It was Sunshine and Moonbeam, the deadliest and most beautiful bounty hunters in all of the Unremembered Realms. "Whoa," Aiden stated, wide-eyed as they turned around away from the counter.

"Nimbus!" both of the ladies yelled out in surprise, before running up and hugging me. "Where have you been? We've been thinking about you!"

"Oh, you know," I said. "Just doing paladin stuff. How have you two been?"

The two sisters let me go and smiled before looking at the rest of my party, their eyes dwindled on Kellepto for a second before Sunshine replied, "Making bounties and bringing criminals to justice."

Moonbeam nodded in agreement; her snow-white hair flowed around her shoulders as her head moved. "We have been tracking a hard-to-catch rogue, perhaps…"

"Never heard of him," Kellepto interrupted, before turning to me. "Not to ruin your reunion, but we came here for Garrot."

Garrot had forgotten why he was here, too. He had removed his pointy wizard hat and was combing his hair with his fingers, hoping to impress Sunshine and Moonbeam with his looks. "Oh, yes," he said, snapping out of it. "Pardon us, ladies."

After a few pleasantries, I said goodbye to my old chums and re-joined the rest of my party, who were talking with Bub and Lar. It was nice seeing the two bounty hunters again, though; I found them to be quite noble. I did find it odd that they both kept winking at me, it must be some kind of bounty hunter signal that I just don't understand.

"Oh, we can fix this up," Bub said, holding up the wand and looking at the illustration from the Gammaland gamebook. "Just come back in a few hours."

"Leave the hat, too," Lar said, admiring the conical-shaped topper with stars all over it. "I have an idea."

When we returned a few hours later, we stood in awe at what the two wizards had made for Garrot. Kellepto was amazed at the price, but I didn't mind. Our Game Master deserved a treat, once-in-a-while.

"We laid the wand across this scored half-tube carved down into this wooden grip," Bub stated. "It's kind of like a crossbow without the cross-section."

"A few small magical gems embedded along the sides hold the Magic Arrow wand into place," Lar added. "The brightness of their glow also lets the user know when the wand is low on charges. That was my idea."

Bub rolled his eyes. "I thought of that years ago," he muttered, before turning to me. "Lar's version had bad side effects; which, took years to correct."

"That's an old wives tale," Lar retorted.

"And how long did it take to dispel the tail your wife grew because of that experiment?" Bub shot back, "A month?"

"Three weeks, actually," Lar stated. "And it was a lovely tail. She said it helped with her balance."

"It even has a holster!" Garrot said, excitedly picking the long piece of leather up from the counter. "That's a nice touch!"

Within moments, Garrot had put on the holster and was quickly drawing his new weapon from it. "And now for the coup de grace," Lar said, reaching down under the counter and pulling out a hat.

"My wizard hat!" Garrot said in an awestruck tone. "You reshaped it!"

"Nice brim," Kellepto said. "I've never seen a hat like that before."

"I guess they're getting popular on the western side of Slaphammer," Bub stated. "We saw a play out there a few years back while visiting Hollowood. A couple of actors were wearing them, and we thought it looked cool."

"The mini-gems along the band around its base have some protection magic on them," Bub stated. "This will make it harder for arrows to hit you."

"Will these items protect me from the Off Grays, Bleep Bloops, or the Urkwan?" Garrot asked, hoping to stump the wizard.

"That depends on how you roll," Bub said with a wink, before pulling open his robe to reveal a Gammaland tunic underneath.

"Whoa," Garrot stated. "You, sir, are awesome!"

"That's just great," Kellepto groaned. "Now, we have two space cases!"

━━━━◆ ◆◆◆ ◆━━━━

Entry 52

Some people don't have good luck, no matter how hard they try. Sure, skill has a lot to do with some things, but I swear some folks just can't take their career to the next level. For instance, whenever Kellepto needs a vacation, she brings in her cousin, Bad Rolley.

This clumsy elf needs constant supervision because nothing ever seems to go his way. If there's a trap, he'll spring it, or if there's a monster to fight, it's almost certain he'll drop his weapon or trip over his own feet. Poor Aiden has to follow Bad Rolley around, so he doesn't die before Kellepto returns. For some reason, he is her favorite cousin.

"Someday his number will be up," Aiden said, casting a Negate Poison spell on the unconscious rogue after he sprung a trap on a treasure chest.

It was a simple orcish trap, too. All the elf had to do was turn the knob, undo a bolt, and push a lever to the "Off" position. Bad Rolley had sneezed while turning the knob and hit the latch before unbolting. "I could've done that," Footpalm harrumphed, looking down at the twitching elf. "This fool can't do anything right! I don't see why I have to share any treasure with this nitwit!"

It always took a while to calm the dwarf down; as a matter-of-fact, most of my party didn't look forward to working with Bad Rolley. But, the upside was it always made us appreciate Kellepto when she returned. Even Footpalm would give her a joyful hug. She'd tell us all about her vacation over dinner, and we'd tell her about our dungeon raids and how much treasure we found. These tales always made her smile. Kellepto would ask how her cousin did, and we'd just smile, and Aiden would say,

"Oh, Bad Rolley's getting better," which isn't a lie because he was always recovering from something.

Kellepto would thank us, then gamble over cards with Bad Rolley the rest of the night. I never understood why he was her favorite cousin. I mean, he was lousy at cards, too.

<hr />

Entry 53

I don't know what it is about shoes, but Kellepto is obsessed. The worst I've ever seen her was when we encountered what I called "The Cruel Boots." We were in Achincorn on our way to get some adventuring supplies when we passed by Friar Martin's Boot's N' More. Kellepto froze like a deer in torchlights when, there, front and center, was the most beautiful pair of boots she claimed she had ever seen.

The rest of the guys moaned, so I let them go ahead without us. They wasted no time and quickly ran off. Sighing, I reluctantly followed her in, holding out my hand; which, she promptly put her travel pack in. Friar Martin, himself, came out and greeted us with a big smile. The white-haired man wordlessly pointed me to the "Waiting" bench, while guiding my giddy friend to the window display.

I sat down on the bench next to an older gentleman who looked like he had been sleeping for a while. He had wisely turned his wife's travel pack as a pillow between his head and shoulder. A line of drool had created a small puddle in one of its grooves and was continuing it's drip down on his leg.

It was kind of gross, but I couldn't take my eyes off of it. The only thing that broke my concentration was when Kellepto's voice seemed to come out of nowhere. "What do you think?" she asked in an unusual tone.

I looked over at her to see her strutting around with the boots on. Wincing with every step. "They look great, but painful."

"No, no," she stuttered. "They match my armor perfectly."

Friar Martin shrugged. "I told her those were two sizes too small," he explained.

"But they are one-of-a-kind!" Kellepto moaned, forcing a crooked smile. "I'll take them!"

Friar Martin rang them up, and we left the store hoping to catch up to the rest of the party. "Don't walk so fast, Nimbus," Kellepto complained as we walked.

I rolled my eyes and slowed up. I knew those boots were going to be trouble. Not only was Kellepto slowed up by the pain, but other women kept stopping her to give compliments. "Those are beautiful!" someone would say, or "Those are to die for!"

I didn't know about any of that, but if she was going to raid a dungeon in those boots, they would be to die for, literally! When we found the others, they were outside the supply store looking over a map. "Nice boots," Aiden said as we approached.

"Oh, I just threw them on," the blushing elf responded.

"With a crowbar," Footpalm commented under his breath to Garrot.

"I heard that, you bald dragon dropping!" she growled while stumbling in his direction.

"It was a joke!" he yelled, hiding behind the wizard. "Your feet are dainty! Like an elf's!"

"I am an elf!" she barked, "and these shoes fit perfectly!"

After calming Kellepto down, we hit the trail in search of the dungeon. Kellepto complained about the distance the whole way, but lost her mind when we figured out there was no dungeon or secret caves there at all. It turned out we had a phony map. "Are you kidding me?" she complained. "I can't believe we walked all this way for nothing! Where did you get that map?"

"From some halfling in Neverspring," Garrot replied. "I had a gut feeling that I could trust him."

Kellepto sat on a fallen tree and began rubbing her calves, "We marched all this way for nothing! Ooh, my feet are…"

We all turned at once to look at her. "Um, are looking lovely in these boots," she mumbled out.

"Great," Garrot stated, pulling out another map. "Because I bought this one off him, too. It's only an eight-mile walk over uneven terrain…"

That's when one of Kellepto's boots hit him in the head.

Entry 54

There are some lessons in life you have to learn for yourself, especially when spending lots of money. For instance, there was one time when Aiden needed some new scale mail armor, so we stopped in at Clozadeal's Armory in Turtlesong. We were looking at a new suit of plate mail out on the showroom floor.

"Oh, she's a beaut, isn't she?" said a happy looking fellow approaching us with his hand extended. "It's the newest model for this upcoming year."

"It is nice," Aiden said, rubbing his hand over the chest plate. "I bet it's pricey."

"Hey," the salesman said. "Let's not say no just yet. Why don't you try it on then take it for a spin?"

I had to agree it was nice, but even I could see it was beyond the cleric's budget. "I don't know," I told the salesman while looking at its high price tag, "It's nice and all, but it seems a little excessive. I mean, what's the return on investment?"

The salesman gave me a wide grin and held up one of the arms. "Feel this," he said, rubbing his fingers inside the armhole. "It's got two layers of undercoating…two!"

Aiden seemed impressed, but I wasn't. I had always heard undercoating was a scam. "This baby has zero miles on it," the salesman continued before grabbing Aiden's shoulder and pointing out the showroom window. "Imagine the looks from all the ladies as you cruise down the sidewalk."

I could see my cleric imagining just that. "I like this," Aiden said, looking at me.

"Does it come with any warranty?" I said, trying to bring things back to reality. "I mean, I don't want this thing to fall apart the minute we walk out the door."

"Of course," the smiling salesman said. "One thousand walking miles, and all repairs from boot to helmet. Listen, friends, if you buy used, there's no guarantee of what will happen. The costs will justify themselves over time."

"Has there been any recalls on this model of armor?" I asked. "I had heard rumors at the tavern down the road."

"It's a great deal, or my name isn't Kenny Clozadeal," he said, slapping Aiden on the back. "Now, how about we head in my office and fill out the paperwork?"

I could tell Aiden was already sold, but I was still hesitant. It was his money, but I wanted to be the voice of reason. "How much are the payments?" I asked before tapping on his old scale mail. "And will you take his old armor as a trade-in?"

Kenny looked at it, slightly lowering his smile. "Oh. Hmmm. Not much resale value in this. Lots of dents and scratches. Let me check the Kenny Bluebook."

When we got into his office, he pushed aside a bowl of walnuts and grabbed a worn-out looking book stuffed with all sorts of notes. I grabbed a handful of the walnuts while he quickly fingered his way through the book then raised an eyebrow. "You're in luck, sir," he said, grinning wider than ever. "It looks like I can give you a little something for that as a trade-in!"

Aiden looked pleased as punch when we finally walked out of the Armory. "Mmmm," he said, happily clanging along next to me. "I love that new armor smell."

The large-nosed cleric was happy as a peach as he strutted down the sidewalk, anxious to show off his new metallic duds to the rest of the crew. That's when we passed by another armory and spotted the exact suit of plate mail in its display window. There was a big "Sale" sticker listed on it. It was about 30% off what Aiden had just paid.

I'd never seen the young cleric so furious. We marched back to Clozadeal's and demanded to see the owner, once again. "Kenny," Aiden began. "I just saw this same suit of armor just down the road for 30% cheaper; I want a discount or something, or I'm going to return this item!"

"No can do, son," replied the salesman. "That will cut into my profit margin. I knew about the sale, kid. After all, where do you think I bought the suit?"

"Are you telling me you're subletting the warranty on this?" I said, not being able to believe this guy's arrogance.

"Mmm," he said, pretending to think, "Yup."

Aiden had turned beet red and started undoing the armor. "I want to return this for a full refund!"

"Whoa, there, Nellie," Kenny said, holding up both hands. "You don't want to do that. This suit has got some mileage on it now; it's now worth half of what it was before…"

"We've only gone a few blocks," Aiden snapped. "Nimbus, I think I'm going to do something rash…"

In the end, it never got that far. I stepped in between the two and said, "We made a deal. Come on, Clozadeal, isn't there something you can do?"

"Sorry, boys," he replied with a smirk, "that's just how the cookie crumbles."

"You mean like this?" I said, removing a walnut and placing it in my inner elbow, just on my bicep.

His eyes grew wide as I crushed the nut by flexing. Moments later, Aiden and I walked out a little happier. He never did get a discount, but he did get a free year's supply of Armory All wax.

Entry 55

Word throughout Brokenpoor was that an evil wizard, named Boombah, had hired a dragon to live with him in a new dungeon he had built in the Bookoo Mountains of Rustwood. We had also heard that he was building a sizable army of orcs and trolls. My party and I decided to scout it out for the people. Even if we couldn't take Boombah out, at least we could confirm the rumors and deliver the information to the king of Rustwood, so he could gather his troops.

There was a sparse gathering of trees along the mountain's ridge. It was by no means a forest, but it did provide decent cover as we snuck up to where we were told the not-so-secret entrance was. Just as we approached, Kellepto waved us back and treaded forward a bit. Her keen eyes had picked something up, so we waited until she bid us ahead with a hand wave.

As we moved closer, I could hear it now, too. It sounded like a grown man sobbing and blowing his nose. We cautiously moved forward until we could see what was going on. There was the wizard, Boombah, crying, and stomping on a book. Then, he would sit down and blow his nose into the sleeve of his wizard's robe. I hated to see a grown man cry, so without really thinking, I stepped out from behind a tree and asked, "Are you alright?"

My party gasped at my foolishness, then slowly revealed themselves, too. I don't think Footpalm gasped as much as he did mutter, I didn't understand what he was saying, but I assumed it wasn't pleasant. To our surprise, the wizard didn't act surprised. He barely even looked up as he walked over and kicked the book he had been stomping. It tumbled in my direction and landed at my feet.

"I give up!" he yelled, more at the sky than at me. "It's impossible!"

"Are you giving up to me?" I asked, slowly picking up the book.

"Sure," he stuttered, choking back his tearful frustration. "Why not. It beats living here anymore!"

I looked at Garrot, and he just shrugged. I turned back to Boombah, who had gotten a far away look in his eyes. "So, tell me, paladin," he began, after wiping a tear away. "Are the jail cells clean in Brokenpoor?"

"Sure," I said. "I've put lots of bad guys away there. They are very neat."

This thought seemed to put a smile on the wizard's face, and he started wandering in circles, muttering to himself about how awesome it would be to be away from this dungeon. That's when I decided to look at the book I had picked up. It read, "How to Dungeon Train Your Dragon." I began to get a clearer picture, now. "So, just how bad is it in there?" I asked.

Boombah looked at me with wide eyes and clenched his teeth. "You wouldn't believe it!" he yelled. "That thing is untrainable! I've tried everything! From rewards to routine times and even whacking it on the nose with a rolled-up scroll! And all that got me was a burned bottom!"

"That creature must have a small bladder, too," he continued. "He'd lift his leg on everything! Trolls smell bad enough as it is without that dumb lizard showering them! Even my army of orcs left. They got sick of being on shovel duty!"

Entry 56

One thing that Footpalm has taught me is that sometimes a good offense is a good defense. Like this one time, when we were camping on a trail we had found deep in the Faerwood Forest. Usually, we would have walked around the forest, but Garrot discovered the path and thought it might be a shortcut to our destination. When I pointed out the "Danger: Keep Out" words carved into a tree, he just scoffed and said that was someone's attempt at keeping the trail clear for themselves.

When Kellepto pointed to the humanoid skull that was bitten in half, the wizard just pshawed. "Don't be such a pessimist," he told her. "You see the skull as half consumed, but I see it as half there! Whatever danger is in there, it's belly is probably half-full."

As silly as this logic was, curiosity got the best of us, and we wandered into the trail, hoping it would end up being the short cut that Garrot had expected. It wasn't. By the time nightfall hit, we were hopelessly lost and muttering to ourselves as we set up camp in the mysteriously dangerous Faerwood Forest. While we sat around our campfire, Garrot sang some tunes he learned on his last visit to Hollowood. I enjoyed them, but Footpalm and Kellepto kept trying to shush him, claiming that he attracts attention.

"You know," Aiden said, tapping me on the shoulder. "He's not all that bad."

As the wizard finished his last number, he removed his hat and bowed. As Aiden and I clapped, I saw the frowns of Kellepto and Footpalm. They were both staring at us, intently. The two were moving their eyes simultaneously in a direction as if trying to signal something without garnering attention. That's when Aiden and I both noticed the glowing red eyes that began to multiply in the firelight! It was more than we could count!

"Thank you, thank you!" Garrot shouted. "I'm here all week, don't forget to tip your waitress."

Garrot sat down on the ground and opened his backpack, utterly unaware of the danger. "I just love camping," he said to us all. "Could there be anything more peaceful?"

We heard a few twigs snap before Kellepto shot up to her feet and said, "Hey guys, do you remember that time we ripped off that dragon's head with our bare hands?"

I had no idea what the elf was talking about, but she was looking at the rest of us strangely. Then Footpalm got a grin and stood up as well. "Sure do," he stated. "And used its blood to comb our hair back? Brilliant!"

"That was okay," Aiden said, suddenly standing up from the log next to me. "I liked it when we ate the pulsing heart of that fog giant Nimbus killed with just a stare!"

"And used its intestines to jump rope!" Footpalm stated, while acting like he was doing just that. "They are such weak and pathetic creatures!"

The noise from the woods seemed to quiet down, and the red eyes were blinking back and forth like they were hesitant. That's when I realized what the rest of the party was doing. I don't like to lie, so I just stood up to my full height, stretched out my arms with a yawn, and then started rubbing my belly. "I'm so hungry right now; I could eat almost anything," which was a true statement.

"You want me to go out into the woods and find us something?" Garrot said, standing back up. "I don't mind."

The clueless wizard still didn't have any idea as to what was going on. "I'm hungry now, too," he stated. "And if we're all just going to sit around and makeup stor…"

Aiden tackled the mage before he finished his sentence. "Why go out?" Kellepto stated, rushing over to help Aiden. "Let's just eat one of our own!"

There was a collective gasp from woods, then the sounds of multiple feet retreating. I didn't know what was out there, but I felt a bit of relief just knowing they left. Garrot struggled away from Aiden and Kellepto's grip and stood up, yelling at them. "You people are crazy! Why are you trying to eat me?!"

"We're not trying to eat you, dolt!" Footpalm said, rolling his eyes. "Besides, everyone knows that if anybody were going to get eaten from our group, it would be Aiden."

"Hey!" the cleric said, while the rest of us smiled at him.

"Calm down," Kellepto said. "It was only a joke."

Garrot ran over and stood in from of Aiden. "Don't worry, buddy, I wouldn't have let them eat all of you. Besides, I think you'd be much too stringy!"

Entry 57

Sometimes adventures can pop up out of nowhere, like this one time when my party and I were traveling through the city of Tidepool. We stopped at a place called the Jolly Thyme Tavern to grab a snack. The selection was terrible and the tavernkeep apologized profusely. According to him, the supply caravan had been mysteriously destroyed somewhere along the trade route.

The thought of wagonloads of snacks stolen or rotting away got my pants in a twist. It takes a lot to get me upset, and this is one of my hot buttons. I told the tavernkeep not to worry, because we were on the job. He thanked us and said that if we were successful, we could keep all the snacks we liked. Kellepto was upset about this job and questioned me as we hit the road. "We're working for food again? Why not just hold a sign on a street corner!"

"Frost cakes, Crunchlers, Moon Bars, Crazy Maroons, and more. Sorry, Kellepto," I explained. "This job is too good to be true!"

"You're a walking stomach," she huffed before marching on ahead.

I didn't mind. The thought of all those delicacies danced through my head in a conga formation that led to my mouth. That, my friends, is a treasure beyond measure! After half a day's travel, Aiden snapped me out of my daydream when he spotted the abandoned caravan wagons sitting in the middle of the road, between vast fields of corn. "Where did everyone go?" he commented.

"And where are the snacks?" I said, checking the wagons.

We poked around for a few minutes before Garrot pointed something out. "Hey," he stated while kneeling on the ground. "Why are there sliced up ears of fresh corn lying everywhere. Did the bandits use ears of corn for weapons?"

"That's odd," Kellepto said, holding up an ear. "This one even has blood on it."

"It's eerie," Aiden said, making everyone groan at the bad joke. "Could they have been assault and buttered?"

He laughed at his joke, while we threw some of the ears at him. The last thing we needed, at the moment, was more corny jokes. "Aw, shucks, guys," he said, jumping behind a wagon, laughing even harder.

We would have continued with our fun, but we began to hear a big gust of wind in the distance. "What in the realms is going on here?" Footpalm asked while jumping up on a wagon to get a better view.

"Hey," the dwarf stated. "There is a dark whirlwind approaching us. It's coming from some farmhouse!"

That's when we saw them. Flying ears of corn! Their yellowness exposed as their leaves expanded out in what looked like a manta ray's wings. "Mantacorn!" I shouted out, before pulling Abbott from its sheath.

Before we knew what was going on, we were surrounded by the whirlwind of animated vegetables. Some flew at us, but we were able to knock them back. I thought we'd be pummeled to death, but then a mysterious figure walked through the wall of corn and approached us.

He was thin with white hair and wore thick horn-rim glasses. He wore mostly farmers' clothes except for his jacket; which, was part of an old Slaphammer military uniform. It was adorned with multiple pins. "My name is Colonel Renn Bocker," he barked. "I've told all you people to quit coming through here and stealing my corn!"

"Whoa there, mister Bocker," I said, holding my hands up. "We're just here investigating what's been happening to the Jolly Thyme's supply caravans."

"You mean the ones who were stealing corn?" he said, pointing to the cornfield. "Don't think I didn't have each one numbered."

"Wow," Kellepto whispered to Garrot. "You wizards are cheap!"

"What kind of dark magic is this?" Footpalm shouted through the sound of the racing whirlwind. "Are you some kind of illusionist?"

"Illusionist?!" Renn replied, spitting on the ground. "I'd rather be an orc's luffa!"

The mage walked over to the whirling wall and grabbed a Mantacorn. The vegetable was now inanimate in his hand as he drew it across his nose, taking a big sniff. "Ahh," he smiled. "I retired from the Slaphammer army to relax and try my hand at farming. With my magical abilities, I've been able to grow the juiciest, most flavorful corn this side of the Hoktu Mountains! So I don't like it when revenuers or interlopers like you come in and try to pick me clean of profits!"

"Oh, we're not here for profits," Garrot said, smiling broadly. "We're here for the snacks!"

My whole party did a facepalm at the wizard's poor choice of words. "Aha!" Renn cried aloud. "So, you were after my corn!"

"That's not what I meant! I meant for Jolly Thyme!" he yelled out as the Mantacorns circled in closer.

"So you admit that you steal for a jolly good time!" the old wizard yelled, waving his hands around. "Attack them, my children! Except for the elf, she's kind of cute!"

"Eew," Kellepto replied. "Get a life you old goat!"

Renn turned red. "Attack her, too!"

"Wait," she yelled, "I think you have good eyes!"

But it was already too late, the cyclone of Mantacorn was closing in on all of us. We quickly formed a reverse huddle and began one of our most practiced maneuvers that we called the "Hackerproof Firewall." Garrot stood in the center, turning in a circle while shooting out a Flame Spell. We hunched in front, just below the flame, but also ready to attack if anything survived the blast. Garrot spun and spun, repeating the spell multiple times! After a minute, we could hear popping noises, and we began to get hit with large, puffy pieces of popcorn!

When the smoke cleared, we were surrounded by huge piles of the aromatic snack. "My profits!" Renn Bocker cried out in anger. "What have you done!"

The wizard started to cast a spell, but I held up a hand. "Wait!" I shouted. "What if these are your profits?!"

Bocker adjusted his glasses, then lowered his hands. "What do you mean, paladin?"

"Jolly Thyme Tavern needs snacks," I began to explain. "You're pretty close. This popcorn could be sold there. It's a win-win!"

The older man smiled, then winked at Kellepto. "This could work! Can you set this up?"

"In a jiffy, pops," Aiden said, giving the wizard the thumbs up.

In the end, it all worked out and everyone was happy…well, except for Kellepto, who had wanted gold instead of snack food for some reason that I couldn't understand.

Entry 58

Sometimes, I'm genuinely amazed at the lengths some dungeon masters will go to keep their operations running. There are raids on the locals, fending off heroes such as us, plundering them for gold or magic items, but there are also some other routes they can take.

For instance, one time, we fought our way through the Dungeon of Negativeno, a rising power in Sunkensod. The dungeon had everything, man-eating Death Globs, Shambling Hounds, and even a few Sporcs (spell-casting orcs). It was a rough go, but we managed to clear the place of all evil. The only problem was that it wasn't very rewarding.

"Where's all the loot?" Kellepto said as she searched the fallen leader's corpse. "I've searched his room eight times!"

"Maybe he ran this place on a tight budget," Garrot explained. "I'm always living delve-to-delve."

"We're missing something," the elf said, inspecting the walls for secret switches. "There has got to be something more!"

"What about all those messages carved into the walls in hallways outside?" Aiden asked. "Remember, we couldn't decipher any of them, so we ignored them."

"I wonder what it says," I commented. "Maybe it gives a clue as to whereabouts of the treasure."

"It's written in some evil tongue," Garrot stated. "None of us speak it, but I might have an idea on how to decipher it."

Following our mage's advice, we went back to the inn. Soon, we were surrounded by dozens of boxes of cereal. Garrot walked around the table, explaining his plan. "It says here on the box that if you send in enough Magic Flakes box tops, you can get a magical decoder ring."

"Are you kidding me?" Kellepto said, slapping her forehead. "This is your plan?!"

"You have a better one?" the wizard smugly stated, crossing his arms and raising an eyebrow. "Cuz' we'd all love to hear it!"

"This garbage better taste good," she complained. "It cost us a fortune!"

It took two weeks for the magical decoder ring to reach the Der Waffle Haus Inn. It was just in time too, because we had just finished the last of all the cereal. "I never want to hear of Magic Flakes again!" Footpalm complained, pushing his empty bowl away and belching. "I'd rather eat one of Garrot's socks!"

Garrot slipped the ring on, and we headed back to Negativeno's Dungeon. We slipped under the Do Not Enter warning tape that I had left on its entrance when we left. We shooed out a couple of druids who had decided to squat there. "Finders keepers, right Jinglemilk?" one said to the other.

"That's right, Flip Flop," the other one answered. "I can dig that."

I held my fist up to the one called Jinglemilk's nose. "I'm a paladin and you are trespassing. Do I need to bring you two in?"

Jinglemilk touched my fist with his fingertip and gulped. "Let's go somewhere else, Flipflop. This cat is a negative vibe merchant."

After they left, we went to a message written on a wall. We were giddy with excitement. "C'mon Garrot, hurry up!" Kellepto said, pushing him forward.

"Yes, yes, of course," he said, holding his hand up with the ring on it.

The ring glowed an eerie green color and slowly, but surely, the symbols turned into letters that we could all read. "Eat more Magic Flakes. A nutritious part of your daily breakfast."

"The messages are all advertisements!" Garrot laughed. "So that's how Negativeno was funding his dungeon! Ain't that a hoot?!"

I swear I could taste the Magic Flakes rise in my throat. I have to admit, though, they do give you lots of energy. Kellepto, Aiden, Footpalm, and I chased Garrot around for almost twenty minutes!

Entry 59

Sometimes ignorance is bliss. Did you know that the free buffet at weddings, funerals, or guild graduation ceremonies are not necessarily open to the public? I did not realize this until I took Aiden with me to an event one time. After he told me it all made sense. "So that's why they are always staring at me," I said to the cleric. "I thought my reputation as a hero just preceded me."

"You've gotten a reputation around here, alright," Aiden replied. "But I don't think it's as a hero!"

I felt quite embarrassed, and I apologized to the new bride after a quick dance. I felt a little humiliated, so I made sure we left after the third course.

Entry 60

"Hold on," the undead creature huffed and puffed. "You guys are too fast!"

We stopped and turned around to see the ghost leaning on a wall of the crypt. Translucent beads of sweat dripped from its forehead. "Phew," it said. "I need to haunt the gym a little more."

"It's a Flabberghast," Aiden said, as we began a casual walk to the exit of the crypt. "Why any cleric raises one of these is beyond me."

"I feel bad for it," Kellepto said, surprisingly. "I think it blew a suspender."

Footpalm grabbed his stomach. "I know I could miss a few meals. Not much grub gets past my food ring!"

We all agreed to help the Flabberghast and went back. "Thanks, guys," it groaned, and started doing some stretches. "But I'll be alright. Things could be worse; I know a skeleton with big bones who was raised from the dead."

We hung out for an hour or two, letting him chase us around, counting his laps, and even helping him with a few sit-ups. I even let him drain a little of my life force for a quick energy boost. "You can do it!" Footpalm would shout at the apparition in his weird dwarven accent.

In the end, we still left with the loot, and that was okay with him. He felt encouraged and told us he would now exist in undeath with a renewed sense of life.

Entry 61

Sometimes Kellepto amazes me with her practical approach to dungeoneering. I remember two specific instances where she got us into a dungeon by just using a bit of common sense. The first time was when we couldn't find the rumored secret entrance to a dungeon just southwest of Dociletoff. "I give up," Garrot said. "They must have an illusionist or something. The door has to be protected by magic!"

"What day is today?" Kellepto asked the group.

"Tuesday," I said. "What difference does that make?"

"It's early in the morning," she responded. "Tuesdays are trash days in this province. Follow me."

The rest of the party still didn't have a clue, but we followed her until we found the dumpster we had passed earlier while looking for the door. "We already looked here," Footpalm grumbled. "And I'm not rooting around through garbage like some druid!"

"Shh…," she whispered, signaling for us to duck behind some bushes.

Sure enough, an evil-looking older man in slippers and a bathrobe, holding a trash sack, emerged from the side of the mountain. We tackled the wizard and eventually cleared out the dungeon before hauling him over to a nearby Redeye Knight outpost.

The other incident was when we were about to raid an encampment of orcs. We were paid to get rid of them by the Mayor of Shamptown. The orc army had grown big enough not only to be a threat, but they had also applied to have their campsite rezoned. It was now a part of the city. Not only was this a brazen maneuver, but when the corrupt city board approved it, the pesky creatures ignored the payments of taxes. "At some point, they are going to pillage, then kill us," the Mayor complained. "But to top it off, they won't even pay their fair share of taxes!"

It wasn't long before we stood outside the large encampment with our weapons at the ready. "There's too many of them," Aiden complained. "I don't care how good our team is; we're easily outnumbered 10-to-1!"

"Maybe there's a better way," Kellepto said. "If we capture the leader, the rest will probably go back to where they came from."

"That's a nice thought," I commented. "But what do we do, march in and say take us to your leader?"

"Nope," she replied, pointing to a mailbox on the side of the road, just outside the camp. "When they got the approval on rezoning, the city had to give them a mailbox.

Kellepto gave me one of her smarty-pants grins and walked over to the box. There were a few letters scattered on the ground. Some looked like they had been left that way for weeks. Also, there were a lot of coupons and some scam mail. She pointed out to us that the mailbox had a raised flag, meaning whoever lived here had left a letter in the box for the postman to pick up. The elf smiled and showed us that all of the mail in the box were replies to contest scams.

"I can't believe in this modern era, people still fall for this," she laughed.

"Those fools," Garrot grinned. "I sent mine in last week; there's no way they are going to beat me."

"What does this have to do with anything?" Footpalm asked, impatiently. "I just want to beat in some orc skulls!"

Kellepto emptied the mailbox and handed the letters to Garrot, except for one. She pulled out a quill and started to write on a sheet of paper. "You may have been chosen as our top prize winner! Recheck your mailbox tomorrow for the big prize!"

She stuffed the note back into the envelope, then back into the mailbox before putting the flag down. We weren't hidden in the woods long before a lowly orc came to check the mail. It read the forged letter before becoming excited, throwing down the empty envelope, and running back into the camp.

"Now we just wait a day," Kellepto said, smugly.

Footpalm was not happy about it at all, but the next day, the elf's theory had proven right. Around noon, the orc chieftain came out to the mailbox clutching the letter with anticipation. What he didn't anticipate was the face full of foot that our dwarven monk repeatedly gave him. Soon, we were back in town, turning the monster in and collecting our reward. When I tried to distribute the gold evenly, Garrot refused his portion happily. "That's just a pittance," he laughed. "You keep it."

We all looked at him like he was crazy. "You see," he said somberly, "I took all the contest registrations that Kellepto mindlessly discarded, erased their names, and put mine in!"

<hr />

€ntry 62

I've warned my party a thousand times never to break the law, even when they think no one is looking. It doesn't seem like this should be a problem, considering we're all pretty good-spirited. But the exception happens to be whenever somebody gets behind the reins of a wagon.

For Kellepto, it's speeding; Garrot never signals; Aiden parks in handicap zones, and one day it was Footpalm who finally got pulled over for running a halt sign. After receiving the ticket, the dwarf was furious. "That's just typical," Footpalm said through clenched teeth. "I just got my portion of our last dungeon raid, and whammo, right down the commode!"

"I told you to come to a full halt," I said. "You never listen."

"I'm fighting this," he replied. "This is entrapment!"

"No, it's not," Kellepto explained. "I'm a rogue, remember? I would have detected it."

"It still makes me mad," Footpalm said, angrily.

"Look on the bright side," Kellepto stated. "At least he didn't notice you weren't in your booster seat!"

<hr />

Entry 63

Sitting in a tavern can be neat because you get to meet all sorts of unique characters. Once, as we sat there killing time by playing a game called "Crampage"; which, is about overeating at buffets. I was just about to roll for the results of a heartburn spell when we heard the squeaks of two halflings who walked past our table.

"Hey, Hank," one said to the other. "Look at the sissies playing a board game."

The other one laughed and said, "Oh, yah. Total waste of time. Let us laugh at them scornfully!"

We looked up and saw the two pointing and snickering. Both were as short as you'd expect, but in great shape with extra-large muscles. "Beat it, twerps," Kellepto said, "You're messing up my concentration. I can't lose to Garrot, again. I'll never hear the end of it."

The two looked at each other, laughing once again. "Games are for girls, right, Hank?" one said.

"That is right, Frank," the other said. "For girls."

"I am a girl," Kellepto said, getting angry. "And one that could pick both you up by the scruff and toss you out of here on your backsides!"

"We thought you were all girls," Hank stated, flexing his muscles. "Or at least girly men!"

"Haha, that is right. Let us flex and show what total pumpage looks like!"

We watched them flexing for about half a minute, before turning back to our game in boredom. "Did somebody hear something?" Aiden said, holding back a chuckle.

"Welcome to the big time," Frank said before kissing his own bicep. "Look back over here, or you'll miss the show."

"I hope we get an adventure soon," I said, yawning loudly. "I had much bigger plans for today."

"We never plan ahead," Hank said. "Because we're already here!"

"Oh, yeah," Frank nodded, "So save the drama for your mama!"

"Buzz off, you two," Footpalm said, throwing a potato nugget at them. "I'm trying to think of my next move!"

"Hah!" they both replied. "We don't think of moves; we only bust them!"

With that said, they started flexing, doing squats, tumbles, and some weird hairy-footed double-knuckle thing where they used their toes to do push-ups. "Feel the burn!" Hank yelled out.

"You wannabe adventurer's better a pack a lunch," Frank huffed. "Cuz' what you've seen is total, double-aught buffness!"

Getting tired of the two, I flexed my arm, showing my large muscle; which, had to be bigger than both their waists, combined. They became wide-eyed for a moment. "You may join us on future quests, muscle-kin!"

"No, thanks," I said, waving to the waitress. "I think I'm going to order a second lunch."

"Haha," Hank said, "Frank and I never eat or sleep; it takes time away from the killing!"

"Let us show them our latest moves," Frank said to Hank.

I was just about to say something, but a desperate looking man with a bag of gold came up and said, "Can you two kill some bugbears that have been raiding our village at night?"

"Are we allowed to use our 'bare hands'?" Hank said, holding up both of them.

"Nice one brother," Frank responded. "Let us go swat them!"

"Wait a minute," I said to the man with the gold. "We're the party you want. Bugbears can be tough; therefore, you need the toughest team in the room."

Just then, our waitress showed up with another round of food. "Here are your Marshmallowy Tiddlywinkles," she said, laying the color-ful concoction of cheese, meat, and cake on the table. "I even added the little umbrellas you like."

She smiled and winked at me, as usual, and turned back toward the kitchen. For once, Hank and Frank were silent. The man with the gold just blinked a few times and then said, "Yeah….um…okay."

So, he handed them the gold and all three left. It was apparent my party was not happy with my last order of food; which, was just bad tim-ing on my part. I have to admit; I was disappointed with this, as well. So much so, I almost canceled my third order!

Entry 64

The one person in our party I have the most admiration for is Aiden. That poor cleric has a lot of patience for his patients. I don't know how many times he's gotten up in the middle of the night to answer silly questions or deal with some ailing members of the crew. Sure, there is the odd time that he'll run out his allotment of daily healings. Which, means he's cobbling together some natural cure out of who knows what to keep one or more of us alive. But, most of the time, Aiden is dealing with offbeat maladies or paranoia.

"I think I have heartworms," Garrot would ask while clutching his chest.

"Again?" Aiden replied, before putting what most clerics called an auditory scope in his ears and putting the cold end on the ailing wizard's chest. "It's not heartworms; it's gas."

"How do you know?" Garrot replied.

" Because I can smell," Aiden said with a frown.

"Phew! That's a relief," the mage said, smiling.

"I bet it is!" Aiden replied.

Then, there are other times with Footpalm the Elflinger. "Doc, I think I may have a major infection!"

Aiden looked him over and said, "I can't find anything wrong with you, other than the big jelly stain on your bottom!"

"How do you know it's jelly? How do you know it's not some dangerous secretion?" the dwarf said, desperately.

"Because it was my sandwich that you sat on," Aiden said, sadly. "I wondered why it was shaped all weird when I came back to our table. Now I think I'm going to be sick!"

Then, there was Kellepto. "Aiden, can you remove a curse?"

"I'm not sure," he replied. "Describe the discomfort."

"It's a pain in my neck, actually," she explained. "Not literally, though. You see, every time I finally get around to eating my special snack from our supply wagon, it's gone."

"Hmmm," Aiden nodded, jotting down a note in a pad. "Sounds suspicious."

They both looked at me. I happened to be standing there, because I came to see Aiden earlier about having a very itchy beard. "You know, Aiden. I've noticed food disappear from my plate at taverns, too," she said, still looking at me. "It's like this curse is always around when I'm adventuring with this very party."

Aiden finished his note and handed it to her. It was a crude drawing of a large bearded man stuffing his face with food. He looked very familiar, so I swore to Kellepto that I would watch over her plate from now on.

Entry 65

The criminal mind never ceases to amaze me. When evil and selfish thoughts take over, it can cloud any common sense you may have. There was a time when we had slain a large group of bandits that had been wreaking havoc along the beaches of Watercliff. They were good fighters, but no match for my crew.

They were all slain, except for one severely wounded guy and their group leader, Malarkus. He had a nice reward on his head, so we looked forward to turning him over to the proper authorities in Watercliff. We had him sitting next to his unconscious friend with both their hands tied in the back of a wagon we rented. I rode in the front with Footpalm, who held the reins. The dwarf sat on an overly stuffed cushion; which, he claimed kept him from getting a sore bottom, but Kellepto kept calling it a 'booster'; which, would infuriate him.

The rest of my party rode in the back with the prisoners, keeping our weapons drawn in case Malarkus attempted an escape. "I'm not such a bad guy," the bandit leader explained. "If you only got to know me, I'm sure you'd let me go."

"I don't think so," Aiden said. "You've committed a lot of bad crimes."

"Is it a crime to want more out of life? To take care of my men and give them a step up in this world?" he said with a sad tone. "Is it such a horrible thing to murder a few wealthy strangers on a beach!?"

"Yes!" my whole party replied at once.

"Tell me, wizard," Malarkus turned to Garrot. "Haven't you ever dreamt of eating a tad better? Am I so wrong to desire a little finger food before the main course?"

"You ate some of your victims," Garrot said in disgust. "You even ate their toes!"

"Mmm…yes! Toe-Fu'd, I call it. Delicious!" he said, licking his lips. "What about you, paladin, you look like you've eaten well. What do you crave?"

"Justice," I responded without turning around. "With a side of spiced potatoes."

"You thought you were an evil genius, Malarkus," Kellepto said, keeping her crossbow aimed at him. "But tomorrow morning at the gallows, you'll just be another blockhead."

Malarkus frowned and turned to Aiden. "Humph. Can you believe what this part of the realms is coming to?" he said. "People like this elf just turn my stomach!"

"Only because you didn't cook them properly," his friend moaned, blinking a few times, before laying his head back down.

"Don't be absurd, Marcum!" Malarkus said, shushing his colleague. "You know I quit eating elves, they never agree with me."

"Or your stomach," Marcum spoke up, once again.

"Quiet you!" Malarkus said, kicking his friend. "Listen, guys; I'm not all that bad!"

"It says here on your wanted poster that you enjoy pushing old ladies off cliffs," Aiden said, pointing to the words written just below his image on the scroll.

"It's a misprint," Malarkus said, sheepishly. "I adore the old bags, I mean, wonderful bags. I was only trying to help them get a clearer view of the rocks below. Is it my fault they can't take a reassuring pat on the back?!"

"It also says you passed wind in libraries, kicked fluffy bunnies, and cheated at hopscotch!" Garrot said in shock. "Those chalked numbers are there for a reason!"

It was no use. Malarkus truly believed he wasn't that bad. He argued the whole ride to Watercliff, and then with his executioner. I don't know why people can't behave, I mean, who wants to end their life with a bunch of lame excuses? Yet up until the very end, the evil Malarkus left this world arguing his head off.

Entry 66

Sometimes, I ask myself why things can't be more cut and dry? When I think I've seen it all or lived through every situation, the Unremembered Realms finds a way to throw me a curveball. Here's a good example of one of these situations that leaves me with a headache.

My party and I had heard rumors that a Dark Cloud elf named Pang was stirring up trouble in a dungeon just south of Horkenspit. Word had it that he had a fondness for traps. People hadn't heard anything from him in weeks, and the people of Horkenspit were worried that the silence might be the calm before the storm.

I was up for the challenge of finding him, and Kellepto seemed pretty happy about this, too. She'd been wanting to practice her trap disarming skills for a while. So, after a day's journey, my party and I found a small trail and followed it through the woods until we reached the dungeon's entrance. When we approached, we were shocked by what we saw. The thing was sealed off by a big round boulder!

To make matters worse, it was covered in dried blood and guts of some humanoids. "That's gross," Kellepto said, inspecting the giant stone. "That must have been some trap."

"Come look at this," Footpalm said. "I think I found who set it off."

Crushed inside the bottom corner was the rotting corpse of some unidentifiable human. There was still a small golden statuette clutched in his left hand and a whip in his right. "That'll help pay for the trip," I said, picking up the statuette. "And maybe even a little trip to the Isle of Fortune for some rest and relaxation!"

Everyone was pretty happy about this, especially Kellepto. She had already picked up the whip and discovered it was magic! "It feels so natural," she said, whipping it around. "It weighs nothing, and for some reason, it feels like I've been trained to use it my whole life! This weapon is going to come in so handy!"

"Well, this guy sure won't be needing either one," Aiden said, inspecting the body. "It looks like he's been here for at least three weeks. The birds have been picking him clean. I wonder why Pang just left him here?"

Just then, a covered wagon appeared from the woods and pulled right in front of us. Painted in large letters on the side of it were the words "Evil Bob's Repair Service." Sitting behind the reins was an overweight human wearing a dirty uniform and sporting a bad combover. We drew our weapons as he grabbed a small toolkit and jumped down.

"Calm down, folks," he said in a gruff voice. "I'm just here to reset the trap for Pang. I'm not looking for trouble."

"Yeah, right," I said. "With a name like Evil Bob, you're asking for it!"

The man just laughed and pointed to the nametag on his uniform. It was located above his left tunic pocket. It read, 'Tim.' "Bob's my dad," he explained. "I'm Tim. I lean more to the neutral side. It's better for business."

This situation had me flummoxed. "How can you justify fighting someone just doing their job, paladin?" he asked, seeing the hesitancy in my stance.

"He's serving evil," Kellepto said, whip at the ready. "I say he is siding with evil. After all, Pang hired him."

"Evil isn't so bad," Tim scoffed. "And it does pay well."

Footpalm decided he'd heard enough, "Let me fling him," the dwarf said, stepping forward. "At least let me break his arm or something."

Tim backed off a few steps and said, "Listen, gang, just let me do my job, and I'll split. Pang's been inside there for three weeks, and I'm sure he's livid!"

"Wait a minute," Kellepto interrupted. "Are you telling me this carcass under the rock sprung the big rock trap, not only killing himself, but trapping Pang and his army inside, as well?"

"Why didn't you get here sooner?" Aiden asked, amazed at the indifferent look on the repairman's face.

"Listen," Tim explained. "We told him we'd be here between one and three weeks. If he chooses to starve to death in between those weeks, that's his business."

"Boy, you are evil!" Kellepto said. "Go ahead, Footpalm, give the ol' boy a fling!"

Tim panicked and started to run, but Kellepto's whip wrapped around his ankles, causing him to fall, knocking the wind out of the repairman. It wasn't long before the dwarven monk had him spinning around before letting him go and sending him crashing through the canvas of his covered wagon.

"Not bad," Aiden said, patting Footpalm's back.

"Not bad my foot," the dwarf proudly stated. "That was superb; it was a direct hit!"

"Right between the B's," Kellepto commented, smiling. "I hope Bob doesn't mind we ruined his sign."

"If he has a complaint," I said, tapping the end of my sword. "He can schedule an appointment. Evil Bob's just got to leave his schedule open for one to three weeks."

Entry 67

My party was raiding the caverns of Sunkensod when I got separated from the group. Garrot insisted that we split up to cover more ground; which, turned out to be a horrible idea. Kellepto and I ended up on our own, captured by these goofy looking creatures that looked like stalagmites. They were tricky because when you got close, they moved like tentacles and wrapped themselves around you.

Once held in place, a group of Smogmen came out and knocked us unconscious. I couldn't believe my eyes when I woke up, because I discovered I was lying in a bed of gold coins! I quickly sat up on my elbows and looked around. At first, I smiled because I saw my friends, not too far away. Then, it dawned on me that they were all trapped inside a cage. They were shouting something and pointing behind me.

I figured it must be something important and slowly turned my head. There, sitting on its haunches behind me, was a huge red dragon. "Finally," it hissed. "You're awake!"

I scurried backward away from it, and that made it laugh. "Don't worry, paladin. I don't plan on eating you…just yet. Besides, I can always snack on your friends!"

"What do you want, dragon?" I said, standing up, brushing off some gold. "Because I am Nimbus "Stormcloud" Slumberdim, and you're not eating me without a fight! Well, it may be indigestion later, but that's still some sort of discomfort!"

The dragon just smirked and lowered its head. "Listen, Nimbus," it began. "I'm glad you showed up. I could possibly use your help. Not long ago, I polymorphed myself into an elf and visited Hollowood. Since then, I've become enraptured in what you call 'Plays'".

I was a bit puzzled at this and shrugged my shoulders to my comrades. They all looked bewildered, too. "You see," the dragon continued. "I think I want to become a playwright. The problem is everyone is scared of me. My horde of orcs, goblins, and lesser beings won't give me a straight answer about the scripts I've written. You, on the other hand, are a paladin. I've heard you won't lie. Is that true?"

All my party was shaking their heads, giving me winks or the shush signal with their mouth and fingers. "That's right," I said, ignoring them. "It's always best to be honest, right guys?"

When the dragon looked over, they quit shaking their heads and began nodding instead, with smiles and thumbs up. Sometimes I wonder how they can be so wishy-washy about things. "So, what happens to your followers who don't like your writing?"

"I eat them," she sighed. "Oh, I know that seems harsh, but I get so emotional when faced with negativity. I guess that's what happens when you're a budding artist."

"You're not making this honesty thing easy, ya' know," I told her. "But I'll do my best."

Excitedly, the dragon ran around in a circle for a moment, giddy to have someone read her play. She handed me a stack of paper written in a tidy script. "Wow," I said. "You have nice handwriting skills."

"Oh, cut it out," she said, blushing. "Go on and read it."

I looked at the cover. "Death of a Swordman, by Trashfire the Dragon."

"Great title, eh?" the dragon said, smirking and raising an eyebrow. "Someday, I hope that when people come out of theaters, after seeing a play, they'll compare it to one of mine to determine if it's good or not. They'll say, 'Oh, that was okay, but that was no Trashfire'."

"What if they don't?" I asked. "What if they don't like it?"

"Then, I'll burn the place down and chew on their guts!" Trashfire said, snarling, before recomposing herself. "I'm sorry, it's just how I handle criticism. Do you think that's a little overboard?"

"Um, just a smidge," I said, holding my finger and thumb close together, so the dragon could see.

"Well, go on, read it," Trashfire said, picking up a golden throne and placing it behind me.

I sat down and started to read, slowing flipping through the pages as the dragon paced in front of me. Once in a while, I'd glance over at my party, who were pacing inside the cage, except for Garrot, who was taking a nap using some gold for a pillow. When I came to the end, I stood up, placed the script on the chair, and faced the dragon.

"That has to be the best play I have ever read," I said. "I found your word choices absolutely stunning!"

Trashfire jumped up in the air, letting out whoops of joy. "I knew it!" she cheered. "I'm going to be famous!"

The look on my party's faces were of pure surprise; they couldn't believe what I had just said. The dragon reached over and lifted the cage off of them. "You all may go," she said, "and feel free to take a little something with you."

They all filled their sacks with some gold coins, gems, and whatever jewelry was within reach. "You may go," the dragon said, showing them the door. "Thank you, Nimbus Slumberdim. You have made this dragon very happy."

I smiled and bowed, then ran out the door, quickly closing it behind me. I leaned against it and let out a big sigh. Kellepto gave me a big hug. "Thank you, Nimbus! I can't believe you'd go through with a lie just to protect us. Is that in the paladin's code or something?"

"I didn't lie," I replied, telling the truth. "It was the best play I ever read. It was also the worst. I've never read a play before."

They all laughed before Garrot chimed in. "But you said the word choices were stunning!"

"They were," I replied. "Stunningly bad."

"This, I have to read for myself!" stated the mage, who tried to reopen the door.

To this day, Garrot is mad that we drug him away from there. But, that's okay; we told him we would make a trip to Hollowood someday, so he could see the play. Word on the street was that everywhere it was performed, it brought down the house. Especially after the reviews!

Entry 68

"Are you awake, Nimbus?" Garrot whispered to me from his side of the tent.

I mumbled a no, but apparently, that was not good enough. Just as I slipped back into unconsciousness, I felt a finger tapping me on the forehead. "Are you awake?"

There went my dream. I had just finished filling my plates at an all-day-buffet when Garrot woke me from that moment of sweet bliss. I blinked a few times. The vision of hot, piled high plates was replaced by my wizard's bugged out eyes and bonged out hair. "I'm too excited to sleep!" he whispered loudly.

"Ugh," I replied, rolling over on my sleeping roll. "At least let me get to the appetizer!"

Of course, it was almost impossible to get back to sleep. The wizard kept rocking back and forth in his spot and muttering. When the blackness finally crept back, I was back in my dream and dipping a golden deep-fried fat cake into some butter. The smell was intoxicating as I lifted the hot piece of food to my lips, and then something grabbed me by my shoulder and shook me. "Nimbus," Garrot whispered. "I thought I heard something!"

As I woke back up, I checked my fingers for the fat cake and sighed. I groaned, "It was only a dream!"

"No, it wasn't," Garrot said. "I heard something moving outside."

"I wasn't talking about you," I said, sitting up. "I was talking about the fat cake."

The wizard looked at me, strangely. Then, he whispered, "I'm hearing voices in the night!"

"Of course you are," I began to say, but the wizard held his finger up to his lips.

"Shhh," he began. "Be quiet!"

"I was quiet; as a matter-of-fact, I was sound asleep!" I said, raising my voice.

Garrot covered his head with his blanket. "Would you peek outside and check? Come on, be a lad."

I wish I hadn't drawn the short straw and been the one who had to accompany Garrot on his secret mission. I always seemed to draw the short straw at times like this. I often wondered why Kellepto, Footpalm, and Aiden winked at each other and giggled every time this happened.

Grumbling, I got off my bedroll and crawled to the flap of the tent to unzip it. I looked outside and didn't see anything unusual. "What do you see? Werewolves? Dragons? Line cutters?!!!" Garrot whispered loudly.

I knew he didn't care about any monsters, but it was the line cutters that had him concerned. "All I see is the same thing we've seen for the last two days, dozens of tents filled with an endless amount of gaming geeks!" I said loudly. "Now, can I go back to sleep!"

"Be quiet!" came a voice from a nearby tent. "Don't make me come over there!"

There was nothing as embarrassing as getting yelled at by the out-of-shape halfling in the tent next to us. The runt looked like he spent more time on his card collections than on his hygiene. "Sorry, Goyder," I apologized, not meaning to be rude.

I tried to go back to sleep once more, but then, out of nowhere, an out-of-tune lute strummed loudly from just outside our tent. A voice cried out in rhythm, "My heart is stuck in the castle, oh baby, don't let your daddy give us a hassle. Your beauty drives me insane, and your dad, the king, is a royal pain!"

My eyes shot open, once again, "Banefire!" I grumbled before sitting up. "I wish someone would smash that bard's lute!"

"I like his music," said Garrot, clapping his hands in sync with the tune. "It draws you right in!"

"But he's been playing the same song, over and over again!" I replied. "The king's daughter this and the king's daughter that! For realms sake, just ask the girl out and go elope or something! Singing about it at three o-clock in the morning isn't getting anything done!"

"My heart is swollen like a fat dragon's belly," the bard continued singing. "That's clear to see through like a cube of jelly! Whoa yeah, baby, baby, baby, yeah, yeah, whoa, baby, baby!"

As I was about to wrap my head in my pillow I heard the song come to an abrupt stop and some yelling. When we stuck our heads out of the flap of our tent we could see Felix Banefire swinging his lute unsuccessfully at Goyder the Halfling, who had his chubby fists balled up and was bouncing around, avoiding each swing of the instrument.

"This is the last time I'm waiting in line with you for a game that you could just buy after the rush of its release!" I huffed, while laying back down. "I don't know why you have to have it on opening day at the Dice Tower Tavern!"

"But it's the Return to Dwarf Mountain," Garrot said, clutching both fists into his chest. "It was one of my favorite games when I was a kid!"

The rest of the night was more of the same. It felt like I hadn't slept a wink in days. But, in the end, I guess it was worth it seeing my party's mage so happy. He got one of the first copies, and even met Eelmonicus, the snakelike dragon from the game. I didn't have the heart to tell him it was just some teenager in a poorly made costume. Garrot was lucky it was me who was with him and not any of the others. None of them would have posed for a sketch with him and Eelmonicus before we left.

I thought it was all over, but for a few months of adventuring, I kept having to hear Garrot sing, "That's clear to see through like a cube of jelly! Whoa yeah, baby, baby, baby, yeah, yeah, whoa, baby, baby!"

Entry 69

I never understood what was so fascinating about Kellepto's books, except for her Manual of Monsters, they aren't about learning new skills or anything pertaining to the history of the Unremembered Realms. Most of these wordy time-killers are light-hearted fantasy romance novels about zombies. She said they were known as RomZom's, and they were trendy in the realms, at the moment. "You just don't understand," she'd tell me, holding one of the books to her chest. "They are stories of true love overcoming all odds, even beyond death!"

"Zombie love," I chuckled. "That's just absurd."

"That's because you're stuck in the real world," she'd snap. "Pardon me for wanting to escape to a place where anything can happen!"

Entry 70

During the winter season in the Unremembered Realms, I tend to sleep a little on the heavy side. I'm glad I travel with a trustworthy team, because sometimes when I wake up, they have to explain things to me. I remember there was a time when we found a catacomb that went deep inside the Hoktu Mountains. We had fought a few monsters and decided we should take a little rest before continuing. I was pretty exhausted, so I fell asleep right away in what we thought was an abandoned orc barracks we found.

When I woke up, I had to push a dead orc off me. From the crossbow bolt sticking out of his eye, I safely assumed that Kellepto had a hand in this. When I sat up, I saw many more dead orcs scattered around.

146

Aiden was healing Footpalm with an injury to his right foot and Kellepto was going over the dead orcs for treasure, while Garrot did a victory dance. "Hey," I said, swinging my legs over the bed. "Why didn't someone wake me up?"

Kellepto just laughed and grabbed a small sack of coins off one of the bodies. "We're highly trained professionals," she claimed. "Not miracle workers!"

There was another time when I woke up on the beach surrounded by dead pirates and a giant squid! I was holding a piece of the mast, or whatever remained of it. "A log sleeping on a log!" Kellepto said, who was sitting next to me, pulling seaweed from her dark hair. "You missed out on all the fun. I hope you at least had a good dream!"

The last thing I remembered was telling the captain of the ship that I was going to turn in because I had grown tired of looking for the pirates who were rumored to be causing trouble in the area. "It was quite a battle," Aiden explained, waving his wet socks over a fire someone made. "The spellcasters were going to town!"

"They thought they had us, but then I pulled out my Boomstick!" Garrot said triumphantly. "I've never seen a ship sink so fast!"

"What about the giant squid?" I asked. "How did it get here?"

"All the combat attracted it," Aiden said, kicking at one of its tentacles. "It brought down our ship so fast that we barely had time to fight it!"

"I don't know how you didn't wake up," Footpalm stated. "It had you in one of its tentacles. It was waving you around like a wee little dolly."

"I was dreaming about being a kid and getting a warm hug from my mother," I explained. "I remember thinking how weird it was when she squirted me with ink!"

The worst incident that happened when I was asleep was when my arch-enemy, an anti-paladin named Clawhammer, showed up to slice me to ribbons. He wore a gauntlet of razor-sharp blades and carried a massive hammer in his other hand. I guess his evil cleric, Harmon, had brought a Ring O' Fire spell down from the sky and tried burning down the inn we were staying at in hopes that my party would run outside, so his team could face us head-on. "Can't anybody read?" Garrot shouted over the top of the blaze. "I put a Do Not Disturb sign on the door!"

Unfortunately for my nemesis, there was a high-stakes bingo game that night in the lobby. Clawhammer's crew was attacked by a horde of elderly grannies who went off their rockers! To make things worse for him, The Black Plunger was also among them. The military genius and war general had retired and was making a living as a civilian in the plumbing trade. Kellepto told me it was hilarious watching the giant armored supervillain running down the street with a plunger stuck to his face being battered with bingo cards, chips, and daubers!

Entry 71

One of the great things about traveling with a wizard is their cantrips. Most people would overlook cantrips; which are minor, non-powerful spells. But, not me, I love them. With the snap of a finger and a Tidepuff (which is a little plant that grows near Tidepool), you can see your laundry washing itself in a barrel of water. It sure beats a tedious and inconvenient visit to a Bog Wizard or a launderette.

It can have its downsides, too, though. Like when Kellepto was in a hurry and threw a red cloak into my wash barrel. It's a good thing I have high boots, or all the other paladins would razz me endlessly about my pink socks!

Another good thing about cantrips for cleaning is that they can be used for drying, too. I think that one is two fingers twisted and a light blow on them. You have to be careful when using a drying cantrip, as well, because too much hot air will shrink your clothes. I know this because I now use a once favored cloak as a bib!

I have to give all the kids out there a warning, though, don't ever accept a challenge to eat a Tidepuff. Not only will they give you a sour stomach, but you'll probably need another one to wash your trousers by the time the mysterious cleaning plant works its way through your bowels!

Entry 72

I remember hearing voices outside of my tent one time when my party was on our way to Turtlesong. We had been traveling down an old trail that Garrot had recommended. When I got my gear on, I stepped outside to see Garrot tending the dying fire, and there was a gentleman who had just left and was walking down the trail. "Who was that?" I asked.

"Some guy named Zyn," Garrot answered. "A Dark Cloud Elf. He was looking for some old lady's house. I guess she makes the best muffins or something. He said they were so good he had to cut off his current quest to follow her for more. I've been watching smoke coming up through the trees to the north, so I pointed him in that direction. He said he was starving."

"Me too," I said. "It's your turn to cook, mage. You better get started before the others wake up."

"No problem," Garrot said. "I just need more firewood."

I patted my magical claymore sword. "I'll be back in a swish."

There was a nice patch of trees off in the direction where the stranger headed, so I walked over and poked around looking for fallen ones. I had only been chopping for ten minutes or so when a little girl in a red cloak interrupted my chores. "Excuse me, woodsman. I'm looking for my grandma's; I'm a little bit lost."

I wiped the sweat from my brow and smiled at her. "I believe there's a place up the road," I stated, then pointed. "My mage saw smoke coming over from that direction."

"Thank you, sir," she replied, before handing me a muffin from her basket, then skipping off.

I watched her red cloak get smaller and smaller as she disappeared into the woods. The muffin was delicious. Probably the best I ever had. Every single crumb was devoured with care. I went back to cutting, but I couldn't stop thinking of that fluffy treat! I decided I had to have the recipe. Aiden just had to make these!

I knew it would regretfully delay breakfast, but I sheathed my sword and left in the direction the girl went. Before long, I could see the cabin in the distance, and then I heard a scream. It must have been her! I ran at breakneck speed until I reached the front door. I checked the knob, but it was locked. Then, I heard shuffling inside, so I started to beat on the door. Before I could bust it off its hinges, the door opened, and standing in it was a genuinely bizarre sight, a werewolf wearing an old lady's robes!

The creature grew wide-eyed at the sight of me. "My what a large man you are," it said in awe.

"The better for rescuing maidens," I replied.

"My what big arms you have," the werewolf stated, nervousness creeping into its voice.

"They're good for pummeling monsters into mush," I said, before pulling Abbott out of its sheath.

"My oh my, that's a sharp-looking sword you have!" it said before making a break and trying to run past me.

Before it could get anywhere, I had stuck out my arm and clothes-lined the wily beast. It did two complete flips, then crashed to the ground with a grunt! A swift punch to the eye rendered it unconscious. I quickly ran into the cabin and saw the girl cowering by a large cooking pot! I had gotten there just in time; the werewolf must have had plans to eat her and her grandmother! "Thank you, woodsman," the little red-cloaked girl said. "Is there any way I can repay you?"

"Just doing my job, ma'am," I replied. "Sorry, I didn't get here soon enough to rescue your grandma."

The girl just smiled. "Oh, he didn't get her," she explained. "She left me a note that she was off picking berries and would be back soon. That nasty werewolf was taunting me with it. He said he was going to cook us both! Please, let me make you a nice breakfast as a way to thank you. My grandma should be back soon, and she wouldn't have it any other way!"

My stomach grumbled, and I agreed. "Can I go get my friends?" I asked. "That wouldn't be imposing too much, would it?"

"Not at all," she beamed. "We'd love to have you all for breakfast!"

I quickly tied the werewolf to a tree, then left to get my friends. When we returned, I found Zyn the Dark Cloud Elf still unconscious and tied tightly to the tree. "Your friend is a true hero," the little girl said to my crew.

"Oh, if there's danger or food," Kellepto said. "Nimbus will sniff it out!"

"Can't be a hero on an empty stomach," the grandmother said, coming out of the cabin carrying two large baskets, filled with food. "Everyone dig in!"

"Wait until you try the muffins," I told my crew. "They are to die for!"

This comment made the girl's grandmother laugh out loud. Every-one else did a slight chuckle, but the older woman laughed so hard that tears came from her eyes, revealing a black mark under one of them! I looked at the man tied to the tree. Then, something dawned on me, and I ran around, slapping the uneaten muffins from my party's hands. "Hey!" Footpalm cried out, angrily. "Have you gone crazy!"

150

The grandmother was baffled and caught off guard. She was about to say something, but I ran over and punched her square in the jaw. This action knocked her back over a pile of firewood, and it collapsed as she fell. My party let out a gasp moments before I kicked the red-cloaked girl in the backside, sending her crashing into a tree! "Nimbus," Kellepto shouted. "Have you gone mad!?"

I pointed to the unconscious grandmother, and they watched in shock as she transformed into a wolf right before our eyes. The same thing happened to the little girl. "How did you know," Aiden said, puzzled.

"I punched the werewolf in the eye earlier," I explained while walking over to untie the obsidian skinned elf tied to the tree.

I held up his face and could see the lavender color of his eyes as they slowly blinked open. "There were no marks. But, grannie's bad makeup job started coming off. They were the real werewolves!"

"They were using their muffin recipe to lure in victims!" Kellepto said, sniffing at the dropped muffin she picked up. "They were using normal ones to lure people in, then knocking them out with these drugged ones!"

In the end, everything worked out. Zyn thanked us for the rescue and after finding his two weapons, a longsword named Talon and a dagger of venom, he promised to take both werewolves to justice in Turtlesong. Later, he returned to our camp to share in the reward from the city for solving quite a few missing person cases. He let us know that the two lycanthropes would be locked up in kennels for the rest of their lives.

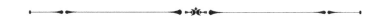

Entry 73

My party had heard rumors of a gathering of orcs along one of the rivers of Two Snake Lake, so we decided to hire a ranger to guide us there. He was a halfling named Yut and had a reputation for knowing the area quite well. As we traveled toward an area he called Crumblestone, he told us of its history. Apparently, many battles had been fought there.

"Most of it has been claimed by the King of Sunkensod to be Provincial Park Land now," Yut stated while throwing a food wrapper on the ground. "But that doesn't mean some thoughtless monsters won't come along and try to ruin it."

"I see," I said, picking up his wrapper.

As we got to the area, I noticed the halfling had a habit of littering, stepping on anthills, or relieving himself on colorful flowers. I started lecturing Yut on not being so thoughtless, but the halfling would cut me off. He would begin to tell a meandering story that didn't necessarily have an ending or point. I was starting to tire of Yut's attitude, but I hoped that we could be a good influence on the little guy. Kellepto, on the other hand, suggested slapping the snot out of him.

We reached Crumblestone by nightfall and made camp in an area that looked like it had been used as a campground recently; there was trash everywhere. "It's one of my favorite spots," Yut explained. "Where you can enjoy the beauty of nature!"

"I should have guessed," I said, shaking my head.

We made camp and had gotten through most of the night peacefully, but then I heard a faint holler. It sounded like a cry for help, so I ran from my tent to find Kellepto and Yut already up. "It's from that way," Kellepto pointed. "North."

I would have woken the others, but we heard the cry again and didn't want to make the person in distress wait. The calls grew louder and louder. When we got about half a mile away, we could hear the cry for help clear as a bell. It wasn't in common tongue, but we could hear it coming from just over the cliff. When we looked over, we could see an orc child had slipped off and was hanging onto a ledge. Thinking quickly, we formed a humanoid chain. I lowered Kellepto by the arm, and then she held Yut. Luckily, it was just enough to grab the orc girl and haul her back up.

The girl jabbered something in orc, but we didn't understand. Then, she hugged us, so we got the idea. The girl then pointed to the woods. That's when dozens of orcs emerged from them with their weapons drawn. The girl ran to an orc of impressive size and looked back at us, hopefully explaining the situation.

The orc, who was obviously their leader, then signaled for the rest of them to lower their weapons, and he approached us. "Thank you," it said in a surprisingly good common tongue. "You saved my daughter. We would be honored if you joined us for breakfast."

We looked at each other and nodded, yes. When we reached their camp, it was huge. Lot's orcs and a smattering of other creatures were going about the place; it looked like a celebration of some sort. "It be our jam-

152

boree," the leader said, showing us around. "It be an annual tradition."

The orc introduced himself as Gurmuffle, and he said we would be his guests of honor. He had even dispatched a crew to bring back the rest of my party. Before we knew it, we were at a big gathering of rickety tables with a wide variety of orcish food set before us. Kellepto looked in horror at a big bowl of gruel mixed with writhing grubs. "I'm not going to eat that," she whispered, frowning at me.

I must admit that I can eat almost anything, and that turned me off. "Me neither," I replied.

The others kindly refused the bowl as it passed, too, except for Yut, who ladled out a heaping spoonful. "Interesting," was the only thing he said.

Then Gurmuffle, who sat next to me, smiled broadly as large sandwiches were set before us. "Mmmmm," he said. "Hot and steaming Mowdung. My favorite!"

Even Yut pushed his plate away this time. Gurmuffle laughed and took a big bite. "Not everyone a big fan of bread, I see!"

The orc waved his hand, and salads were brought out. We smiled and thanked Gurmuffle. He just shook his head. "How you grow so big on rabbit food?!"

This whole event was strange; we were actually getting to see a life in the day of an orc gathering. We watched them play games, converse, and relax and have a good time. I had always assumed the creatures just sat around thinking of ways to kill other humanoids, which they still did, but it wasn't their only focus.

The strangest thing that happened before they let us go was the beauty contest. This tradition must have been Gurmuffle's favorite, because he made us sit in the front row. The big orc asked me to be a judge, which made me nervous, but luckily Yut chimed in, "I'll do it!"

The halfling quickly scrambled to one of the judge's seats near the makeshift stage. Orc female after orc female came out demonstrating all sorts of abilities, alongside showing off what must be considered beauty amongst the orcs. Offkey singing, horrible poetry, passing wind, and scab picking were just a few of the things we had to endure. Aiden and Kellepto couldn't even watch, but Footpalm, Garrot, and I couldn't stop. It was like watching a head-on wagon crash; we couldn't look away.

Like most halflings, Yut was a weirdo, so he cheered through the whole thing. I swear he winked at every female on the stage. Finally, it ended, and Yut strolled back as happy as could be after they announced a winner. "I think she likes me," he said proudly. "She gave me her number."

He held up one of the small necklace signs that each contestant wore. It had the number scrawled on it in some animal blood. At the end of the day, we said goodbye to Gurmuffle and his daughter. The orcs were sad to see us go. They didn't get to hang out with other humanoids often, either, so it was a change of pace for them, too.

"Well, that was different," Footpalm said as we walked down a trail away from the camp. "I enjoyed myself, well, except for the food."

"I didn't like it," Kellepto said. "The only good thing I can say about it is that it's over."

"The best thing about it," Yut stated while holding up his little sign with the number ten on it. "Is that it's annual!"

<hr>

€ntry 74

The notoriously evil Swogglehorn laughed in our faces as his group of highly-trained warriors circled us. "Tonight," he stated, as he paced in front of me, his black plate mail armor shining in the moonlight, "Is the night where I shall kill you and your crew. I will tote your heads through the nearest villages, letting them know that my army is unstoppable!"

His men let out a triumphant cheer as he approached me and pointed his armored finger in my face. "Tonight, the first domino will fall in the destruction of all things good," he continued. "I shall become the most feared man in all of the Unremembered Realms!"

Before he could rant on any further, a small knife flew from out of, what seemed like, nowhere and embedded itself in his eye. With a small gurgle, he crumpled to the ground. His troops let out a gasp. "Wow," Kellepto said, stepping forward. "That was easy."

The troops all started to shrug and murmur amongst themselves. "That was a total let down," "What a loser," and "What a bummer," were a few things we heard before they started to leave.

"Good shot," I told Kellepto. "I wasn't expecting that."

"Neither was he!" she laughed.

"Remind me to stay on your good side," I grimaced, watching her retrieve the knife from Swogglehorn's eye socket.

"Don't be forgetting to wash that blade," Footpalm commented.

With a laugh, she gave the dwarf a small curtsy and said, "Well, that just wouldn't be ladylike."

Entry 75

While traveling just to the north of the city of Achincorn, I remembered that it was Kellepto's birthday. So, the guys chipped in and sent her to the town for one of their famous foot massages. "Thank you," she said. "But it's no big deal, please don't make too big of a fuss. I'll have hundreds more."

Little did she know, that when she went to sleep in her tent the night before, everyone sat around the fire, figuring out what nice things we could do for our favorite rogue. "I'll get some chocolate," Aiden volunteered.

"I'll get the flowers," Footpalm stated. "I think I saw a nice patch nearby."

"I'll get her those nice shoes from Achincorn she was looking at the other day," Garrot said. "I don't know what good fancy shoes like that would do on adventures, though. I'll never understand women."

"She's a rogue, pinecone brain," Footpalm laughed. "Those are used for trapping of a different kind!"

We all laughed, except for the mage, who still looked confused. "I'm writing the poem," I said. "Kellepto loves poetry."

With our plan all set, everyone took off. I went to my tent, retrieved a piece of parchment and my quill, and sat pondering what I could write. It's a good thing I brought extra because most of my attempts at the poem ended up crumpled and tossed in the fire. Finally, I came up with this:

"May your traps be sprung, so monsters turn blue, may you stomp your enemies to death with the heels of your new shoes."

I would have continued, but I was getting a bit misty-eyed. I hoped the poem wasn't too mushy; Kellepto gets uncomfortable when I get too sentimental. I rolled up my masterpiece and tied it with a little ribbon, then sat and waited. I got bored fast and decided to see if I could find Footpalm and help him pick flowers. I went in the direction he went and luckily spotted his footprints; which, led off the trail a little. It wasn't long until I found him lying down in a colorful patch of beautiful flowers.

"Sleeping on the job, eh?" I said, walking up beside him.

I knelt to wake him up and noticed that his eyes were still open! He was slowly blinking, and drool was coming from his mouth! My eyes started to become heavy, too, so I laid down next to him. Before I began to doze out, I noticed small flowery tendrils had embedded themselves in the dwarf's skin where it was exposed. I also noticed the ground beneath me was crunchy. I weakly brushed some of the flowers aside and saw, to my horror, that the field here wasn't made out of dirt, but rotting humanoid bones! After that, I completely blacked out!

I woke up a short time later to the smell of smoke and burning chocolate! I quickly sat up, pulling green tendrils from my face. A fire was burning all around me, and a whining hiss was coming from the flowers. Footpalm was sitting up as well, along with Aiden, who was trying to stamp out the box of chocolates he had purchased. He must have found us here and tried to help! The same was true for Garrot; he was slapping the flames with a shopping bag, trying to make his way to us!

On our way back to camp Garrot said he found the three of us asleep in the field of Tarnations; which, he said was a type of man-eating flower. "I couldn't come in to get you or I'd of been under their spell, too," he explained. "So I figured a nice little Flame Spell would take care of the problem. Besides, if any of you got burned a little, Aiden could cure you."

"Good thinking, Garrot," Aiden said thankfully. "But I can't cure the gifts."

When Kellepto got back to camp, she saw us charred up and still smoldering. We sang a birthday song as she approached and handed her each one of our gifts. "I can't leave you guys alone for five minutes," she chuckled.

She opened the stomped and melted chocolates, sniffed a handful of burnt flowers, read a couple of the leftover lines of my poem, and held up the charred remains of the shoes she had wanted. "Well," she said, "This turned out better than last year!"

Entry 76

Out of nowhere, when I began ordering appetizers at taverns, I started getting attacked by food thieving imps called Distraktions. Garrot pointed them out, saying the magical creatures were nearly impossible to catch.

I'd never seen one, but Garrot insisted they were there. Whenever a big plate of my food arrived, the mage would point behind me and yell, "Look! A Distraktion!"

No matter how fast I turned, I'd always miss them. And when I turned back to my plate, a few pieces of my appetizer were missing. "What did it look like?" I asked.

It must have been horrible, because the wizard was so scared he covered his mouth with his hands and just shrugged. "Did anybody else see the creature?" I asked, feeling a bit perturbed.

But they just chuckled and ignored me, getting back to their food. I swore an oath to one day discover what these creatures were and bring them to justice. Just as I stood up and swore the oath, I realized what had happened. From that point on, I just went along with Garrot's little gag and ordered extra. I didn't mind; the mage seemed to get a kick out of this ongoing joke.

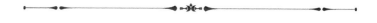

Entry 77

When I first joined the RedEye Knights, I was assigned to an older, more experienced partner named Sargeant Splinterwood. We met in Chief Gallowdrop's office, where he introduced us. "Splint," he began. "This is your new partner, Nimbus Slumberdim."

"What kind of name is that?" the Sargeant huffed. "No offense, kid, but your moniker should strike fear in the heart of every scofflaw on the street!"

I just shrugged while he looked me over. I towered over the old dwarven knight, but his stern glare held me in place. Thunder cracked in the distance as a recent storm had just moved away, leaving the hot summer night steamy and uncomfortable. "I'm calling you Stormcloud," he said, "Because you're way up there!"

It sounded good to me, so I just gave him a nod. He could've called me anything, and I would have agreed to it. The old dwarf looked like a scrapper and not someone you'd want to disagree with too often.

After getting assigned my two light sabers and some armor with the Redeye insignia stamped into the metal, we headed out of the RedEye Temple and began walking our beat. "How long have you been a Red-eye?" I asked.

"Long enough, kid," he said, stroking his beard. "I'm hoping to re-tire soon. Why did you sign up?"

"I want to wipe the evil off of my boots on the curb of justice!" I proudly said, sticking out my chest.

Splinterwood let out a big laugh and said, "I like your attitude, Stormcloud. Plus, you're big as a bugbear!"

"Wait until you see me eat!" I commented back; which, made him laugh harder.

As we walked, he explained, "There is a lot of breaking and entering by bandits, chasing away graffiti-painting elves, transient druids, and a whole bunch of other things for which to keep your eyes open."

It wasn't long before we were called upon to break up a fight at an all-hours café. A large barbarian gal and a pudgy halfling covered in soup were screaming at each other. I thought the large gal was going to squash the little fellow, so we stepped in between them. "This is none of your business," squeaked the halfling. "Now beat it, flatfoots!"

"Whoa, there mister," I said. "We're just here to protect you."

The two laughed in our faces. "Obviously, you've never been in love," the halfling stated, wiping soup from his face with his sleeve. "Let's get out of here, babe."

"Sure thing, sugar foot," the barbarian gal replied.

She picked him up, tucked him under her arm like a news scroll and walked out. The halfling just winked at us as he was carried out. The Sargeant and I just looked at each other and shrugged. "That was strange," I stated as we walked out.

"Anything can happen in this town, rookie," he said. "And it usually does."

We walked by one of the city parks, and it was reasonably quiet—just a couple of druids sleeping on benches, and a stray dog or two. But then, out of nowhere, two large groups emerged from alleys on opposing sides of the park. "Uh oh," Splinterwood said, stopping in his tracks. "Two rival gangs. This situation is more than we can handle without some reinforcements!"

He signaled for me to follow him, and we ducked behind a bench where there was a sleeping druid. "The ones coming from the west side are the Crypts," he said, pointing to the gang. "They're mostly zombies, with a few ghoul friends and even a ghasp or two. Rumor has it they've been expanding."

"Who are the other ones?" I asked, looking eastward.

"Those are the Bludz," Splinterwood whispered. "They are made up of some ghouls and a few vampire drones that serve Thurston Furblud. They mostly find victims to haul over to the old vamp to snack on."

I thought there was going to be an all-out brawl when the two groups met face-to-face, but there wasn't. Instead, two leaders stepped forward and began to chat. Then, from the Crypts, came a roguish looking figure dressed in mostly black. The rogue's hands were tied behind his back and he was acting like this obvious trade didn't bother him at all. A ghoul representing the Bludz pulled out a sack of what looked like gold and pointed at the prisoner. It was at this moment that the sleeping druid we were hiding behind began breaking wind, loudly!

The monsters and prisoner all looked in our direction for a moment. The two gangs both turned back to their discussion, but the prisoner did not. He stared in our direction long and hard; his one eye seemed to have a greenish glow. I noticed him staring at us, or could it have been the sleeping druid?

He started nodding his head like he knew we were there. The two gangs weren't paying all that much attention and continued their discussion. He kept staring and staring as if waiting for something. When the druid let out a loud snore, the prisoner shouted out, "Fumblegums! Wake up, you idiot!"

With a couple of grumbles, the druid sat up on the bench and muttered, "Wuth goin' on, did we win?"

When he stood up, his druidic robe fell onto the bench, and it revealed that he wasn't a druid at all but a cleric! The rogue then kicked the leader of the Bludz in a bad place and threw his back against the leader of the Crypts, who was completely caught off guard. "Hold on, Gwai Lo, I got thith!"

Both gangs had started to close in on us, but the cleric lifted a holy symbol that evaporated gang members on both sides! With a grin, the sarge and I jumped out, brandishing our lightweight sabers. We started hacking the remaining undead to bits, allowing the cleric to reach his friend and untie his bonds.

Undead gang members started to flee, as the vampiric drones started yelling, "Busted, man, run!"

The minute the rogue heard this, he looked at us in surprise, then grabbed the cleric and began to run off. Before they disappeared down a southern alley, the rogue turned around and gave us a quick salute. I didn't get a good look at him, but I did notice he was now holding the sack of gold that the gangs had exchanged earlier. I was going to point it out to the sergeant, but he started blowing his alarm whistle, so other RedEye Knights in the area would come to our aid. I've always hoped to meet the rogue and his cleric friend with the weird lisp one day and thank them for their help with the gangs. They were both heroes in my book!

Sargeant Splinterwood and I both got commendation awards for the bust, and I thought this was pretty great for my first day on the job!

€nτry 78

Watching my whole party die in front of me was horrible. The expressions on their faces burned a hole in my heart that I swear I'll never forget. I had told Garrot about the maneuver we were planning and even he had his doubts. "Are you sure this is even possible?" he asked.

But I was extremely confident, and Kellepto said it was worth the chance. Boy, was I wrong! Nothing went right, and in the end, everyone had met their fate, and it was all my fault.

Footpalm threw the gameboard in frustration after Garrot rolled the exact dice he needed to wipe out all of our characters. "In your face, good guys!" he cried out triumphantly.

"Nimbus! I can't believe it!" the dwarf cried out, pulling on his beard and storming off. "I only had two more moves before I reached the Inner Sanctum!"

Kellepto just patted my back before leaving, and Aiden just stared at me, looking perturbed. I wouldn't have felt so bad, but the Dungeon Escape game was over six hours long, and even longer with Footpalm's endless bathroom breaks. "Don't skip my turn!" he'd yell out from the woods.

I tried to apologize to the dwarf, but once again, he had gone back out into the woods. I don't know why he eats so much garbage. "You can't delay the inedible," I yelled out into the woods.

"Quiet you!" he yelled back. "After tonight's game, this is the only relief I get!"

Entry 79

I love capturing villains and bringing them to justice, and once-in-a-while, I hit the jackpot and find some cool magic items. One time, we defeated Granny Schmidt. She was an evil cleric and rising threat that had wormed her way into the temple of the Blooming Orchard; which, was just on the outskirts of Brayburn in Dragonshelm.

Clerics from Lhentil's Keep told Aiden about this bad apple, so we went to investigate. Unwilling to turn herself in, we had to storm the temple and fight with her minions, called the Jonnaguards. It wasn't easy, but we eventually split them into pieces. One guard, named Crispus, was captured and he told us of a secret door she used as a place to hide out.

We found Granny Schmidt hiding exactly where he described. "I'm just a little old grandmother," she claimed, looking up from her desk. "Look, I've made a fresh pie…"

Without thinking, I stepped forward to see the plump and aromatic treat. That's when she kicked the desk over and cast a Concussive Blast spell, blowing everyone off their feet!

"The pie!" I yelled, trying to grab it as it flew past me.

Everyone crashed into various pieces of furniture, breaking most of it to bits. The crazed cleric then did a triple flip in the air, landing next to Aiden and smashing him in the chest with her mace. The loud crunch in his armor did not sound good. Then, with the wave of her hand, a Force Hammer appeared in the air and smashed Kellepto, Garrot, and I, sending us flying once again.

The only thing that stopped Granny Schmidt was Footpalm. He had caught the pie in mid-air, did a tumble, then jumped up, bounced off a wall, and jammed the pie into her face before she could bring her Force Hammer spell upon him! She stumbled backward blindly and fell over a barrel. "My hip!" she cried out. "I've fallen! I don't think I can get up!"

Bruised and battered, we all managed to get back up and subdue the elderly powerhouse. We tied Granny to a chair where she spat at us while calling us all sorts of unrepeatable things. Eventually, we stuck an apple in her mouth to keep her quiet, but it just fell out with her dentures still clamped onto it. At that point, she kept trying to insult us, but we didn't understand her without her teeth. What is a shmelly phile of foo, anyway?

After searching her, Kellepto found a Minor Ring of Strength, a Circlet of Tumbling, and what Granny Schmidt called a Change Purse. Kellepto donned them all. "This is amazing," she said, "I feel stronger, more agile, and I have somewhere to put my spare change!"

"No, no, no, yoof ool," Granny said, angrily. "Tha purth detech whut you want to wear and gifs it to you. Nothin magical, but at leetht yoo never hath to go thopping again."

Every one of the boys cheered at that. "Don't' get too excited, fellas," Kellepto said. "You're all still going shopping with me!"

There was a collective groan. "You see, boys," she stated. "Your time and patience with me is one of the greatest treasures a girl like me has."

"Then give me Ring of Strength," Footpalm said, reaching out.

"Yeah, right!" Kellepto laughed, sarcastically, before hitting him with her purse.

Entry 80

We had been in the dungeon of Fillbuster for two days before we finally found his anti-chamber. We were beat-up, bruised, tired, and nearly depleted of strength when we decided to proceed, anyway. My party just wanted to get the job over with and head back to Port Laudervale for a much-needed vacation.

"So, you've found me," Fillbuster said from his throne. "It is of no matter. My troops will be here in just a few seconds."

It was a nice sized room with lots of elegant furniture. Rich tapestries covered the walls and a beautiful assortment of foods sat on a desk, along with maps of the area. "Your troops aren't coming," Kellepto remarked. "As a matter of fact, they fell to pieces when we encountered them!"

She held out her dagger and let green blood drip onto the floor. Fillbuster looked shocked. "My trolls!" he yelled, losing his composure.

"You can surrender peacefully," I started to say, but then was cut off by Kellepto.

"Or die," she cut in, starting to move toward him.

"Whoa, whoa, whoa," Fillbuster said, holding both hands up. "You didn't get to hear my evil speech, yet."

This comment didn't stop any of us from moving forward. "You," Fillbuster yelled, pointing at me. "You're a paladin. Y..y..you know I'm allowed one evil speech…it's in your Oaths and Regulations Handbook!"

My party stopped and looked at me. The villain had me there. Had I forgotten this was even a thing? I took off my pack, pulled out the book, and looked through the index. "Hmmm…Earning Gold…Eating Etiquette… ah, here it is, Evil Speeches," I said before flipping to the proper page. "And thou shalt listen to the end of an evildoers speech, showing politeness."

"Wow," Garrot said. "That stinks."

"Oh, brother," Footpalm said, grabbing a banana off the guy's desk. "Hurry up, will you? I'm hungry."

"Go ahead," I said, sighing. "We're listening."

This legality seemed to make Fillbuster happy. "Ahem," he began by clearing his throat. "Ever since I was an evil child, I wanted to be a bully, but no one cared. Most of the kids at my school didn't want me to bully them. My analyst said this was some form of oppression and I needed to get it all out of my system. I suppose I just needed to release my inner tyrant…."

After the seventh hour of this long-winded meandering and nonsensical speech, Aiden and Footpalm had fallen asleep on the floor. Garrot was transfixed, even raising his hand to ask questions. Kellepto, on the other hand, kept pacing around me. "Can I hit him on the head with a brick?" she kept asking me.

"Who? Fillbuster or Garrot?" I replied with a chuckle.

She grinned for a moment, as if contemplating. "Good question," she replied.

At the tenth hour, Fillbuster's voice was starting to get hoarse. I did notice that he would periodically glance at the door with hope in his eyes. We, on the other hand, had eaten all the food off his desk, drank his water, and were in the middle of our third round of cards. "Are you guys listening to me anymore?" Fillbuster asked, becoming irate. "Because I've only begun! This speech was only the beginning!"

A few hours later, he was kneeling on the floor, nearly out of breath. "And that, paladin, is how I'm going to defeat you and take over the Unremembered Realms!" he pointed at the door before collapsing on the floor.

We all looked at the door, then back at him. "If you're waiting for your trolls, they are not coming," Kellepto said.

"B...b..but they just needed time to regenerate..." he muttered.

"They don't' regenerate if you burn them," I said. "Now, can we go?"

Fillbuster passed out on the floor. So, we tied him up before I slung him over my shoulder. As we left, Kellepto turned to me and asked, "Can I borrow your handbook later?"

"As long you don't rip it up, stomp on it, then throw it in a fire," I stated.

"Never mind," she grumpily said, while closing the door behind us.

Entry 81

One time, I got separated from my party somewhere outside of Blisterfoot. I was knocked unconscious after spotting swamp giant tracks on the trail I was on. When I finally came to, I was sitting in a cooking pot with some vegetables floating all around me. I saw a large female swamp giant wearing an apron and chopping some gigantic onions on a table close by. That's when I heard a door slam. 'Where have you been? Out with the boys again?"

"No," an ugly male giant replied, stepping into the room. "I was out grinding bones for bread, you old nag!"

"Humph," she scoffed. "Don't bowl me over with romance, Romeo. Why don't you ever think of bringing me flowers, anymore?"

He threw the bag of bone flour on the table. "I did bring flour," he said, proudly. "I even mashed up a few dwarves in here."

"Dwarves give me gas," she griped. "I tell you all the time, but you never pay attention, do you?"

"That's because you tell me everything all the time," he retorted. "You never stop talking! I'd need a notebook as thick as my head to write down everything you say in just one day!"

She gave him a glare with her one good eye and he grumbled before sitting down at the table. "Where's my dinner?" he said, tying a dirty napkin around his neck.

"I just started cooking him," she stated, returning to her onions. "It'll be a little while."

He looked at me, sitting in the pot, and licked his lips. My hands were tied behind me, so that I couldn't move around. "Paladin, again?" he complained. "That's the second one this week! Ugh. I'm so sick of paladins!"

"We eat what we trap you big baby!" she snapped. "And you better eat him all this time. You know there are starving giants in Darkenbleak who'd love to have paladin for dinner!"

"Just don't burn him, like you did the last one," he stated. "You know I hate the flavor when they are overcooked; they're too chewy. And for the realm's sake, would it kill you to add a little salt?"

"You know what the shaman said," she stated. "You're supposed to be watching your blood pressure!"

"Don't you tell me what to eat, woman!" he said, slamming his fist on the table. "I do what I want, and furthermore…"

"You two sure do fight a lot," I interrupted. "Why did you ever get married?"

They both looked at me like I was crazy. "Quiet, paladin," the female giant warned. "This is none of your business."

"No, really," I stated. "Did you always fight? Or was there something that appealed to you about him?"

She appeared reluctant to answer, at first, but then she cracked a small smile. "Well, there was one thing," she said, looking off in the distance, as if in a dream. "John used to write me poems when we were courting."

"Oh, Mary," he said, cracking a smile, himself. "You remember those?"

"Your good eye," she began, reciting one of the poems, "reminds me of a dark lake, filled with mud. Your hair, matted with crud!"

"I forgot about that one!" the husband chuckled. "I guess you did inspire me!"

"Oh, John!" the wife cried out.

"Oh, Mary!" he responded.

They quickly embraced and started dancing around the room. In the process, the duo knocked over the cauldron I was in and spilled me out onto the floor. I quickly ran out and through woods, until luckily, I found the rest of my party who were looking for me. "Why are you running around the woods in your underpants?" Garrot asked.

Fortunately, they had found my gear; which, had been discarded. "And why do you smell like stew?" Kellepto asked.

"It's a long, crazy story," I said, "but aren't all love stories that way?"

<hr />

Entry 82

Like most adventurers, my party and I decided it was time to raid the most famous dungeon in the Unremembered Realms, the Temple of Temperamental Evil. The massive structure was built long before anyone remembers and has been the target of many heroes for generations. Rumors surrounding the place are endless, and to my knowledge, no one had ever been successful at clearing it out.

Kellepto wanted to search for secret entrances, but the rest of us outvoted her. "Let's just use the front doors," I said, walking up the massive flight of steps. "There's nothing like a grand entrance!"

She wasn't happy, but went along with the vote. After a quick check for traps, she grabbed a door ring on one side; then I did the same on the other. Slowly we pulled the massive twenty-foot doors open. We stood in the doorway, amazed at the size of the place. The entry room itself must have been at least a hundred feet deep and maybe just as wide. Massive marble columns rose thirty feet in the air. Paintings, tapestries, and stairwells were all illuminated in the moonlight; which, poured in like eerie milk in a haunted bowl of cereal.

No monsters or other kinds of evildoers were in sight, but we could see multiple doors in different areas that probably led to where the action was. As we cautiously took our first step in, something happened that we never suspected. First, we heard a small click; which, I realized later must have been a pressure plate on the floor. Then, there was a series of loud pops and flashes. Lights erupted all around us, causing us to be temporarily blinded. I felt something gently hitting my skin, and when my eyes adjusted, I could see what it was- confetti!

All around us, the small bits of colorful paper fell, along with balloons and the sounds of music, clangs, rattles, whizz poppers, and slide

horns. From the ceiling unfurled a tapestry that read, "Congratulations."
Before we knew it, we were surrounded by all sorts of deadly monsters
wearing party hats and smiling. Emerging from the horde was a lich in a
moldy black robe. "Welcome to the temple," it hissed. "You are the
10,000th adventurers to try to raid us!"

We stood there dumbfounded for a minute, not understanding what
was going on or what to do. That is, until Garrot started jumping up and
down with his arms in the air, "We won! We won!"

After a few hand or claw shakes, we were escorted to a table where
we were given a small trophy, a sack of gold, and official certificates marking our accomplishment. First, we posed for a few sketches with some of
the monsters. Then, we were even interviewed for their dungeon news
scroll, "The Temperamental Times."

"You guys are going to be on the cover!" the lich beamed, proudly.

After doing some mingling and hearing a few choruses of "They're
some jolly good fellows," we were escorted back out.

"You are all welcome back any time," the lich stated, while his minions slowly closed the door. "But just to warn you, you will be lifeless
husks on the floor of my dining room."

I would have returned the polite threat, but frankly, I was still a little
stunned at the situation.

Entry 83

The one thing I have learned in life is that justice always finds a way,
and if we all just obeyed the law, we would be much better off. That's
what I thought the day I left the courthouse in Neverspring. My team and
I had been hired by local authorities to deliver an accused elven mobster
named Crumbs Capeesh to the courthouse for his trial.

It was rumored that Crumbs had made a mess of things in Dirtspill.
He had murdered a local politician at the Whittlewood Tavern, a favored
place among the locals. The problem was, even though there were countless witnesses, they either wound up changing their stories, missing, or
dead by mysterious suicide, like repeatedly stabbing themselves to death
in the back of the head.

I had my suspicions about Crumbs, but he seemed to be confident the court would rule in his favor. "This one's in the bag," he laughed, while riding in the back of the wagon. "When this is over, and you deliver me back home to Neverspring, I'll buy you all lunch."

"No thanks," Kellepto told him, with a sneer. "Our job will be to drop you off outside the Dirtspill city limit. From there, you are on your own, dirt bag."

Crumbs just smiled at her, showing off his yellowing, crooked teeth. As we approached the courthouse, we became surrounded by hundreds of protestors who wanted justice. A lot of them held signs, nooses, and other instruments of pain. Crumbs just laughed and stuck his tongue out at them. After walking him inside, we all took our place in the courtroom and watched one of the biggest circuses I had ever seen.

The obviously corrupt judge would cut off the nervous-looking prosecutor, who mumbled most of his accusations, and would only refer to the defendant as "the kind and honorable Mr. Capeesh." Actions like these made me suspicious about this being an honest trial. The jury box wasn't any better. Even Garrot noticed that half of them bore scars, wore mob-style clothes, and hissed and booed whenever a witness for the prosecution would take the stand.

Kelllepto got fed up and walked out of the court about halfway through; I didn't blame her. But somewhere in my heart, I always believed justice would find a way; it is all part of my paladin's code. By the time the trial ended and the jury came back with the "not guilty" verdict, I was a little disturbed. "The guy should run for Mayor," Aiden stated, angrily. "You'd think this bum was a saint!"

As we left the courthouse, we were met at the steps by hundreds of boos and jeers. Food was thrown, and spit was spat, all the usual I expected from such an unpopular decision. Still, we managed to make it to the wagon where we were to escort Crumbs Capeesh to safety. "The law was law," I yelled out to the people, "It must always be obeyed!"

Of course, it didn't help that Crumbs taunted the people, dancing, shaking his rump, and taking bows along the way, "Welcome to mob justice!" he yelled out.

I'm big, and my team is tough, but the crowd was stirred up into a frenzy! Luckily, Kellepto was waiting for us at the bottom of the stairs with the wagon. We all loaded on and slowly turned around, making sure not to hurt any of the protestors. "I have men waiting for me a few miles out at the city limits. You can leave me there, paladin."

I sighed and snapped the reins lightly to get the horses moving. We had only gone about fifteen feet when Kellepto took the reins from me and shouted, "Whoa!"

"What's going on here?" Crumbs asked. "Why did we stop?"

"Yeah, Kellepto. What is the deal?" I also asked.

The rogue pulled out a scroll and unrolled it. It was an officially stamped city document. "It's a temporary rezoning permit," she smiled. "Officially signed by the City Commissioner. We are now at the city limits."

Mr. Capeesh's face turned beet red. "What!?" he screamed. "Take me to him right now!'

"Oh," Kellepto said. "He's not feeling too well right now, so I doubt that it's you he wants to see."

"Take me, now!" he hollered as the wagon shook from the angry multitude of people around us.

"My job was to take you to the city limits," I said. "I believe it was a nice ride, now get out."

"I can help him out," Footpalm the Elflinger said eagerly, grabbing the elf by the arm. "Right this way, sir!"

Before Crumbs could react, he was flung like a ragdoll over the awaiting crowd. "Welcome to mob justice," Garrot shouted out to him as the mobster landed in so many awaiting arms. "That was a great stroke of luck," I said happily to Kellepto. "How did you get the City Commissioner to rezone on such short notice? I was convinced mobsters poisoned his mind."

"That's close," she replied. "However they got to him, I don't know. So, I thought I'd sit down and have a cup of tea with him. Then, out of the blue, he filled out this temporary rezoning form that I requested."

"You certainly have a way with words," I beamed, "I just don't know how you do it, Kellepto."

"A lady has to have her secrets," she said, twisting an empty vial between her fingers. "Now, let's get out of here."

Entry 84

While making our way across some plains near Skull Hollow, we came to Dip Valley, where two hills created a path that you were required to pass through. Bandits and other neer-do-wells loved to do ambushes there, but we decided to take a chance going through, instead of spending an extra day walking around the place. Soon, we were at Stone Pass, where somebody had rolled a bunch of stones down, not only to narrow the pass, but to give them a place to hide.

"Watch out," I told the rest of the party, "and be ready for anything."

Just as I finished the warning, an arrow hit me in the chest but glanced off my chest plate and stuck in the dirt next to me. My party scrambled behind Garrot and he cast a Deflector Shield spell. A few more arrows came at us, but were bounced away with no problem.

"Your shield won't last forever," said a musclebound orc, stepping out from behind the rocks. "Pay the toll, or we take your skulls!"

Kellepto jumped out from behind the shield and fired her crossbow at the orc. He knocked the bolt away from him with little effort. He laughed. "We have all day," he yelled.

"These aren't ordinary orcs," Kellepto said. "I spotted a duty mark on his shoulder."

"What's a duty mark?" Footpalm asked.

"They are special forces from Skull Hollow, called the Skull Riders," she replied. "I've heard of them before. This unit is made up of Slinky Sly, Scarity, Shutterspy, Roadapple, and Rainbow Smash."

"Which one is the leader?" I asked.

"From what I heard, it's Rainbow Smash, who've we've just seen. But originally, it was Slinky Sly, who organized the party."

"How is the Deflector Shield, Garrot?" I asked.

"It's strong, but won't last forever!" the mage replied.

Arrows, sling stones, and few throwing knives struck the shield, causing it to flicker a bit. I was just about to ask Aiden for any suggestions, but the cleric started a small chant. Then, from out of nowhere, a Ring-o-Fire appeared above the enemies' hiding spot. I loved that spell; it came in handy in times like this. But before I got my hopes too high, Roadapple, their shaman, cast a shield of his own above them, blocking the flames.

The day dragged on and more spells were cast, arrows were shot, and taunts were exchanged. Eventually, Garrot's spell finally flickered out. That's when Rainbow Smash jumped out from behind a boulder and yelled, "Fire!"

"Were out of arrows," Shutterspy replied.

"And spell components," Roadapple added.

Furious, Rainbow Smash stepped out from the rocks and stomped forward. He halted about thirty feet from us. "We're all out of arrows, do you mind if I grab some back?"

"Kind of," I said, stepping a few feet toward him, drawing Abbott from its sheath. "But feel free to go ahead and try taking some!"

"Tough guy with a sword, eh?" the orc said. "How about we duke it out and see who wins this fight? If we win, you'll be taken prisoner back to Skull Hollow, and if you win, you get to pass without paying the toll."

Rainbow Smash was as big as I was, but this didn't deter me, at all. I looked forward to a good brawl now and again. I placed Abbott back and unlatched the scabbard from my belt, before tossing it to the ground. Then, we quickly started grappling one another. Before long, we were surrounded by cheers and jeers from both of our parties.

I have to admit that we were both evenly matched. Every blow, stomp, kick, and punch was met or given back with equal force. The day wore on, and we kept fighting. Then, after a brief pause to catch our respective breath, we both noticed the cheering and jeering had stopped. When we released each other from our maneuvering clutches, we couldn't believe what we saw. Both of our parties eating lunch and playing cards!

"What in the Realms!?" Rainbow Smash panted.

"Hey, guys," I said. "You're supposed to be cheering me on!"

"You two are taking too long," Garrot said.

"Yeah, we were getting hungry," Scarity added. "Plus, we were bored!"

Bloodied, bruised, and beaten, we stumbled over to the group. Rainbow Smash and I sat down and grabbed some sandwiches. It was hard to eat with a busted lip, but I managed. After a loud belch, the big orc said, "Listen. You guys are all right. Forget about the toll, go ahead and pass."

He held out his hand and I shook it. "Thanks," I said, grateful to find a solution to the situation. "Hey, just what was the toll, anyways?"

"Two gold pieces," he replied.

I couldn't believe it; I would have paid that before any of this fighting had begun! "Why didn't you tell me that to begin with?!"

"You never asked!" the big orc replied.

Entry 85

"Never gamble your money away by playing Hide-and-Seek with illusionists!" Garrot angrily yelled, slamming the door behind him. "I just
lost everything!"

Everyone at the inn laughed as the mage stomped up the stairs in
just his long underwear. "At least he had the back flap buttoned this
time," Kellepto chuckled.

We drew straws to see who had to track down the illusionists to re-
purchase all of our wizard's gear. Footpalm ended up with the short one
and left. When he came back a half-hour later, he too was in his boxer
shorts and a stained undershirt. "I don't want to hear a word!" he said,
stomping his way upstairs to our room.

Aiden scoffed at him. "Never send an elflinger when you can send a
cleric!"

The healer was back within a half-hour wrapped in a blanket.
"You've been fleeced!" Kellepto cried out, laughing.

Aiden stuck his tongue out at her and went upstairs just like all the
others.

I was next out the door and was pretty confident that I could get
everyone's stuff back. When I came back, minus my gear, Kelletpo was
waiting at the door. "Nice sackcloth, Nimbus," Kellepto commented
about my new clothes. "They still smell like potatoes."

"Very funny," I told her. "You're our last hope. They're a tricky trio of
illusionists. Be careful, because Henning, their leader, is full of surprises!"

One hour later, Kellepto came back with all our gear piled in a
wagon. I wanted to scold her, because I had a feeling she played unfairly,
but I was just too happy to have my kilt back. "Cupcakes?" I asked, picking my gear up.

"Everyone loves cupcakes," she smiled, her eyebrow raised.

"Until they stumble away from their hiding places seeking the antidote!" Garrot laughed, placing his hat back on.

Entry 86

I love a good old-fashioned dungeon delve. Monsters to fight, treasures to find, and sometimes you get declared a local hero. Sure, there's a chance that you'll be burned to a crisp, absorbed slowly over time in a Jelly Cube, or bitten in half by a dragon. But, at the end of the day, hopefully, you've done some good, had some fun, and stopped a few monsters from taking over the realms. That's why it's so frustrating to go into a dungeon, ready to fight, and find a "sick day" sign on the door.

"This stinks," Kellepto remarked after reading the sign. "I was looking forward to this."

"You'd think they'd have a cleric around," Aiden said. "Or even a few potions. Even we carry a few at all times."

"Maybe we could heal them," Garrot said. "Then, we could go in for a fair scrap."

We all agreed, and I pounded on the door. "Go away," a voice sounded from behind the door. "We're all under the weather and need a few days."

"We have a cleric and would like to help," I said.

We heard a click, and the door opened just enough for a slobgoblin to stick his head out. A long trail of purplish snot was smeared across his nose. "You would do that?"

"Sure," I replied. "We traveled over three days to get here, and I don't feel like going back and waiting a week before traveling back, again."

"Or you could just give us all your treasure," Kellepto said, stepping up to him real close, pulling out her dagger.

The slobgoblin sneezed on her, spraying her with purplish goo. "Uuuugghhh!" she said, stepping back a few feet.

"Sorry, miss," it said, wiping its nose. "I told you we were feeling poorly."

"Well, since I have to cast a cure disease spell on Kellepto, I might as well do a bunch of you," Aiden said.

After telling us to hold on and closing the door, the slobgoblin returned to let us all in. We were led through most of the dungeon, and Aiden did his best to cure them. I even used my daily allotment of small healing spells from my magic sword, Abbott. Garrot also heated some of the goofy oils that he claimed would heal them. By the end of the day, we cured the whole lot. There were some slobgoblins, a bugbear name Jim, a couple dozen kobolds, and even a Jelly Cube that was off colored. Their leader, a gnoll named Fetchstick, thanked us profusely and promised to give us a fair fight later when we broke back in.

By the time we finished, everyone was feeling good and ready for a scrap. We were led back out, and a slobgoblin removed the sign and locked the door after our exit. "See you in a few minutes!" the slobgoblin said cheerfully.

"We'll be right….achoo…there….achoo," I sneezed.

I looked over at Aiden, and he was pale. It was the same thing with Footpalm. "Oh, brother," I said. "Don't tell me we're all out of curing spells and potions."

Aiden nodded. "No new spells without some rest."

"This is just super," Footpalm said through a series of coughs. "No good deed goes unpunished!"

I looked, now bleary-eyed over at Garrot, who was smiling broadly, and not looking sick at all. "I told you my oils work!" he beamed.

<hr />

Entry 87

Larper Valley was in peril. The undead had started appearing infrequently and attacking the townsfolk, as if out of nowhere. At first, it was no big deal, a random zombie, a few skeletons, and maybe even a ghast or two. Then, they started appearing in higher numbers, so the main council, the Larper Valley PTA, sent messengers out to the King of Rippenwind asking for assistance.

The king was busy facing other challenges, so he put out the call for local heroes to help. When we got to the town, we found everyone in the city doing their part to stop the oncoming threat. Mayor Feauxfidor happily greeted us. "Welcome to Larper Valley," he stated. "We're very grateful that you're here. Our forces are being overwhelmed by these horrid creatures!"

"That's because you don't use real weapons," Kellepto said, observing a man run by with a foam sword.

"We are a peaceful people," Feauxfidor explained. "We don't like to kill, but these creatures are already dead, and they want to eat our brains and nosh on our souls!"

These Larpers needed protection quickly, and that's what we were there to do. We started showing the people of the town our weapons and how effective they were against zombies. They couldn't believe their eyes! We immediately began making them weapons, like clubs and spears. "Real weapons seem to be much more effective," the Mayor said, while inspecting the townsfolk as Footpalm trained them in fighting moves.

"Do you know where the undead are coming from?" I asked the Mayor over dinner around a campfire. "Have you found the source?"

"Rumor has it that they are coming from the south," he began, "and that they are being summoned through some sort of magic portal by an angry halfling cleric named Leapshin."

"How did you find that out?" Aiden asked.

"We sent someone to scout it out," Mayor Feauxfidor said, setting down his fork. "A fellow named Schlingel. He's quite talented at sneaking around. We know because we arrested him after he broke into the First Bank of Larper Valley!"

"Why would you trust him?" I asked. "He sounds a tad unscrupulous."

"We don't have that kind of skill," the Mayor explained. "But we promised him freedom and a little bit of gold. So, he went out and came back, letting us know what was happening. He discovered the source of the undead horde and the portal they are coming through!"

"Where is he, now?" I asked.

"Behind you," Schlingel said, stepping out a shadow, wearing a dark cloak.

That caught us off guard and we stood up, except for Footpalm, who just kept eating. "How did you do that?" I asked, hand on the hilt of my sword.

"I didn't even detect him!" Kellepto said, looking concerned. "He's good!"

"Thank you," Schlingel replied. "Now, let's talk about gold…"

The rogue was about five feet tall and thin with greasy black hair that hung over his eyes. He sat down next to me and grabbed a chunk of chicken off Kellepto's plate. "Thanks," he said, winking at her.

She was just about to say something, but Feauxfidor cut her off. "We're paying Schlingel to lead your group to this evil cleric, so you can destroy the portal and bring her in."

"How are we supposed to do that?" Garrot asked.

"With this," Schlingel said, setting down a gray ball with a cross on top. "It's called a Heavenly Handbomb. We'll run up, throw it at the gate, and the undead portal will be blown to dust!"

The rogue let out an evil laugh that creeped us all out. "Don't worry, big guy," he whispered, leaning over to me. "I talked Feaufidor into paying upfront. So, if things go south, we can always run off and split the treasure!"

I didn't like the way this guy thought, so I gave him a big frown and he backed off. "Why didn't you just have him do it?" I asked Feauxfidor.

"It's magical, so it needs a spellcaster," the Mayor explained. "A quick toss, a few simple words, and kapow! No more portal!"

"Not a problem," Garrot stated, grabbing the explosive and putting it in a brown sack. "The plan is simple; what could possibly go wrong?"

The Mayor handed me a sack of gold and jewels. "This will make it worth your time," he said proudly.

It wasn't long until we were moving quickly down the hidden trails that Schlingel had marked. We tried to be as quiet as possible, because we eventually encountered the zombie horde and had to circle them. There were all sorts of the undead too- humans, elves, orcs, and even a valley giant who looked kind of bummed.

After about an hour, we could see the glow of the portal as it shined brightly through the trees of the forest. I was glad there was a full moon to help us see as well. We stepped gingerly through some brush and knelt at the edge of a clearing. We could see the halfling cleric, Leapshin, was in some kind of trance and chanting. A new zombie would pop out of the portal every few minutes and start shambling northward.

Kellepto came up to me and patted me on the back. "What's the plan, Nimbus?"

"We'll rush Leapshin, and then plant the bomb," Schlingel whispered, answering her.

"Great," Kellepto said. "I'll let the others know."

She ran over to Garrot, then the others. Soon, we all nodded and did a quiet count of three before rushing in shouting for her to freeze. She looked up at us, smiling, and pointed all around. Dozens of zombies appeared from the edge of the woods and surrounded us all. Leapshin laughed as we all fell into a defensive position.

"I have to hand it to you," the halfling said. "You do great work!"

Kellepto embraced me for a moment. "Were trapped! Nimbus, what are we going to do?"

I was shocked. Kellepto never acted like that, and I had never heard her lose her cool before. Before I had a chance to think of what to say, Schlingel approached me with his dagger extended. "Give me the bag, paladin!"

"What, wait? You're with Leapshin?!" I said, confused.

"That's right, you dimwits," he snarled. "I thought the people of Larper Valley were of below-average intelligence, but you guys almost take the cake!"

"Almost?" Footpalm asked.

"That's right," he grinned. "I stole a cake earlier, too, you ignorant rube!"

Being surrounded by a large number of undead, I didn't feel like I had a choice. My mind raced, but I couldn't come up with a plan of action, so I reached down to my belt and unlatched the bag, handing Schlingel our treasure. He grabbed it and ran over to Leapshin. "You're a genius, Schlingel!" Leapshin said. "Letting yourself get caught trying to rob their bank, so you could fool them into giving you a bunch of treasure while I provided the distraction!"

Leapshin and Schlingel both did a quick bow. "So long, chumps!" Schlingel laughed while stepping into the edge of the portal with the halfling. "I hate for this to end this way."

He winked at Kellepto, who gave him a wink back, which looked like it surprised him. "Garrot," she said. "Go boom…"

Garrot immediately said some magical mumbo jumbo, and the bag Schlingel was holding exploded! Leapshin and the traitorous rogue's blood and guts flew everywhere, spraying us and the undead. The portal evaporated before our eyes! The zombies were distracted by the flying guts and started to eat the pieces scattered all around.

My team used this distraction to get ourselves in a better position to start slaughtering the undead. Within a short time, we had hacked the undead to pieces before falling to the ground in near exhaustion. When I caught my breath, I smiled at Kellepto, who was covered with zombie goo. "You switched the bags…" I panted.

"Yup," she laughed.

She pretended to swoon for a moment. "Nimbus, save me!"

"I should have known," I laughed.

Entry 88

One of my favorite things about adventuring is sitting down to eat and finding out what Aiden has packed for our lunches. The cleric takes special pride in making us all something we enjoy.

Kellepto usually gets mixed berries with oats on the side, mixed with a twigling of cinnamon. Once in awhile, she'll get a chocolate-covered fruitnip wrapped in a small purple flower. We were threatened at dagger point that we better not tell anyone about it, so reader be warned.

Garrot gets one main thing every day, nutbutter and picklejam sandwiches. Most people would turn their nose up just at the smell, but like the wizard claims, "They are a 'dillight'!"

Footpalm is more difficult, as he is the pickiest of all of us. He is often pleasantly surprised at what the cleric prepares for him. Butterbread sticks and corn pudding, fish eyes smothered in chilled hot sauce, and maybe even marbled crumblecake. These are examples of what the dwarf will be picking out of his beard throughout the day.

Me? I'm the cleanup crew. I eat whatever's left, because I like it all. If it's consumable, I'm there with a fork and a grin. Aiden doesn't forget me, though. If I'm still hungry, there's usually half a turkey tucked away for me, and even a whole pie for dessert.

You may wonder how we carry all this food around, and the answer is simple: magic! After a significant financial payout from a dungeon, we all agreed to pay a visit to the Palm Eye Finger Magic Shop in Neverspring. The owners, Bub and Lar, custom made an item for us that I had long dreamed about, a Frigid Air Box, or FAB, as I call it. It's like a Sack of Holding but keeps food chilled and fresh. It can hold a nearly endless supply of delicious food!

I like the easy to carry handle and light weight of the device, but it's Garrot who got the biggest kick when they illustrated the outside of it with action scenes from his favorite game, Gammaland.

Entry 89

"You've got to help!" the farmer said, running up to us at the Tilting Table Tavern in Watercliff. "My wife is trapped inside a cave, and an ogre is attacking her!"

We jumped up off our chairs, nearly knocking the table over. "Tell us where she's at!"

"Hmmm….let me see. I haven't been there much before, and I'm feeling a bit frustrated. Was it by the big tree with small rocks or the big rocks by the small tree? It may be by the big tree; my wife loves big trees. You know, we used to carve our initials in big trees. It was always so romantic. She used to say to me, 'Kibbitz, can you carve our name into that big tree?', and I'd say, 'anything for you, Daloopa, my love.'"

"That's nice," I said, feeling antsy, "but where is she?"

He stared off for a moment, and then started talking again. "I know we were exploring along the coast, trying to find a good place to have lunch. We love to listen to the waves on the beach as they come crashing in. It reminds us of how we first met. I was thrown overboard off a ship, and Daloopa was picking seashells."

"Thrown overboard?" Kellepto asked, trying to figure out what he was babbling about.

"Oh, yes," he said, sitting down. "I was in the Barrendry Naval Core for many, many, days. That is, until they decided to throw me off the ship for talking too much."

"And for all that lying and stealing…" the tavernkeep shouted out from behind the counter.

"But if they hadn't, I never would have met my beloved Daloopa," he continued, while ignoring the tavernkeep. "I swore I'd get my revenge. But Daloopa, bless her soul, is a kind person and talked me out of it. She has always been there for me. I remember one time…"

"Excuse me," I said, trying to cut off another rambling story, but it was no good, he just kept going.

He leaned forward, "One time, we were waiting behind this rogue halfling in a supply store. It looked like he was buying a massive amount of scrolls. 'There for making fake maps to sell to rubes,' he laughed when I asked. I thought that was dishonest, so I was going to let the little runt have a piece of my mind, but Daloopa stopped me. She pointed out the deadly looking dagger he wore, so I let that go."

The farmer kept talking and talking, so we eventually sat back down, impatiently waiting for him to get around to telling us where the cave was. After a few hours, Footpalm wanted to fling him out the window, but I couldn't let him do it. If there were a rescue, my paladin's code wouldn't let me ignore it. "Where is she!?" Kellepto yelled out of impatience, slamming her fist on the table, interrupting one of the man's stories.

"Where is who," he asked.

"Daloopa!" we all shouted at him at the same time.

The farmer chuckled, "Silly me, I almost forgot," then he looked off. "Well, actually, there is a long story about this whole thing…"

Footpalm leaped over the table, clutching the farmer by his collar, "Tell me, or I'll fling you up the chimney!"

"Over the hill, down the road about two miles, by the big tree overlooking the ocean!"

We all rushed out the door, dragging the farmer along with us. He never stopped talking, even when we stopped along the way to catch our breath and get our bearings. It was hard not to let Footpalm fling the guy, but we had to press forward, if we wanted to make a successful rescue. It wasn't long after that when we spotted the top of the big tree, and then the ogre under it.

As we approached, we noticed the ogre was sitting down, resting his head on the palm of one of his hands with his elbow on one leg. He looked incredibly bored. In front of him was the farmer's wife, who was talking to him. "Kibbitz," she said, spotting her husband. "You've come to rescue me!"

"Of course, my Daloopa," he said, running up and embracing her.

"She never shuts up," the ogre grunted at us, moving his hand, making his fingers and his thumb simulating a mouth moving.

"We know the feeling," I said, feeling sorry for the big monster.

"Daloopa thinks it's important that you know what happened here," Kibbitz said. "Does everyone have a moment?"

To this day, I don't think my group has ever run so fast from anything! To my surprise, the ogre passed us by like we were standing still! "Why are we running?" Garrot asked, panting heavily, "I kind of wanted to know!"

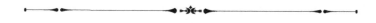

Entry 90

You meet all sorts of unusual people while waiting around at taverns. One of the most unique I met was a halfling rogue in the Ogglewart Tavern in Miftenmad. My party was supposed to meet me there later for dinner, but I decided to go in and get a pre-dinner meal to get warmed up. I saw the little guy sitting at a table by himself, and he had a personalized mug in front of him that read "Spare Change."

I pulled a silver piece out of my pocket and dropped it in as I walked past, and he said, "Thanks, mister."

I walked over to the tavernkeep and gave my order, then turned around to look for a good place to sit. That's when I saw the halfling waving me over. I nodded to him and went over, pulled a chair, and sat down. When I did, a waitress showed up with the halflings food, a top-notch meal, indeed. "Keep the change," he said when paying her with my silver piece.

"Can you afford this?" I asked.

"Sure I can," he replied. "Watch."

Sure enough, after a few minutes, a couple of elves walked in, spotted his cup, and dropped in their spare change. "See," he said. "It's not a problem. Can I pay for yours?"

"Why are you begging for change if you have enough money?" I asked, a little bit disturbed by all of this.

"I'm not begging for change," he replied. "My nickname is Spare Change. I got this personalized mug as a gift, and people keep putting money in it. I don't even have to ask."

"It doesn't seem right," I said, "I think people misunderstand."

"Listen, mister," he began. "I graduated at the bottom of my class at the Crimson Roof Thieves Guild. I'm a lousy rogue. My parents were ashamed that I barely passed, so they bought me this mug instead of a proper thieves kit. But honestly, in my opinion, this is better than any thieves kit. Except for this way, I do not have to pickpocket; which, I'm lousy at anyway!"

I wasn't sure what to think about the situation, but he did pay for my meal and bought us some hot tea to wash it down. "I'll be right back," he said, after spotting a couple of dwarves leave their seats. "Time to cushion surf!"

Spare Change ran over, searched the cushions in their stall, and held up a copper piece for me to see. He was grinning ear-to-ear. Now I know how he got the nickname, Spare Change!

When he came back, he grabbed his mug and headed out for some fresh air by the front door. It wasn't long before he came back in with a mug full of coins. Later, my party joined me at our booth, and we had a pleasant time. "If you need a place to stay," the halfling said, finishing the last bite of his meal. "You can stay at my place."

"Can you fit us all in?" I asked.

"It's a sixteen-room estate over by the mayor's house," he laughed. "I think I can squeeze you in!"

"I'm thinking about changing my name," Kellepto said, admiring this halflings ability to make money.

I think we all wanted to, at that point!

Entry 91

The first time I met Kellepto was when I was still working for the Red Eye Knights. Due to a misfiling of paperwork, the Red Eye's recruitment office was forced to share space with another group doing the same thing. The problem was that it was an evil organization that recruited thugs for various groups looking to cause mischief throughout the Unremembered Realms.

Foulwinds, Inc. had a Dragonborn rep, named Plagwyrm, whose desk was right across from mine. He would always try to lure my recruits over to his side with easy solutions and get rich quick schemes. "Why be a Red Eye Knight when the easy money is with extortion, blackmail, and robbery!" he'd say.

All I could offer is hard work, honesty, and a clean conscience. So, let's just say many people crossed lines to work for whatever organization Foulwinds, Inc. was recruiting for that day. The newly hired prospect would always have to walk by me to leave, though, so I'd hold up a drawing of the gallows I made and say, "See you soon."

This drawing turned one or two people back to my side, but most of the time, I was met with laughter or derision. But, that was okay, one or two was better than nothing, and I always seemed to end up with the beings with the most potential, and that's what brings me back to my memory of the first time I met Kellepto. She had been on a large wagon full of Crimson Guard Thieves Guild graduates. They poured in the door, chattering with excitement, hoping to land jobs and start their careers as rogues.

Two of them rushed up to Plagwyrm's desk right away. One was large and muscular; the other was thin and slimy looking. "I'm Appichat," the thin one said, "and this is Onquay. We need jobs, and we'll do anything, as long we get rich!"

"Yeah, rich," the larger one agreed.

"What if it means robbing, stabbing, or stealing candy from small children?" Plagwyrm asked.

"Easy pickings," Appichat said. "Sign us up!"

When they walked by, I held up my drawing; they both laughed. "Being a villain means life on easy street," Onquay sneered. "We'll be feared by all!"

"No," I said. "You'll be puppets for some goon and eventually pay the price for all your crimes. You'll see. I have taken your kind to gallows plenty of times!"

"We're too smart for that," Appichat said, smugly. "Nobody outwits us!"

That's when I saw a pretty elf gal leaning against the back wall by the door. She was observing the scene. While I signed up a few recruits, the line for Plagwyrm was much longer. Soon, everyone had signed their names, and the place had emptied. "What are you doing?" I asked.

"Waiting for a couple of friends," she replied. "They promised they would be here. They jumped off the wagon near the town's fountain."

"Why wait for them?" Plagwyrm stated. "Come sit down, sign up, and soon you'll be rich and famous!"

Something was different about her, and I could sense the good in her. "You can always join the Red Eye Knights and use your abilities to help the side of good."

"I don't want to be a knight," she said. "I'm a rogue."

"The Red Eye Knights hire rogues all the time," I said. "We need them for secret missions and things like that. We hire clerics and mages, too."

"The hours are hard and the pay is terrible," Plagwyrm cut in. "After a few years working for someone like Elfalfuh, the elven crime boss, you could earn the rank of captain and be telling others what to do."

"It is hard work; I have to admit," I told her. "But stopping evil and bringing justice to the realms brings satisfaction that money just can't buy!"

"All that work is too hard," Plagwyrm cut in. "Join one of my groups, and you'll be rich beyond your wildest dreams!"

Kellepto walked up to Plagwyrm's desk, put her palms down on it, and leaned in. "I'm a rogue; you don't think I know a scam when I see it?"

She turned and walked over to me. "I kind of like being a free agent," she said. "But I do like the idea of serving the greater good. What's your name?"

"Nimbus Slumberdim," I said. "People call me Stormcloud."

Little did I know that just a couple of months later that she would be joining my team. She was shocked that I was no longer a Red Eye Knight, but pleased she didn't have to join an organization. Kellepto liked that I was now a paladin fighting on my own for the good of the realms.

Entry 92

There was a lot of small talk going on about the halfling village of Littlefoot, so we decided to head over and investigate. A halfling named Shordy had been forming some cult, so we thought we'd check it out. "Be Little!" was their motto and they were firing up halflings left and right not only to have pride in their size, but to take their tiny inner rage out on others.

We had just left the town of Mazenhog, where we arrested a couple of their Shordy thugs. They had been taunting their vertical oppressors and kicking their shins before running away. By the time we got to Little-foot, we saw halflings going about their lives, like nothing happened. We spotted an old halfling lady removing cultist flyers from the town's bulletin board and decided to approach her. "We've been hired by Mazenhog officials to stop the Shordy Cultists before they cause too much trouble," I said. "Can you tell us where Shordy is?"

"You're too late, paladin," the woman said. "The whole movement was cut off at the knees by bad finances."

"Don't tell me the money came up short," Kellepto said, confirming our suspicion that Shordy was a con artist.

"All of us fell for it, too," the old woman griped. "He claimed we had little faith, then took off with all our gold!"

We followed some tracks we found and located the treacherous runt sitting in front of a campfire, eating shrimp. Shordy put up a wee fight, but he gave up after Kellepto punched him in the nose.

I reminded him of his crimes, he claimed that those were just "tall tales," and that he'd be back on the street in a limited amount of time. "That may be true," Kellepto told him. "But, your story will be a short one if we hear of you trying this, again."

Entry 93

When I was a kid, dealing with bullies was never a problem on account of my size. Even if the brutes were as big as I was, I still enjoyed giving them a good scrapping. My father was a fighter and he had taught all of his children to go toe-to-toe with evil in any form. Sadly, not everyone has had my advantages, and I can't be everywhere at once to defend the less fortunate. But, I do remember one time when I helped out a kid named Nerbles.

I had come to the park with my big brother, Stratus, and my little sister, Mary Lynn. They went off to play on the beach while I chose to look for other kids for which to play. That's when I spotted Nerbles. He had been sitting at a bench in the park, sobbing and feeling sorry for himself. "What's the matter?" I asked, as I went over and sat next to him.

The skinny kid wiped his eyes and put the glasses back on his head, before replying, "Big Dirk says this is his park now. Then, he punched me in front of all the other kids! Now he says I can't come back and that all my friends are his."

Seeing the tears pour over his blackened and swollen eye had me steaming. "I'll handle, Big Dirk," I said. "I'll make him apologize!"

"It doesn't matter," Nerbles said. "All my friends think I'm a wimp, now and Big Dirk will just come back when you're not around."

"Hmmm, you're probably right," I said, leaning back on the bench.

That's when an idea hit me. I explained everything to Nerbles, and he happily agreed. Ten minutes later, he marched back into the park to-

185

ward Big Dirk and his scared friends. I waited quietly in some nearby bushes.

"Hey, Big Dirk," Nerbles said nervously. "Get out of my park and leave my friends and me alone!"

Big Dirk was big, but not nearly as big as I was. "What are you going to do about it, you baby? Cry at me? How about I punch you in your other eye?!"

"It was a lucky punch," Nerbles said. "I was caught off guard, and now I think I'm going to give you a jolly good thrashing!"

Before Big Dirk could respond, I leaped from the bushes and ran over. "What's going on here?! I'm the new king of this park! This park belongs to me! Do any of you have a problem with that?!"

Big Dirk's eyes were as big as saucers. "N..n..no problem here…" he stuttered, holding up his hands.

The other kids cowered in fear, shaking their heads as well—all except for Nerbles. "I have a problem with it," he said, standing up to me. "This park belongs to no one. Leave now or face my wrath!"

I did the best fake laugh I could, "This, I have to see!"

I ran up to him with my fist raised, and I heard everyone there gasp. That's when Nerbles clenched his fist and fake punched me in the stomach. I crumpled to the ground pretending to writhe in agony. "Oooo….I wasn't expecting such strength!"

Nerbles turned to Big Dirk and showed him his fist. The bully let out a shriek and ran off as fast as he could. Nerbles' friends let out a cheer and surrounded him, patting him on the back, before carrying him off on their shoulders.

The kid gave me a big smile as they left, and I sat up, giving him a wave goodbye. I enjoyed the feeling of that moment, and I never really got over it.

Entry 94

I've never understood how Footpalm the Elflinger became a monk. I have always been under the impression that monks are patient, peaceful, and at one with their surroundings. From the moment he wakes up, he's complaining of aches and pains and his need for coffee. Then, at night, he brags to no end of his accomplishments; he does not exude what you would call a spiritualized balance.

Footplam claims he does his meditations in the bathroom; which, must be true because he is in there for an hour every time. You can hear his joints pop whenever Kellepto offers to do light stretching with him. As a matter-of-fact, whenever another monk passes him on the street and nods, he sticks his tongue out, belches, or says, "What are you looking at?"

I finally asked him about his behavior one day when we were alone by the fire while on a mission to Skull Hollow. "How come you don't act like the rest of the monks we meet?" I asked. "They all seem so at peace."

"It's all about zen," he stated. "As a young acolyte, they told us to pursue what brought us inner peace. Me? I like complaining, oversleeping, eating whatever I want, and flinging elves."

"But what about insulting or being rude to other monks?" I said.

"Yeah, that too," he said while poking a stick in the flames. "It's how I find balance."

"Then why do the other monks give you a look of disdain?" I said.

"That's their way of accepting my path," Footpalm replied.

"I think he slept through the philosophy part of his training," Kellepto said, sitting down next to him.

"I was finding my zen!" the dwarf growled.

Entry 95

I love Winterfest. From the minute I sense the chill coming, I get that festive spirit that only happens at this time of year. From the ways in which towns decorate their streets with boughs of holly to the colorful magic lights that I see wizards trying to unravel and hang up around lantern poles.

Even dungeons around this time tend to get in the spirit of the season. I remember this one time when we raided the dungeon of Iceminster the Cold, and he went all out. Monsters made out of snow, evil creatures' socks lining hallways with care, and even chimes that played popular Winterfest songs when you walked in.

Not that these decorations or activities couldn't be dangerous, though. I remember Aiden getting a pretty big zap after walking under some Magic Missiletoe. Even then, he was in a good Winterfest spirit when we visited him in the recovery room at the temple.

Entry 96

I usually love small towns. The communities are tight-knit, and everyone knows everything about one another. When dangers arise, heroes like my team are contacted early, and damage control occurs. Not every town has heroes. That's why we roam from place to place. Most of these towns are happy to see us coming—all except Tudemoor, in the province of Rustwood.

"Excuse me," I said to the tavernkeep when we arrived in town. "We're heroes passing by and we heard rumors that some orcs are getting ready to raid your town. We're here to help."

"We didn't ask for your help!" the old dwarf replied, looking up at me while polishing a glass. "If you're not going to order, scram!"

We found it a bit odd, but he was a dwarf, who are cantankerous, anyway. Feeling a little perturbed, we sat down after placing our order. A human farmer and an elven bard were playing a card game at a table near ours. "Excuse me, fellas," I said. "We're here to help the citizens of Tudemoor with its upcoming orc problem. Have you heard anything about their movements?"

"Of course we have, do we look like fools?!" the elf sneered, rolling his eyes, before turning back to his hand.

"We're only trying to be helpful," Aiden stated, obviously perplexed.

"Helpful isn't going to help," the farmer spat back at him.

"Um, yes it is," Kellepto cut in, her temper was flaring. "That's exactly what it means!"

"Buzz off," the farmer shot back. "Hmmm…maybe I should rephrase it so your pointy ears can hear it better. Shoo!"

By this point, everyone at our table was upset, but I reminded them that as heroes of the Unremembered Realms, we had a job to do, no matter how we, or even the town felt. "Let's not forget the children guys; what about the children?" I said, knowing it would win their hearts.

They let out a collective groan and agreed. We ate our meal in relative peace, then decided to patrol the town, making sure things were safe. "What are you guys doing here," a cute little halfling child said to us as we passed through a park.

"We're heroes looking to protect you," I replied, kneeling with a smile.

"Who invited you?" the bright-eyed boy replied, "because we sure didn't!"

With that said, a bunch of other children who had been playing with him began throwing sticks and rocks at us. Frustrated, we stomped away before any of us lost our cool. "What is it with this town?!" Kellepto said, rubbing her arm where a small rock had struck her. "I am out of here!"

"But what about the chil...." I started to say, but was cut off by a look from the elf.

So, we left town and decided to let the chips fall where they may. This whole situation was giving me a headache, anyway, or maybe it was from the stone that hit me on the head; I couldn't tell. We took a moment to apply some small bandages to the bumps and scratches.

About a mile out from Tudemoor, we stumbled across the orc encampment. "Hold it, right there," an orc shouted, running out to us, "or face the wrath of the mighty Buckfang Horde, the scourge of the..."

"If you're going to raid the town of Tudemoor, forget about it," I said, cutting him off. "They wouldn't even let us protect them!"

The orcs that had begun surrounding us babbled amongst themselves, "They must be tough," the leader said, while looking at our bandages. "It looks like they beat you up pretty good."

"And this was just their children!" I said, frustrated.

With a look of fear, the leader started chatting with a shaman who had walked up. "Paladins do not lie," he told the leader.

With a few more grunts and a few arguments, the orcs gave up on their task, packed up their gear, and headed off in another direction. I felt pretty good, as we made off toward our next destination, knowing that we had managed to save the day, once again. Or was it the children of Tudemoor? I still don't know; the whole situation made my head hurt.

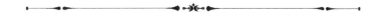

Entry 97

The Unremembered Realms is full of danger, so you have to be careful at all times. There are monsters of all descriptions, traps ready to go off, and even cursed magic items! For example, one time, while passing around the Faerwood Forest, Kellepto spotted the corpse of a slobgoblin leaning against a tree a little way into the woods. It had a neck bite that looked incredibly gruesome.

Curiosity got the best of us, so we went in to investigate. We could see a group of something had come through, because of the snapped branches and an occasional body part scattered along the way. We also kept finding half-eaten carrots.

Then, we found a clearing deep into the forest and saw three dead slobgoblins lying in front of a cave. "I've got a bad feeling about this," Footpalm warned.

"These bodies are old," Aiden said, kneeling over one. "I'd say they've been here for a few months."

"Looks like the work of a Hoppalopper," Kellepto said while flipping through her Realms Manual of Monsters. "Footpalm is probably right, they are pretty deadly, and probably best left alone."

"I agree," I said, after poking one of the bodies with the end of my sword. "Let's just go."

As we all started to leave, Kellepto said, "Wait a minute, where's Garrot?"

"I'm in here!" he shouted from inside the cave. "Come on in! I've found something!"

His voice sounded a little off, but we had no choice, we had to go in and get him out and see whatever he had found. So, we all stepped into the darkness. Footpalm's eyes adjusted easily, because he was a dwarf, then Kellepto's did, as well. They led Aiden and me down about twenty-five feet and around a corner. That's when we saw a light about another twenty-feet down. Some kind of magical illumination had been cast on a small stone embedded on the wall at another corner. A couple of more dead slobgoblins were lying around rotting on the floor.

More of these lights were in the room we entered. The room was filled with cobwebs, bones, and half eaten carrots. A broken up treasure chest lined one wall, and we could see Garrot's back as he was leaning over the rotting body of some kind of humanoid. "Hey guys," he said, turning around. "Look what I found!"

We all gasped as he turned around and pointed at his two front teeth; they were elongated and resembled a rabbits! Not only that, his ears had grown long, white, and furry and his feet were now huge, as well! Long whiskers shot out from around his nose and his eyes now had a slight tinge of red. "I don't think it's a Hoppalopper."

"What did you do, Garrot?!" Kellepto asked, approaching him cautiously. "What happened?!"

"I got curious," he replied, wiggling his new whiskers. "So, I came in here to investigate. I found this body with this note attached. Man, I'm hungry. Did anyone bring a carrot?"

"Foolish wizard!" Footpalm harumphed. "You could have gotten us all killed, you long-eared oaf!"

"What note?" I asked.

Garrot handed me a small piece of parchment. I read it aloud, "To whom it may concern. I have discovered an ancient item of great power, called the Teeth of the Harebringer. The power it has given me is not worth all of the side effects, plus the fleas are unbearable! I've hidden here, because many now hunt me. I've tried every sort of magic to painlessly remove the teeth, and nothing works! I'm ending it all, before I hurt anyone else. Please don't touch the teeth on my body, they will implant themselves in you, and you will be cursed, as well."

I couldn't make out the name, but the message was clear, this was a cursed item, and Garrot was it's newest host! "You hare brain! Why didn't you follow the instructions on the note?!" Footpalm said, angrily.

Garrot shrugged his shoulders. "I didn't read the note, first. I saw a body lying here with a self-inflicted crossbow bolt to the head. I was just about to pick the note up when I noticed the large teeth. They seemed to have a magical aura, so I touched them. Then, poof! Here I am!"

"I've heard of these teeth," Kellepto said. "They are a thing of legend around where I grew up. They're powerful, but they slowly drive you insane."

"Well, that's not far to go," Footpalm said.

"How do I get these things out?" Garrot whined. "You have to help me!"

From that point on, we tried everything. Aiden started first, casting all sorts of healing spells and whatnot. Then, we took him from city to city asking questions, hearing rumors, and spending a ton of gold on carrots. Finally, we bounced our friend into the *Palm Eye Finger Magic Shop* to see if Bub and Lar could help.

The old wizards were excited to see Garrot and ran up to him, right away. "Are those the Teeth of the Harebringer?!" Lar asked, holding up a magnifying glass. "Amazing!"

"I've only read about them in books," Bub said, before running back behind the counter and opening cabinets.

"You two can fix me, right?" Garrot asked, hoping the famous wizards knew something about removing the cursed item.

"Not without a lot of experimentation!" Bub said, happily, pulling out a large box and setting it on the counter.

When he sat it down, an assortment of rusty tools fell out. There were grinders, pokers, twirly hand-crankable thingamajigs, and a mess of other things. Garrot saw this and immediately fainted, falling face-first on the floor. "You two are butchers!" I cried out, surprised that these two were capable of this kind of madness.

"No, no, no," Lar explained. "Our plumber, M.T. Chamberpott, was here earlier and left his tools. He accidentally sat them down on our thin book of curse removals."

We let out a sigh of relief and helped Garrot up into a chair. But something had changed, the teeth were now on the floor! They had gotten knocked out when he landed face first! "Don't touch the teeth," Kellepto warned the mages, who came to see.

"We know," they said, picking up the teeth with a pair of tweezers and setting them in a jar full of green liquid. "These things are highly volatile!"

Garrot's ears had shrunken back and his eyes returned to their normal shade of color. His feet happened to stay to a few sizes larger, though, and he still had the whiskers. "What happened?" he mumbled. "Did they do it? Am I cured?"

"No and maybe," Bub said, walking over holding the jar. "There's a tiny chip missing from one of these. I think the piece is still in his mouth!"

In the end, we found out there was nothing we could do. So, the two wizards asked us to take the teeth to Mound Doom and throw them in the lava; which, we did. Garrot wasn't bothered. "Girls like whiskers," Kellepto told him, and I think she was right.

He could see a little better, run a little faster, and could jump farther than before. The only real side effect was that he got cranky whenever he didn't get his nightly cup of carrot juice.

Entry 98

It's not easy building a good reputation; I do my best to follow the golden rules of adventuring. But, there are those out there who, through nefarious means, try to use my reputation for their financial gain. Like the time we were in the town of Swindleton and my team and I stopped to have a bite to eat at Ol' Shrivey's Tavern.

While chatting with a waitress, she developed a look of shock at the mere mention of my name. "You're Nimbus 'Stormcloud' Slumberdim?" she asked, "The mighty paladin?"

"Why, yes," I said, happily. "I'm glad to see my reputation exceeds me."

In a swift move, she sat down her tray, ran behind the counter, and through the kitchen doors. "Wow," Kellepto said. "You've never gotten that reaction before!"

I was a little surprised, myself. "Wow," I commented. "I have a good feeling about this town. Something tells me the folks here appreciate heroes. I bet she went to tell the owner who we are and wants us to pose for a sketch or something."

"If they don't have a parade for us," Garrot started, "Let's make our own!"

"That never really works out well for us," Footpalm told the wizard. "Remember Nabiscove, Mossborough, and Achincorn?!"

"This time would be different," Garrot replied, coolly. "I got some new moves."

Before we could respond to Garrot's dream parade idea, I felt a hand on my shoulder. When I turned around, I could see it was the tavern owner Ol' Shrively, and beside him was a town constable. "This is the one," Ol' Shrively said. "He's the one pretending to be Nimbus Slumberdim!"

"He doesn't seem to fit the description," the constable said. "He's a lot more muscular!"

I didn't know what was going on, so I stood up. "And a little taller, too," the constable said, looking up at me. "Now, everything's beginning to make a lot more sense."

"I'd like to know what's going on here," I stated, feeling confused.

"If you come to the station, I can explain," the constable stated.

We followed him and were soon sitting in a small waiting area outside the jail cells. The constable, whose name was Numwall, appeared with a stack of papers in a filing envelope. He pulled out some of the documents revealing a sketch of a puny halfling, some IOU's, and a lengthy tab from Ol' Shrively's Tavern. "It seems the heroic paladin the whole town had lost faith in was an imposter all along!" Numwall stated, handing us the sketch.

"This is a halfling," Footpalm stated. "How in the realms did you confuse him with that pipsqueak?!"

"He had some tall tales," Numwall responded. "Besides that, we've never met you before. We've only heard stories."

Kellepto studied the sketch and jumped up from her chair. "I know this guy! He was a fellow student at the Crimson Roof Thieves Guild! His name is Blott, and his favorite scam was leeching off other people's reputations!"

I felt violated. My identity had been stolen by someone who didn't look or act anything like me! "My reputation will be ruined," I said, feeling frustrated.

"Don't worry about it," Numwall stated. "I'll see to it that this 'Blott' is struck from your record and make sure you're all in the clear."

I reached into my pack and pulled out all the gold I had on me. "No point in all these others suffering," I said. "This should settle all the debts."

Kellepto nearly fainted when I did this, and I had my hand out because I had already anticipated her reaction. "Our gold!" she said, wide-eyed, as Numwall cheerfully tucked the money under his desk.

"Wait until I get my hands on that little creep," she said, stewing.

It turns out that she didn't have to wait long. As we were getting ready to leave, a halfling heavily resembling the sketch of Blott walked in and shouted, "Constable! Ol' Shrively has informed me there's an imposter in town trying to steal my identity!"

He then looked over in our direction, and his eyes grew wide. He now realized he'd been set up by the tavernkeeper. "And tell them nobody gets away with imitating...um...Dragonbeast the Devastator!"

For a second, I almost believed him, because I had heard the stories of how short the Unremembered Realms mightiest hero was. But,

Kellepto yelled out, "That's Blott! Get him!"

I have to give Blott credit; he was indeed fast, but not fast enough. After diving under apple carts, jumping over barrels, and weaving in and out of people, he finally tripped over a stairstep and crashed to the ground. "You've got the wrong guy!" he kept yelling, as I drug him back to the jailhouse. "I'm not who you think!"

"I remember exactly who you are," Kellepto said sharply, "classmate!"

Blott seemed confused for a minute, then a look of dread came over his face. "It's not me," he yelled again. "I'm my twin cousin!"

In the end, my reputation was saved, and Blott was put in jail by Numwall. We invited the constable to Ol' Shrively's for dinner that night, where he told us Blott informed him that Blott wasn't his real name. He was Murfee, an undercover agent working for the King of Eaglespaw, and he was willing to name names. It seemed the halfling was ready to name any name, except for his own.

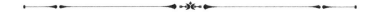

Entry 99

After giving in to Kellepto's wishes, we spent a couple of days at the Dragondrop Mail in Barrendry. The guys knew we were in trouble when the first thing she bought was not one, but two Sacks of Holding! We spent hour after hour following her from store to store, hoping it would be the last. I'm a patient guy, but I swear the shoes she made me look at were sticking their tongues out at me!

This delirium cleared when she sat down on the bench between us all out in the hallway and declared, "I'm done! Hey, do you guys need help picking out anything?"

We left so fast I don't think any of us was paying attention to our direction, and we ended up heading east, straight into the Barrendry Desert! By the time we slowed down, we knew we were lost, and that can be very dangerous in this part of the realms! We quickly consumed our water and rations and were in pretty rough shape when the sun reached the highest point in the sky. "Look!" Aiden shouted, wiping sweat off his face. There's an outcropping of rocks with what looks like a cave!"

We didn't even care about any danger, we just trudged over and ran in, collapsing in the shade that the cave provided. After a few minutes of letting our eyes adjust, we were shocked to see skeletons of all sorts of humanoids scattered all over the place. I jumped up to my feet, ready to fight, but then realized that these were not undead, just regular, good ol' fashioned bones.

"These skeletons look weird," Footpalm stated, walking around inspecting them. "It appears some are slumped over, while other ones were trying to show them...their shoes?"

"They must have been other travelers coming out of the mall," Garrot stated, bending down and picking a shoe off one of their feet.

"That's a good idea," Kellepto said. "We could kill time by going through all the shoes I just bought. I want your opinions. We might have to take some back."

"I say we endure the desert a little while longer," Footpalm stated, heading out the door.

The rest of us followed, with Kellepto tagging along behind us, babbling on about straps, latches, and buckles. We hadn't gone far when we spotted a man sitting on a rock in the middle of the sand, holding a stick with a string tied to the end of it. His line was cast in the dirt. "Shh..." he said. "Yer scaring the fish!"

As we slowly stepped over to him, we watched him hold a canteen up to his lips, and he took long gulps. "Ahh..." he said. "So refreshing! Do you want some?"

"Yes! If you don't mind," I replied.

He held it out, so I let Kellepto go up and take the first drink. She had a strange look on her face when she returned. "The canteen is empty," she said. "I think the sun has fried this old kook's brain!"

"Why are you out here?" Aiden asked, playing along. "It's a bit late in the day for fishing, don't you think?"

The old man spat on the ground and smiled. "Are you kidding?! It was either this or watch my wife try on shoes back at the cave! That woman drives me bonkers!"

"Well, there goes that hope!" Footpalm griped. "We might as well start fishing with this lunatic!"

"From the looks of the others," Kellepto said, "I'd say this is the one fish who got away."

It was a bad joke, but it made the old man laugh. "Yeah, that's right!"

All of a sudden, Kellepto said she could hear the distinct sound of a

196

harness. "Garrot, launch a fireball straight up," she said, grabbing the wizard.

After shooting the spell off, the sound picked up enough that we all began to hear it. Then, over a dune appeared a small caravan, headed our way. "Huzzah!" we all shouted, hugging one another and the old man. When it stopped, an old woman waved, "Harold! I've been looking all over for you!"

"I thought you were still in the cave, Maude!" he replied, walking up to the wagon, holding his hands far apart. "You should have seen the size of the fish I caught!"

"We found her a few miles out carrying a bag of shoes," the captain of the caravan said. "Thanks for sending up a signal. You guys need a ride?"

"We sure do," I said, happily. "Where you headed?"

"The Dragondrop Mall," he replied. "We need to do some shopping."

"Whoo-hoo!" Kellepto said, cheering. "I need to make some exchanges!"

It took the driver ten minutes before he was able to catch up with the rest of us, as we ran deeper into the desert.

Entry 100

While traveling to the town of Stablewind, we came upon a house that was sitting out in the middle of nowhere. It was a nice looking place and well kept. "Maybe they won't mind friendly visitor's looking for a place to sleep?" I said to the party. "The sun's almost set, and Stablewind is still half a day away."

We were met at the front door by an older man with thick glasses that were part of some weird headgear. Multiple circular pieces of glass could be rotated in and out. He carried a thick book with a leather cover that was decorated with an assortment of colorful gemstones. They twinkled almost as much as Kellepto's eyes after seeing them.

We explained our situation, and he was more than happy to have us as guests. "There's plenty of room here," he said, guiding us through the place.

It was neat and tidy, without a spec of dust. Knickknacks of all sorts decorated the rooms, including various kinds of neatly polished weapons. They were each hung on the walls like trophies. "Where did you get all of these?" Kellepto asked, impressed with his collection.

"Oh, things just fall into my hands," he replied with a warm smile.

"Who is this guy?" Garrot whispered loudly to Footpalm from behind me.

"Oldmunn," the old man said, hearing him, as well.

"We can see that," I said, feeling a bit embarrassed about Garrot's rudeness. "But you look good for your age."

"No, no, no," he laughed. "Oldmunn is my name. I have to admit that it made my younger years difficult at school. But as the years went by, I grew into it."

He motioned for us to follow along. The most noticeable thing about his house was his vast collection of books and scrolls. Rows and rows of them filled the rooms. "What book are you reading?" he asked, spotting my journal sticking out of my pack.

"Actually," I explained. "It's my journal. I'm writing it."

"Fascinating," Oldmunn said, rubbing his neatly cropped white beard. "Perhaps, you'll let me glance at it?"

"Oh, I don't know," I told him. "I'm a bit shy about anybody reading it, because then everyone in the realms would know all about me."

Oldmunn politely nodded. "You shouldn't be embarrassed," he said. "There's nothing like reading a good autobiography, after all, what is life but a bunch of small stories collected into one place? As a matter-of-fact, I'm putting together a book, myself."

He held up the book he was holding for us all to see. "It's my big book of heroes. It has a collection of the mightiest adventurers in all of the Unremembered Realms."

When Oldmunn opened the book, the page he turned to was an exquisite full-color drawing of a cleric in full plate mail, and there was text to go with it. Aiden gasped, "That's Cornfeddles the Cleric! He disappeared over five years ago! I would love to read his story!"

"You'll have your turn with the book," Oldmunn said, gently closing it. "But for now, how about a nice warm meal?"

I didn't have to be asked twice about that. Oldmunn left us alone in a study room while he went to prepare our food. We spent a little time inspecting the niceties and browsing through some of the well-dusted tomes. "Wow," Garrot said. "He's got books on everything."

"I don't like this," Kellepto said. "This old coot gives me the creeps."

"Don't be absurd," Aiden stated. "He's legit. I mean, he even has the biography of Cornfeddles. That means my personal hero probably sat in this very chair that I'm in now, telling him his life story! Amazing!"

After a short time, the kindly old man came into the room with a large tray of food on a cart. We all dug in, except for Kellepto, who claimed not to be hungry and excused herself to lie down. If I had not been so eager to stuff my face, I'd have noticed something was bothering her. Instead, the others and I enjoyed the hot buttery rolls, the steaming veggies, and tender brisket that had been prepared. It was truly amazing. The food was so good that it made my head spin, and then spin some more, and then the room became hazy. All I remember is flashes of green light and sounds of furniture crashing. Then, everything went black.

When I finally came to, Kellepto was putting a cork back in one of her antidote vials. I'd been poisoned! I shook off the grogginess and looked around. Every one of my party was missing, except for Kellepto, who stood before me in really sorry shape. Burn marks were all over her leather armor, and she had some blood caked on the side of her head. She held her side and coughed. "It's a good thing I followed my gut," she explained.

"And a bad thing I followed mine," I said, standing up slowly. "What happened?"

She stepped back and showed me Oldmunn, who was bound and gagged, sitting on a chair. "This guy collects heroes," she coughed. "In his book."

"I know that," I said. "Oldmunn told us."

She held the book up and turned it to a page. To my amazement, there was a drawing of Footpalm in it with some text. Then, she flipped to Garrot, then Aiden. "He uses magic to trap them in his book," she explained. "I came back in the room just in time; he was just about to have you absorbed into it!"

Oldmunn groaned in his chair. It was evident that Kellepto did quite a number on him. "How did he do it?" I asked.

"I don't know," she replied. "But there has to be a way to reverse this!"

We both walked over to the old man. "Ugh," he stated after she removed his gag. "I've been poisoned!"

"Turn about is fair play," Kellepto said, twisting her crossbow bolt in his shoulder.

Oldmunn screamed. "My poison wasn't deadly! It only rendered them unconscious! I wanted you all in my collection!"

"How do you reverse it?" I asked. "How do we get our friends out?"

"I'll never tell," he groaned. "They're mine!"

"Not for long," Kellepto said. "My poisons are slow, but not that slow. You got about a half-hour before your body goes to room temperature, if you know what I mean."

"Fine! Fine!" he moaned. "Go to the page. Say their name, then close the book, and then tap the gems on the front, one at a time, in a counterclockwise direction. That's the opposite of how I got them in there."

"Let's test this out," Kellepto said, smiling. "Before we turn him into Stablewind authorities."

The elf poured some antidote into his mouth, then grabbed the Book of Heroes from the floor where it was laying. She tapped the gems in a clockwise motion and then opened it to a blank page. "Oldmunn," she uttered.

With a bright green flash, the old man disappeared, then reappeared as a drawing in the book. He did not look happy. "Can you get our team out?" I asked.

"Let's try," she said, before beginning the process.

One by one, each member of our team appeared before us. They were ecstatic. "I'm so glad to out of there!" Footpalm said. "It was so weird; I could see you staring down at me. It's like I was still alive, but unable to move or call out!"

Aiden helped Kellepto to a chair and started casting an assortment of healing spells on her, while the rest of us had a look around. "Hey, Nimbus," Garrot said. "This place would make a nice getaway for us. It doesn't have an owner now."

"That's a thought," I said. "We'll run that by the authorities in Stablewind, they might just go along with that when we show up with an army of heroes from that book!"

We ran back to the main room where Kellepto and Aiden were. "Hey, Garrot came up with a great idea I want to run by everyone," I said. "Wait a minute. Where's Footpalm?"

"He said he had to use the outhouse," Aiden said. "I guess that food was affecting him. I wouldn't bother him, at the moment. He took a book to read with him."

After explaining Garrot's idea, we started looking around for the Book of Heroes. "Where did I set that book…" Kellepto said, before she became wide-eyed. "Footpalm!"

Just as she spoke his name, he reappeared in the doorway with a big grin. "What a great book!"

"Don't tell me," I said, feeling my stomach flip.

"What?" he replied. "There was no bog roll, so I used the next best thing!"

Aiden turned green and looked like he was about to faint. The dwarf laughed, loudly. "Don't worry; I only got stuck on one page; the heroes are fine!"

"Oldmunn," I said, flipping through the book, only to see his page torn out. "If we get this house, something tells me he's going to be seeing a lot more of us!"

The next day, we arrived in Stablewind with a numerous bunch of famous heroes from the book. We were the heroes of the day, and the people of town voted to let us have the house, as a way to say thank you. "It will make a fine place to go when we need time off," I told Stablewind's Mayor.

We stayed at our new place a few more days, before we rode off in search of new adventures. I couldn't help but to think of how fun our journeys had been so far. I always knew that as long as I had my friends with me, wherever we headed next would be good, awfully good.

EPILOGUE

"Finding the giant is going to impossible," I said, looking down the hallway and it's vast number of doors. "We're going to be here all night!"

"Here it is," Garrot said, pushing open a door with a big sign on it that read, 'Giant's Room - Go Away.'

"Ugh," I said, feeling frustrated.

Luckily for us, the giant was sound asleep, which was a good thing. The room was filled with all sorts of treasures, with the snaggle-toothed giant laying in the midst of it all. "We're never going to find the ancient artifact in all of this," I whispered.

"There it is!" Garrot pointed to a dais by the ogres head.

"Would you cut that out!" I said, feeling frustrated. "Stick it in your backpack, Garrot. Then let's split before this thing wakes up."

We collected some treasure and left the room. That's when we realized that Garrot wasn't with us. "What's keeping that crazy wizard?" Foot-palm said, angrily. "I'm getting hungry, and we still have to fight our way back out!"

Garrot appeared and closed the door slowly behind him. He wasn't giggling and wiping shaving cream off his hand onto his robes. "You don't want to know," he chuckled.

"I don't think this is the best time for one of your pranks," Kellepto warned.

"He'll never know it was," Garrot laughed. "It's not like we're ever coming back!"

The Hall of Heroes

I would like to thank these fellow adventurers who, in one way or another, have decided to journey with me through the Unremembered Realms. Their support has helped this journal happen!

Javier A Verdin aka "Felix Banefire"
Sjef Haan (Netherlands)
Nick Belton
Adam Ziembiec
Esapekka Eriksson
Twyste
Eugene Schmitz RN
Ian "Hawkshot" Holmer
Louis MarioN Lipp
DebbieD
Lefty72
Mirranda Prowell
Christopher White
Terri the terrible
John "AcesofDeath7" Mullens
Emily Burt
Balki
Ranthar Darkfire
Skylar Little
Alexei Pawlowski
Ecaroh Reed
Joseph M. Nahas - Zyn Thadalix
Evita
Candice Lindenmayer
Judykins

Steven Callen
UncLovesBrdGames
Drew & Rebel Lippert
Benjamin "the Medic" Morris
Artimisia Pendalwood
Rick Ohnemus
Dan the Man
Rathtwinian
Jappa
Gruk'Naw The Cursed
Josh H. - The Storyteller
kurt ballien
Lake Leafty
Igan Bersk
Chloe Haikio
Jenni D Strand
Victor Von Hamden
Weefster
Alaura
Jeff Lickert
Carly Marie Coleman
Isaac Gleeth
Joel Warner
Steve McEntire

THIS BOOK IS INDEPENDENTLY PUBLISHED,
IT WOULD BE A HUGE HELP TO THE AUTHOR
IF YOU COULD PLEASE TAKE A MOMENT
AND REVIEW THIS BOOK ON YOUR
FAVORITE BOOK SITE LIKE AMAZON.COM,
GOODREADS.COM, OR AUDIBLE.COM.
PLEASE GIVE THIS BOOK SERIES
A MENTION ON YOUR FAVORITE
SOCIAL MEDIA AS WELL.

THE UNREMEMBERED REALMS™

ALSO AVAILABLE FROM
THE UNREMEMBERED REALMS:
JOURNAL OF AN OUTLAW: BOOK ONE
JOURNAL OF AN OUTLAW: BOOK TWO
JOURNAL OF AN OUTLAW: BOOK THREE

THE UNREMEMBERED REALMS GAMES:
THE FORBIDDEN TREASURE OF MIFTENMAD
THE FUMBLECRIT WARS
GAMBLE AT THE GALLOWS

COMING SOON:
JOURNAL OF AN OUTLAW: BOOK IV
JOURNAL OF A LOUNGE LIZARDMAN MUSIC CD
THE TEMPLE OF TEMPERAMENTAL EVIL GAME
PERIL AT PURGEWATER GAME
THE GAME ROOM'S THRONE

JOIN THE EMAIL LIST FOR PRODUCT UPDATES
AND BOOK SIGNING LOCATIONS!
WWW.THEUNREMEMBEREDREALMS.COM
AND FILL OUT A SHORT SIGN-UP FORM.

ABOUT THE AUTHOR

Mick McArt is the author the Unremembered Realms comedy fantasy series of books. He was inspired to write the books and create this world because of his love of Dungeons & Dragons. Mick is also an illustrator and author of children's books, his most popular being the "Tales of Wordishure" series.

Thanks to massive support at his book signings and crowdfunding on Kickstarter, Mick has also become a game designer, with a number of games being composed based on the Unremembered Realms.

Mick is also working on a Homeschool Art Curriculum for all ages and a role playing system for the Unremembered Realms. Micks family include his wife Erica, and their children Micah, Jonah, and Emerald. They currently live in Midland, Michigan.

Mick earned a Bachelor of Fine Arts degree from Central Michigan University in 1997 and a Masters degree from Saginaw Valley State University in 2006.

Made in the USA
Monee, IL
18 July 2021

73426379R00118